Four Days in Villach

Four Days in Villach

A Novel

Arthur Aughey

SHORELANDS PUBLISHING

Arthur Aughey is Emeritus Professor at Ulster University and has published widely in the fields of Irish and British Politics. He was a Senior Leverhulme Fellow and is a former member of the Northern Ireland Community Relations Council and the British Council's Northern Ireland Committee. This is his first novel.

Thanks to Sky Aughey, Sharon Glenn, Kathleen McCracken, Daniela Pinter, Verena Pohn, Franz Sattlegger and Mary Sattlegger.

Published in the UK by SP (Shorelands Publishing) 2021

ISBN: 978-1-7399568-0-6

Typesetting: Derek Rowlinson

Cover image: Arthur Aughey

A Shorelands Publishing Book

Today I shall find something I thought lost forever; there are such days.

Peter Handke *My Year in No-Man's-Bay*

What I like about you, and I have no idea why, is my memories.

Alain-Fournier *Le Grand Meaulnes*

As professor emeritus, you ought to know why it hurts. But you don't know. You know so much and you don't know anything.

Ingmar Bergman *Wild Strawberries*

In old age we long less for the happiness of our youth than for the wishes of our youth.

Marie von Ebner-Eschenbach *Aphorisms*

Conte

The First Day

The First Day

My confidence must be in things unseen, Edward Sweeney thought to himself. If ever he needed faith in benign providence it was right now. When the *Austrian Airlines* De Havilland Dash 8 had departed an unseasonably warm Vienna, the sky had been cloudless, and when airborne, the autumnal light of early evening had given the Danube plain a soft, dreamy sheen. But over the Central Alps, the captain warned of turbulence, the seatbelt signs came on again, the cabin crew abandoned attempts to serve coffee and retreated to strap themselves into their seats at the front. Unable to fly above the Alpine currents, the turboprop rose and fell, was shaken and stirred. The laughter and chatter of fellow passengers ebbed, bodies formerly at ease held stiffly, hands gripping armrests, the insouciant looks of some seeming to reveal their disquiet more obviously than those who stared fixedly ahead.

Sweeney was glad to have a St Christopher medal in his pocket, given to him so long ago. He admitted being superstitious in carrying this token of pewter with its doggerel, 'Protect us on our travels wherever we may roam'. It secured for him a fragment of comfort in a shuddering aircraft assailed by forces much greater than human reason. An illusion, defective thinking, yet he was content for illusion and irrationality to deliver hope not fear. After all, here he was, still alive after years of roaming, aware there was no logic in his conclusion. He turned over the St Christopher in his fingers and looked out at what he thought was now Styria, its forested mountainsides partly enveloped in thin mist and cloud. Above the gashing of steep mountain passes, sheer rocky faces loomed darkly. Rather than being in some ravine down there, he was glad to be inside the Dash, to be tossed about with these others, their lives woven together in a shared fate, and to say to the elements, 'Do what you will'. He had to smile at such bravado he rarely felt.

Suddenly everything changed. The turbulence passed, the sky cleared, conversation resumed as the aircraft began its descent over the gently undulating landscape of Carinthia's lake-land. The mountainous dark and grey had given way to smooth patterns of green, brown and liquid blue. How calm and luminous this terrain appeared as the flight path took him towards Klagenfurt Airport, above farm buildings scattered amid ploughed fields and pasture; and suburban homes with their neat little gardened plots and tarmac roads pencilled between villages. Sweeney had never flown into Klagenfurt before. In summer he had travelled to Carinthia by car and in winter by train after flying into Vienna. This aerial perspective was entirely novel and the gentleness of the landscape surprised him. After the tempestuous passage over Styrian mountains, he couldn't help but feel embraced by the tranquility of everything he saw. It was a romantic fallacy, of course, yet another of his superstitions, but for the first time since leaving home (on impulse and so unlike him) he considered his decision to revisit Villach to be the correct one.

The loud retro thrust of the propellers died away as the plane taxied in after landing, coming to a stop on the apron a few hundred meters from the terminal building. As he made his way towards the exit door, filing out politely with fellow passengers to the muffled notes of *The Blue Danube Waltz*, he prepared for the flight attendants his, '*Auf wiedersehen, Danke*'. On his journey so far he hadn't yet spoken a word of German. When he got to the exit, the senior stewardess looked at him directly but, before he could speak, she smiled and said in English, 'Goodbye, sir, and thank you. Please take care when leaving the aircraft.' She patted the top of her head and nodded towards the exit door. He considered it only good manners to respond to her in English, 'Thank you, goodbye'.

Sweeney was annoyed. How did she know he wasn't Austrian? Was it his eyes? Was it his face? Did he look too small, too lean to be a local? He used to think, when he compared his physique to that of the average Carinthian male, that they were taller, heavier and more imposing than he. Had the woman noticed those physical differences? Then it dawned on him suddenly. It hadn't been physique or looks but his British Academy canvas shoulder bag. It must have looked like a sign around his neck saying, 'No German please, I only speak English.' We keep a balance sheet in life, constantly registering small gains and small losses, and he knew that he'd just notched up a loss. And thus distracted, he bumped his head against the padding on the exit. '*Hoppala*', he heard the stewardess say and turned to her with a look of apology for his clumsiness, but she was already speaking to another passenger. Once outside the aircraft, Sweeney was no longer her professional concern. He collected his bag from a luggage trolley on the tarmac, around which stood a group of Carinthian baggage handlers, taller, heavier and more imposing than he.

It was six-thirty and he couldn't believe how warm it was. He felt overdressed in his dark, heavy, *Marks and Spencer* Italian-styled 'luxury overcoat with cashmere' (as the label on the inside pocket declared). 'Your undertaker's coat', his daughter Sara had teased when she first saw him wearing it, 'and you have the face to go with it' she'd added. He'd bought it especially for his visit, expecting the weather to be inclement. He'd never been in Carinthia at this time of the year and had assumed it would be much colder.

Twenty-five years had passed since his last visit and he'd made a wager on time being kind to him. Gregor von Rezzori advised you must never embark on the search for time lost in the spirit of nostalgic tourism, but even von Rezzori had found it impossible to avoid the self-same spirit. Sweeney would admit he was on a sentimental journey, but he'd convinced himself, with one of those turns of phrase academics loved, that when you reach a certain age most journeys have become sentimental ones. He knew he might find only disappointment, but he also knew such melancholy was half sweet. The journey was not only a pilgrimage to a place, but also, he hoped, reconciliation with his past (he was tempted to say 'redemption'). Pulling his bag along the tarmac, he stopped and lingered briefly to look beyond the Dash to the Southern Alps. Behind their peaks was Slovenia and further to the west lay the border with Italy and Friuli-Venezia Giulia. The sun was setting and the imposing presence of the mountains appeared tamed. He remembered the weather had not been so kind on his first visit here and if Sweeney had been asked why he'd decided to return after such a gap, he would have replied 'a coincidence of book, rain and umbrella'. He would have used the word 'coincidence' if he'd never been convinced out of his belief that there was no such thing as *mere* coincidence (another of his superstitions). He didn't think it had been mere coincidence this time either.

. . . .

That April he'd spent a morning in Belfast and as usual had wandered into Keats and Chapman second-hand book-shop. Amid a jumble of curiosities, he'd found a 1928 edition of *A Wayfarer in Austria* by G. E. R. Gedye, 'Late Times

Correspondent for Central Europe' as the title page described him. Still in its original Methuen wrapper, the book was slightly edge-worn, but in remarkably good condition. The back cover claimed it to be the first English language travel-book on Austria and Sweeney was attracted by the idea of the 'wayfarer', alone with map in hand, adventurous in spirit, discovering strange places and encountering curious customs. He'd looked forward (as the front cover promised) to strolling 'through the gay streets', pausing at 'convenient café tables' and enjoying the 'little-known delights' of Austria. He'd hoped Carinthia would feature prominently, but was disappointed to discover, as he usually did in Austrian travel guides, that the province was mainly somewhere to pass through, to be remarked on briefly, and the parts Sweeney had known merited little reference. He'd found no image of his own experience in Gedye's wayfaring.

Book in hand, he'd walked as far as the corner of Rosemary Street when there was an unexpectedly heavy shower of rain. He'd stepped into a narrow shop doorway for shelter and was joined almost immediately by two young office workers, a woman and a man, likely on their coffee break, both jacketless, yellow identification lanyards dangling against her white blouse and his pink shirt. As she'd fussed in her shoulder bag, the young woman said to Sweeney, 'You can never tell what this weather's going to do, can you?'

'It's certainly changeable', he'd replied, 'you don't want to get wet through, that's for sure.'

She'd agreed it was good advice. The young man didn't speak, only kept his eyes on his companion and Sweeney's view on the weather (and probably on anything else) appeared to be of no interest to him. He'd been impatient to get on and Sweeney couldn't help feeling the man considered he, rather than the rain, was responsible for the delay. Out of her bag the woman finally pulled a small umbrella. 'I always come prepared, don't I?' and like a child held it up for Sweeney's inspection. He'd been charmed by her innocent nature.

'Very wise, I always keep losing umbrellas.'

'Oh, I know, it's so easy to do, isn't it?'

The man had said, possessively, impatiently, 'Here, let me take it'. He'd managed to manoeuvre the woman so that her back was to Sweeney, opened the umbrella, held it aloft with one hand and with the other pressed her out of the doorway into the street. The woman turned to look back at him, 'Make sure you stay dry, won't you?'

'I'll do my best,' and he'd given her a farewell wave, wondering if she finished every sentence with a question. Under their shared cover they had walked at pace, close together, almost entwined but, Sweeney had been pleased to note, uncomfortably out of step. And, alone again in the doorway, the heft of the book in his hand, seeing the raindrops bounce on the pavement and watching the two of them under the umbrella, how could he not think of Sonja?

The spring weather in Carinthia all those years ago had been as cool and wet as Belfast's, grey skies obscuring the mountains for days on end. A young academic at the beginning of his career, Sweeney had sat for the best part of a week in a functional, stuffy seminar room which might have been anywhere. He'd been attending a conference on modern European literature at the University of Klagenfurt, slightly bored, as he normally was, with the ritual proceedings of papers delivered and arcane points discussed. He would gaze out of the partially steamed-up window imagining hidden peaks, but the clouds had never lifted. When the rain did stop intermittently, they'd hung on, heavy and sullen. But in the end he'd been grateful, for the weather had brought them together.

Expecting incompetence in German by English-speaking participants (an expectation well-founded), the conference organizers had recruited research students from the university to act as guides and interpreters for the various panels. It was how he'd come to meet Sonja Maier, his panel's 'facilitator', at coffee in the morning and at regular breaks during the daily sessions. When time had seemed leaden from the unrelenting rain and the gentle tedium of the day, her presence had lifted his mood. Standing together, warming themselves by a radiator or at one of the windows looking out on the campus, they'd struck a comradely relationship, which in its egalitarian character was, at that time anyway, distinctly un-Austrian. In Klagenfurt, formality had been the rule and deference of student towards teacher was still expected. In their case, an easy acquaintance had been natural and unexceptional. The age gap between them was only a few years and Sweeney still hadn't fully exchanged the mentality of the graduate student for tenured academic. If he'd enjoyed speaking irreverently of his scholarly profession and colleagues, she'd seemed to appreciate being worthy of his confidences. If she'd raised his spirits, he'd made her laugh and they'd sought each other out day by day. It was spring after all, but spring can be a season of false hope and a wet spring in Carinthia seemed to hold out little of promise. Happily for him, its promise was fulfilled.

Perhaps their brief encounters would have remained comradely and nothing more but for the night of the conference dinner. It hadn't been planned as a gala affair and panels were left to make their own arrangements. Sonja had been asked to make a recommendation and everyone had been happy enough to leave to her the task of translating recommendation into a firm booking. And why shouldn't she come along too, they'd asked, the generosity of their invitation only qualified by the expectation she would take them to the restaurant, explain what they were ordering and make sure no one got lost on the way back. They'd become comfortable with their dependence on her and *Wayfarers in Austria* they certainly hadn't been. After dinner they'd walked back to the university along the Lend Canal, Sweeney and Sonja slightly ahead of the rest, chatting inconsequentially, but also, so Sweeney recalled, both aware of an approaching finality, an imminent separation. It had been dark, the street light vaporous in the fine rain which began to fall once more. Out of her shoulder bag Sonja had produced a collapsible umbrella and unfurled it. 'Would you like to share?' she'd asked.

'Let me carry it', he'd said, stretching across to take it from her. Sweeney had raised the umbrella high above their heads, but its angle hadn't protected them sufficiently, making walking together awkward as they were forced to adjust their strides to avoid getting wet. Sonja had lowered his arm, slipped her own around it, moved close beside him and their bodies had touched for the first time. There is a line of Katherine Mansfield's about there being something peculiarly intimate about sharing an umbrella, a little daring even. So it had proved in their case too, Sonja's practical move becoming a romantic gesture and they'd looked at one another differently, as if a tacit contract had been made between them. They hadn't spoken, only kept walking, but he'd realized they now understood each other without words, German or English, it was irrelevant, and their commonplace story of 'boy meets girl' had become something more. It had been the first time he'd ever been moved so profoundly.

Close behind them they'd heard the raised voices, the intermittent and exaggerated laughter of the others who hadn't worn well their slight intoxication. With a shock of recognition he sensed a force of exclusion protecting their self-absorption, the claims of the world, colleagues and academic papers, all practical details, momentarily banished. Sweeney had felt far away from it all, imagining his life transformed emotionally and opening out into another culture. The woman holding his arm, sharing an umbrella, had promised both. In the rain of that spring evening, it had become obvious to him he could do nothing but surrender to the fact, deciding to see their relationship as fated. He was more comfortable with fate than with choice (yet another superstition) and the irresponsibility of such belief was lost on him at the time.

On this autumnal evening, he stood again on Carinthian soil. Trying to settle his conscience, almost as a prayer to himself, he said 'to reach something good one must also have gone astray' and suppressing the apprehensions besetting him once more, turned, walked on and entered the terminal building.

. . . .

At the front of Arrivals, taxis were lined up. There was no queue and he walked to the first car in the rank, a black Mercedes saloon, its diesel engine idling. The driver, who had been leaning with his back to the front passenger door and smoking a cigarette, listening to his car radio through the lowered window, rushed to open the boot, took Sweeney's case from him and slid it inside. He had a stocky build, a bushy moustache, close-cropped hair and looked to be in his late forties. Cigarette between his lips, squinting to avoid the smoke, he opened the rear door and as Sweeney got into the back seat, stubbed out his butt on the footpath. The radio was tuned to a local station and Sweeney could hear, playing softly, a folksy song with a rock beat. Before the driver turned it off, he made out the phrase '*Ich steh auf Bergbauernbuam*' which he translated as 'I prefer mountain farm boys'. He liked the female singer's voice and the energy of the music. Seated behind the wheel, the driver looked over his shoulder, his forearm resting on the passenger seat and looked at Sweeney to give him a destination.

He said, '*Bahnhof, bitte*'. The driver continued to look at him, and asked, '*Hauptbahnhof?*'

'*Ja, Hauptbahnhof*,' Sweeney confirmed, considering the question another linguistic defeat and cursed himself. He couldn't blame the British Academy bag. He should have known to say 'central station' and not 'station' for he remembered too late that there was at least one other railway halt between the airport terminal and the city centre. All of a sudden he was very tired and the mistake added to his mental fatigue. It had been a long trip and he had no wish to get into conversation – though in his limited experience of Carinthian taxi drivers, they weren't particularly talkative. It would be clear enough to the man he wasn't an Austrian and certainly not a Carinthian, so he relaxed into his seat, content to remain in silence.

The taxi left the airport perimeter and eased into light local traffic. After a short distance they passed the graveyard at Annabichl and Sweeney recalled what Uwe Johnson had written about it on All Souls Day in 1973 when he'd travelled to attend the funeral of his friend, the writer Ingeborg Bachmann. All Souls Day, Johnson had been surprised to discover, was not simply a festival of the dead, but also a celebration of life. He'd overheard a conversation on the street in which one woman had announced to another, 'The cemetery is the place to be!' Johnson had liked that expression but, when he'd read it, Sweeney could only think of the old joke from his schooldays, 'Look, there's the cemetery. People are dying to get in there.' He considered the phrase and the joke to stem from the same desire to put death in its place, keeping horror at bay. Tonight there was no one he could see at the cemetery.

The traffic became heavier as the scattered suburban housing and small shops of Annabichl gave way to the grander façades of Klagenfurt's public buildings. When the mobile phone rang on the taxi's blue tooth, Sweeney heard the voice of a young woman. 'Oh, excuse me please', the driver said and there followed a conversation in thick Carinthian dialects, the girlish voice punctuated by the driver's laughing responses. After a few minutes, as the taxi stopped at a set of traffic lights, the call ended. The driver looked over his shoulder with a big grin, inviting Sweeney to share in his pleasure. 'My daughter', he pointed to the dashboard. 'She is studying at university.' He turned back to concentrate at the road junction, turned left across the traffic and along a road which followed the path of the railway tracks, fenced off on the left. To the right was a large structure set back from the road in its own grounds. 'My youngest son goes to the school there.' The driver pointed towards the building. 'He wants to become an engineer. My eldest still hopes to be a professional footballer.' The driver laughed at his son's sporting ambition, but the nature of his laugh suggested he didn't rule out the possibility of the boy succeeding. His genial optimism was impressive and, if Sweeney had been that sort of person, infectious. If he'd known any contemporary Austrian footballers, he would have made some encouraging remark, but he hadn't and he didn't. The only footballers he could think of were from the 1980s – Hans Krankl and Herbert Prohaska – but their playing careers would long be over, and anyway, Sweeney couldn't remember which clubs they'd played for. Raising his voice, the driver continued, 'Family is important, isn't it?' and Sweeney could see him checking for a reaction in the rear-view mirror. 'It is important to have roots,' he continued, and in case Sweeney hadn't understood the German word '*Wurzeln*', he gestured downward with his hand, wiggling the fingers to demonstrate 'roots'. But Sweeney had understood.

How could he respond except by saying yes – even if his expression became distant, thinking the tone of his answer sounded feeble. He noticed the driver eyeing him and sensed the man found his answer unconvincing too, though he nodded approvingly. Likely he was used to lonesome travellers, those in transit from nothing to nothing and Sweeney was suddenly annoyed at what he took to be the man's presumption. Politeness forbade him to show any irritation and just as quickly he shrugged off his suspicion as ridiculous. Why should it matter to him if the taxi driver presumed his rootlessness? Yet the briefest glimpse of that sceptical look in the mirror had unsettled him. Clearly the man enjoyed the role of *paterfamilias* and, yes, the evidence, Sweeney admitted, was on his side – family roots are a 'good thing' and his own innate conservatism concurred. But was it always true? He'd immersed himself in enough Austrian literature recently, reading a lot of Thomas Bernhard, as well as Elfriede Jelinek, and they would beg to differ. But he had neither the German words nor the inclination to discuss the merits of family life. Anyway, he was hardly an example of someone who had acted as if family had been important to him. To his own daughter, yes, he could say that he had tried to be a caring father. He was proud of his daughter, like the man in the front seat was of his. It was one of the few things in his life that Sweeney could say with certainty. Yet there was little depth beyond the immediacy of the father-daughter relationship, no hinterland populated by relatives, aunts, uncles, cousins. Did he feel deprived? Did he feel he had missed out on something true and good? He had never thought about his life this way and he'd no evidence that Sara thought about it any differently. She'd never said anything to make him think otherwise – but he'd never asked her and that was typical of him too. Anyway, the driver appeared happy to move on from the joys of family life, for he asked, 'Where are you going?'

'Villach.'

'Ah, Villach – the train you see?' A Railjet Intercity express, coaches in its red, grey and black livery, was making sedate progress, outpaced by the taxi. Sweeney could hear its wheels click-clacking over the points and its brakes screeching as the locomotive approached the Hauptbahnhof. 'It's for Villach,' the driver said. Looking at the clock on the dashboard, he tapped it, 'You have ten minutes, no problem.' He turned his head slightly and repeated, 'Ten minutes, don't worry.' Sweeney wasn't worried. He couldn't be sure, but he suspected the information about the train wasn't correct at all. He didn't believe it was intended to mislead. The man would have been aware trains to Villach were frequent and whether this Railjet was the right connection or not, his fare wouldn't have long to wait. Sweeney knew because he'd checked the timetable before leaving home. He could only respond to the man's dubious reassurance by saying, '*Danke*'.

A few moments later they pulled up at the rank outside the Hauptbahnhof. When he'd paid the fare with a decent tip, Sweeney was obliged to act as if the Railjet was indeed his connection. The driver stood by the door of his cab and, smiling reassuringly, gestured with his hand to prompt him to hurry. Sweeney gave him the thumbs up and entered at a jog through the automatic glass doors of the main concourse, awkwardly pulling his case along behind him. When out of sight, he stopped and glanced at the large electronic timetable over the platform entrance, flashing lights indicating imminent departures. There was no sign of a Railjet to Villach. However, there was a regional train in twenty minutes and he didn't mind the wait.

. . . .

After buying a ticket from an automated machine he took in the surroundings. He couldn't remember much about Klagenfurt Hauptbahnhof and the building had obviously undergone significant modernization since he'd last been here. He knew the tourist guidebooks highlighted the impressive cubist frescoes in the main hall by Giselbert Hoke. They were striking, distinctive, and certainly not what you would expect from the station's dull, brown, barrack-like exterior. However, it was not the Hoke frescoes that captured his attention, but *Bäckerei Wienerroither*, running the length of the opposite side of the busy concourse. The brightly lit, striking yellow presence said as much about Austria as any artwork could. For if Hoke represented the creative side of Carinthian life, *Bäckerei Wienerroither* embodied its pleasurable every day. The range of delicacies under glass at the counter, or stacked high on shelving behind, was spectacular – breads, all varieties of filled rolls, pastries and cakes. As he strolled by the counter, Sweeney recited to himself their names like a found poem – *Polsterzipf, Reindling, Schaumrollen, Krapfen, Nussschrecken, Zwetschgenfleck* – and there was a café attached, he remembered there was always a café attached. He hadn't eaten anything substantial all day, and the blend of sweet, savoury, and buttery, as well as the aroma of fresh coffee, almost overwhelmed his senses. He was tempted to choose something, but decided against it.

His immediate objective was the *Tabak* directly across from *Bäckerei Wienerroither*. He never smoked cigarettes at home, disliking English brands, their taste and aftertaste. But there'd been one brand of cigarette he did smoke when in Austria, the German brand *HB*. He'd only smoked because all Carinthians seemed to do so and he'd wanted to fit in (however impossible and however absurd the wish seemed to him today). He couldn't remember why he'd chosen *HB*. Perhaps he'd seen someone else with a packet, it was the name he'd remembered and had known what to ask for. These cigarettes had become an integral part of his Austrian past, his memory associated them with pleasure and he considered it a memory worth testing. At his age, he thought, what had he got to lose? In the *Tabak* a colourful array of brands was displayed openly behind the counter. At home all cigarettes were hidden behind sliding closed screens, a bit like the old days (or so he'd been told) when gentlemen would be invited behind a curtain to browse pornographic magazines. At the counter he asked the young female assistant for a pack of *HB*.

'Normal or king size?' she asked in German.

'Normal, please, and can I have a lighter as well?' He'd had to search his mental dictionary to find the German word for lighter. *Zünder* was what emerged from the depths and, whether it was the correct word or not, the assistant understood what he'd meant. It was his first linguistic success of the day. She picked one from a rack, tested the flame and put it on top of the cigarettes. Sweeney handed over the cash, took his change, and in German said, 'thank you and goodbye'. 'Enjoy', the woman replied in English. It was a common response at home and Sweeney disliked it. But here it was different and he considered it a courtesy.

Outside the station was a *Raucherzone*, a smoking area, only a few steps away from the entrance, which was nothing more than a metal dustbin with a cover to extinguish butts. He opened the pack, eased out a first cigarette with his fingernails, put it to his lips and lit up. The first drag was cautious and he experienced a brief light-headedness. The second he inhaled deeply and exhaled slowly. Remarkably, after all these years, it seemed natural. Leaning casually on the handle of his case, he observed locals going by to catch their trains. He smoked the cigarette to the filter and, when he stubbed it out, decided to light another and linger longer.

Darkness had fallen rapidly, the street lights were glowing yellow in the still night, yet it remained warm. He made out across the road on the corner of the square one of the cultural attractions of Klagenfurt, the *Musil Haus* and it being Austria, Sweeney wasn't certain if it was a museum with a coffee house or a coffee house with a museum. As a student he'd tried to read the three volumes of Robert Musil's *The Man without Qualities*. He'd enjoyed the first book, less so the second and, possibly like many, had never made it to the end of the third. Perhaps the failure was appropriate enough for Musil had failed to finish his own trilogy. Sweeney remembered Ulrich, the main character in the trilogy, had taken '*ein Urlaub von seinem Leben*', a holiday from his life, to gain a new angle of vision on the world. In Sweeney's conceit, he was engaged on the same enterprise.

He had sympathy for Ulrich's character albeit he considered himself more a man without direction – more accurately, he considered himself a man reluctant to exert his will and consequently allowing himself to drift with events, accommodating to circumstances, adapting to realities without thinking it possible – or worthwhile – to act upon things and change them. His ever-present temptation was to avoid rather than to confront, evasiveness he'd learned to conceal, usually successfully, behind a front of graciousness and civility. Strategies of avoidance were therapeutic, a form of practical self-help, keeping clear of situations which invited stress and dodging black clouds of emotional pressure. Understanding himself (or believing he did) was not necessarily sufficient protection against the world. There were times when seeing the traps, understanding the difficulties and anticipating the painful consequences, his defences had been disarmed by lack of resolution and on these occasions he could only despise himself for being weak. He knew that masterful inactivity, accomplished evasion, served him well until he was compelled to make a choice and in those crucial moments he would doubt his judgment. In that regard, he was certainly an Ulrich, yet for now, at least, he was happy to dismiss such concerns, for here was a labyrinth of manners and emotions which could only depress him if he entered. He consoled himself with the thought that smoking would be part of his 'holiday from life' and intended to enjoy it.

Musil had only been born here, but Klagenfurt was claiming him as its number one son and in an age of cultural tourism, why shouldn't it? Sceptical of post imperial Austria's 'culture of cultural politics', Musil had believed it was the German language which gave provinces like Carinthia access to the wider world and not anything as nebulous as 'Austrian-ness'. If Musil were alive today, Sweeney wondered, would he be happy with the cultural politics of the *Musil Haus?* By the entrance was a photographic mural and it amused Sweeney to see the great man appeared to be wearing what looked like a dark, heavy, Italian-styled luxury overcoat and looking very much like an undertaker. He noticed too that Klagenfurt had reclaimed Ingeborg Bachmann, her portrait on the wall beside Musil's. Bachmann had once written, '*Man musste überhaupt ein Fremder sein, um einen Ort wie Klagenfurt länger al seine Stunde erträglich zu finden*' – you need to be a foreigner to find a place like Klagenfurt bearable for more than an hour. She'd been convinced, if you got away, you could not – and would not want to – come back. He supposed Bachmann had every right to say she'd no idea what people in Carinthia had to be proud of or why they would want to attract the world's attention. She was from here and she had got away. Yet she had returned, to Annabichel, to the cemetery, not for an hour, but for all eternity. Klagenfurt had forgiven her everything and he visualized her in the café with a strong black coffee and, between smoking cigarettes and eating cake, thinking of escape once more. Sweeney didn't intend to spend any longer than was necessary in Klagenfurt either. He finished his second cigarette, headed through the concourse and onto the platform to catch his train to Villach.

The regional connection from Friesach pulled in on time – sleek, red, modern, aerodynamic and almost empty. Sweeney got aboard, slung his case into the overhead shelving and took a seat by the window. No other passengers were in his carriage. Leaving Klagenfurt, the train skirted the Wörthersee, lights from houses and hotels fronting the lake shimmering across its dark, untroubled surface. On the summit of the Pyramidenkögel, the tower, shining in the night, reminded him of a flaring beacon. He had read it described as a '*Himmelsleiter aus gestapelten Ellipsen*' – a ladder reaching to Heaven by elliptical stacking, art and engineering connecting Carinthians to God. He appreciated this conception. Automatic bilingual announcements informed him regularly of '*nächster Halt*/next stop', a female voice announcing the name of each station – Krumpendorf, Pörtschach, Töschling, Velden, Lind-Rosegg, Föderlach. He liked the cheery, positive inflection her voice gave to each name as if to say, 'Here is your station. Your journey's over. Aren't you glad to be home?' On this particular train no one got off and no one got on. Then he heard Villach Seebach, finally Villach Hauptbahnhof – *Endstation* – and the female voice told him the train would go no further. He took down his case and stepped off. He had arrived – again.

. . . .

Outside the station he crossed the road on the Bahnhofplatz, passing waiting taxis as well as town service buses, their engines running and doors open. On the square, two policemen in conversation were leaning against a squad car while late shoppers bustled in and out of a *Billa* supermarket. Further along, a large neon sign announced Hotel City where he had booked a room for the next few days.

The reception area of the hotel was a bright, if confined, space. To the right of the entrance was a lift, before it a couch on which had been set a number of silver embroidered cushions. Before it on a glass table were scattered newspapers and glossy magazines. To the left was a curved wooden counter fronted with decorative padding and behind it, at a desk facing out into the square, sat a young woman in her early twenties consulting a large computer screen. The receptionist was dressed in a white blouse and dark trousers which Sweeney assumed was the hotel's uniform, for on the back of her chair hung a matching dark jacket. Swivelling around, she rose to welcome Sweeney, smiled at him and spread her hands out on the counter. She had straw blonde, shoulder-length hair and a fresh, round face with the milky complexion of youthful health. He knew everyone in the tourist industry spoke excellent English, but Sweeney was determined to make another effort with his sketchy German.

'*Guten Abend. Ich habe eine Reservierung*'.

'*Die Name, bitte?*'

He slid his passport across the counter, opened at the appropriate page. Seeing the passport and his name, the receptionist immediately spoke to him in English. 'Ah, yes. Professor Sweeney. Welcome to Hotel City. You are staying with us for four nights, yes?'

It seemed absurd to answer in German so he replied, 'Yes.'

'Have you stayed with us before?'

'No.'

'In that case, let me say we are delighted you have chosen Hotel City.' Her expression of welcome looked genuine. If the words were formulaic, probably learned by rote at some training course, nevertheless he willingly embraced her unforced charm.

His compatriot, Oliver Goldsmith, had once written of 'the rude Carinthian boor/against the houseless stranger shuts the door'. Goldsmith's intention in the poem had not been to condemn the foreigner, but to challenge the 'patriot's boast' that wherever you go the best country is always one's own. Though patriots flatter, Goldsmith had written, the wise traveller will acknowledge the world's blessings are more equally shared. 'As different good, by art and nature given/to different nations makes their blessing even'. Sweeney was sure there were plenty of boors in Villach – they were everywhere and certainly he'd

encountered enough of them at home – but his friendly receptionist at Hotel City wasn't one of them.

'Please can I have your home address here, your nationality and your signature here … and here.' She tapped a finger
at the relevant boxes on the hotel registration form. When
Sweeney had signed, she handed over his key, telling him the
room number and the times for breakfast. The receptionist
shuffled various papers into order, stapled them together and
slid the passport across to him. 'Is there anything else I can
help you with, Professor Sweeney?' Her expression was open
and inviting, her steady gaze prompting a response on his part.
Out of politeness he wanted to say something further and to
enjoy her charm a little longer, but his imagination failed him.

'No. Thank you. I think you've explained everything,' he said
and was about to turn away when out of nowhere the German
word for lift – *Aufzug* – popped into his head. 'Oh, can you
tell me where the lift is?' he asked in German, knowing exactly
where it was.

The receptionist seemed pleased, but equally amused. Maybe
'lift' or 'elevator' was the term German speakers used today, an
international term, and '*Aufzug*' could be a quaint anachronism?
He'd noticed already English was everywhere, written and spoken, much more so than he remembered. The young woman
pointed to the '*Aufzug*' and Sweeney pretended to notice it for
the first time. But she continued to speak in English, 'The lift
is there, Professor. You are in Room 506', she repeated. 'It's on
the top floor. I hope you enjoy your time with us in Villach'
and Sweeney liked to imagine by 'us' she meant the people of
Villach, not just the staff at the hotel.

He pulled his bag across to the lift, pressed the button to
ascend, and the sliding doors opened straight away. Before entering, he looked back to the desk, but the young woman had returned already to the computer screen, her attention re-absorbed

by whatever task Sweeney's arrival had interrupted. He pushed the button for the fifth floor. The lift was enclosed in a transparent glass capsule, probably a feature of a recent renovation. He looked out over the Bahnhofplatz. The taxis were silent in their rank, one remaining bus with a couple of passengers on board continued to idle; the lights in the window of the café on the corner were lit, some customers sitting or standing at tables on the pavement under its awning; but pedestrians were scarce on the square, the policemen had gone and few cars passed along the street in front of the station.

Hotel City designated Room 506 an 'economy single' and, opening the door, Sweeney found a neat bathroom to the right of the entrance beside which was a built-in wardrobe and a personal safe. Further along the wall was a mock leather sofa. To the right was a single bed, above which at the far end of the room hung a flat screen television. Against the window looking onto the Bahnhofplatz stood a writing desk, on it a metal reading lamp and before it a cushioned chair. Sweeney deposited his luggage and shoulder bag, looked around at everything a second time and was happy to settle for the unpretentious comforts he found here. Everything suited and he was sure the room would become his retreat.

Fatigued, he'd passed the point where hunger was insistent. By now he had no desire to go out and find somewhere and something to eat. He lifted his case onto the luggage bench beside the wardrobe, unzipped it and searched inside. He'd been given a cheese sandwich on the *Lufthansa* flight from Dublin to Vienna which he hadn't eaten, but stowed away. He lifted it out from where it was wedged between socks and shirts. It would do him. On the small fridge he saw a tray with teabags, coffee and a kettle. He selected an English breakfast tea and boiled some water in the kettle. As the tea was brewing, he switched on the television and flicked through a number of channels.

He could find only advertisements – smiling families at their 'bio' breakfasts, satisfied shoppers selecting their food from supermarket aisles stocked with 'only the best quality', excited youths in love with their mobile phones, sleek cars driven by smug and equally sleek men and women who seemed to have the roads to themselves, pharmacists in long white coats holding some preparation for indigestion – all very familiar and yet at the same time distinctively Austrian. And what appeared to him distinctive was the cleanliness, the Alpine scenery, the perfection of the breakfast, lunch or dinner table, but, above all, the brightness, the sharpness of colours. Teeth looked whiter, the skies bluer, the cars redder, and the vegetables greener. His television at home was far from the latest model he'd admit, but unless a previous guest in Room 506 had changed the contrast settings, the difference was striking. Since he was last here, had there been some aesthetic shift towards brilliant hues? He couldn't remember Austrian life being so vivid before.

He searched for the correct word to describe the impression these advertisements made and the first which came to mind was '*Kitsch*'. But he considered the one he was probably looking for was *Gemütlich*, an ordered cosiness, everything in its proper place, a material world designed for human contentment and by human art arranged accordingly. He switched off the adverts, put the remote control on the table, grabbed his overcoat from where he'd tossed it on the bed and hung it up. If the weather remained as warm as today's he wouldn't need it again and the prospect of dispensing with his undertaker's attire cheered him. When he'd finished the sandwich – it had turned out to be surprisingly tasty – and drunk his cup of tea, it was time for a final cigarette before bed.

Hotel City was quiet. When he opened his door and walked along the corridor he couldn't hear any sound coming from other rooms, no muffled advertising chatter. Nor could he hear his own footsteps for the carpeting absorbed the sound of his tread. The hotel didn't feel ghostly. It was Sweeney who felt spectral, the light, insubstantial sensation one has after a long day's travelling, when mental and physical energies are spent. Back in the lobby, the receptionist looked up from her computer and, anticipating a query, stood and moved to the counter. Her expression was once more encouraging, her large eyes inviting a request, smiling in anticipation of Sweeney saying something, whether remarkably interesting or remarkably banal, it didn't seem to matter. But he could think of nothing. All he could do was to show her the packet of *HB* in one hand, the lighter in the other and indicate the door. Her look conveyed a conspiratorial understanding, a slightly apologetic face as if to say, I know you need to satisfy your habit, I'm sorry the hotel is smoke free and you have to go outside. Sweeney would have liked to explain his smoking wasn't a need, but a choice, and she shouldn't be apologetic because he preferred to smoke outside. Even if he'd had the right words, likely the receptionist would have seen no reason why he should need to explain himself. She kept those soft eyes fixed on him and, as he went past, he made a slightly deferential bow. He wasn't sure to what he was deferring; whether, as a stranger and a guest, he was deferring to her language and nationality or whether, as a much older man, he was deferring to her youth and vitality.

To one side of the entrance he discovered a tall metal table with a circular top, like those found in bars. On it, an empty cup with dregs of coffee had been forgotten or abandoned, around its rim a faint trace of red lipstick. Beside the table was a waist-high metal bin, its top filled with sand, a thicket of cigarette butts planted there. The hotel must have been much busier than it seemed. Sweeney lit a cigarette and, resting his elbows on the table, blew out the smoke, watching it slowly drift upwards and vanish into the darkness. Have I any right to be here, having been away for so long, he asked himself. Asking the question was meaningless, he knew, and yet it was a question that he thought required some answer. Maybe if Villach had been the place of his birth and he'd rejected it (as Bachman had rejected Klagenfurt), a *Heimat* he could no longer tolerate, which was stifling him or destroying him (the subject of so many Austrian novels he'd read recently), perhaps the question of 'right' would be appropriate. None of these things applied to him. He'd felt at home in Villach, unable to erase traces of affection still carried and his affinities of imagined adoption remained strong. More importantly, the memory of Sonja was stronger still. The comfort such feelings of connection brought him was qualified immediately by the fatalism which accompanied him in life, whispering, 'If you do seek atonement, prepare for disappointment.' Nevertheless, he sensed the stillness around him tonight was benign. What connected Sweeney to past and present, enchanted and real, mysterious and familiar was half memory, half dream and in his present ruminative mood he wasn't sure which things were dream and which were memory. Echoes and fantasy, fantasy and echoes, all mixed together.

Philip Larkin had written of his time in Belfast how his strangeness had made sense, how being elsewhere had underwritten his existence. Sweeney had felt the same about Villach, the strangeness of the language, of the customs, of the humour, of the climate, of the town's location, had made him feel self-aware in a way he'd never experienced before. He'd relished those different smells, tastes, atmospheres, sights and sounds, sensory impressions which appeared to validate his individuality and his difference. You could say he'd never been so alive (and he was tempted to add, 'or since'). And in a curious reversal (again like Larkin) he'd sometimes resented the way in which the conventions of home absorbed his existence. If his sceptical voice asked, but surely this elsewhere could have been anywhere, he would reply, yes, of course it could have been. But it hadn't been *merely* anywhere. It had been here, it had been Villach. He had none of his usual hesitation indulging the lyrical side of his mind and to imagine Villach poetically.

He glanced into the hotel and saw the receptionist concentrating on some paperwork. He looked back across the square and glimpsed a dark-haired young man in T-shirt and jeans entering the Hauptbahnhof. This young man could have been me once, Sweeney thought, and he recalled an experience of one summer's night. It was only the briefest encounter, yet it had remained with him ever since.

. . . .

It had been his first time staying with Sonja and her family. One night it was so hot he'd found it impossible to rest. Part of the reason was he had begun sleeping with her. They had behaved chastely when he'd first arrived, keeping to separate rooms and Sweeney, whatever his desires, had no wish either to disturb the harmony of the family home or to outrage parental propriety. In the end it had been Sonja who'd taken the initiative and her parents hadn't objected whatever they may have believed privately. Morality had found it impossible to resist the argument of the age. 'Look, mother,' he'd imagined Sonja saying, 'it's the 1980s and not the 1950s.' Later he'd come to a different conclusion. As he got to know them better, he was convinced her parents had never expected things should be any different, human nature being what it is, men and women being what they are.

In their shared bedroom Sweeney and Sonja became entangled in gentle pleasure and whispered tenderness, for they hadn't lost all consideration for their elders. It was physical and emotional intensity hitherto strange to him and he could never have guessed the grace it brought. But that night his body had been defeated by the relentless summer heat and his longing to remain close to her had been undone by insufferable restlessness. The bedclothes had been tossed aside, they'd sprawled apart in their nakedness, but for Sweeney sleep would not come. He'd felt his sighing and turning was frustrating her, no matter how often she would touch his arm and mumble, 'Poor Eddie, you're really suffering', before dozing off again. Finally, she'd raised herself on her elbow and sighed, 'You stay here and try to get some peace. I'll go sleep on the balcony.'

'No, no', he'd mumbled, 'it's your room. I'll go out to the balcony.' He'd never slept outdoors in his life before, but judged himself honour bound to make the sacrifice.

'Don't be silly. I've done it many times. It was an adventure when I was a child. I'll lie on the lounger out there. I'll put on a nightgown if you're worried about a peeping Tom.' But she hadn't risen. She'd fallen back on the bed as if the effort to speak had exhausted her.

'I won't hear of it,' he'd declared firmly and out of character. 'It will be a novelty. And there's a first time for everything.' He hated using banalities, didn't mean any of it, but couldn't think of anything else to say.

She'd turned to lie on her front, raised her hand a fraction and he'd heard a faint, '*Schatzi*, darling', but she'd fallen asleep again almost instantly.

He'd got out of bed, put on his underclothes, taken one of the sheets lying on the floor, opened her bedroom door and tiptoed out along the corridor to the wooden balcony which overlooked the garden. He'd considered the space, contemplated the lounger and decided it might be better to take a walk to get some air instead. He'd gone back to his own bedroom, put on a T-shirt, jeans, a pair of trainers and, careful not to disturb anyone, had left by the side door. Akko, Sonja's German

The First Day

Shepherd, flat out on his blankets in the hallway and usually alert to every movement in the house, hadn't bothered to lift his head, but only followed Sweeney's exit with his eyes, the dog sensing there'd be no threats about on such a hot night. He had used the key Sonja's parents had given him to let himself out. 'You can come and go as you please,' Sonja's father had told him. 'Thank you, that's very considerate of you', Sweeney had replied, delighted at the trust placed in him.

It was around two in the morning. He'd walked from Sonja's house in the Perau district by the only route he knew – towards the railway station along the Ossiacherzeile, about a mile across the Stadtpark and through the centre of town. The sultry air had been thick, but sensuous, like an opiate taking him outside time altogether, the darkness almost erotic. There'd been perfect quiet, no one else on the streets, nothing seemed to stir and there was no traffic, not even a taxi. By the time he'd reached the station his T-shirt was soaked with sweat and he'd gone to one of the outer platforms seeking whatever cool air might drift from the mountains along the railway track. But there had been none. A small maintenance crew, their overalls rolled to the waist, their white singlets greasy, hard hats in hand, wiping their brows had been discussing the night's work detail. One or two uniformed railway staff could be seen, trying to look occupied and Sweeney, finding no relief from the heat, had decided he should go back. Just then the Mostar-Dalmacija sleeper traveling from Sarajevo had pulled in on its journey to Stuttgart. Its arrival had been the occasion for the railway staff to walk briskly as the train came to a juddering halt, taking charge of the loading and unloading of trolleys on the platform. The livery of the Yugoslav rail carriages was grey and light blue and the grime of the journey had been thickly smeared along their sides. The windows were curtained in faded brown fabric, but no passenger appeared to stir.

Then he'd noticed one blind pull back hesitantly, a pair of eyes peering out, confused and searching. It was a young woman. In her face he'd seen as much need of undisturbed rest as his probably showed and he'd recognized the weariness of a journey which must have seemed interminable. Once the woman had noticed the blue metal plaque on a pillar announcing 'Villach', her confusion seemed to disappear and her face had relaxed. The train had reached Austria, another border crossed, another country reached and, as she'd looked along the platform, her gaze fell on Sweeney, his presence surprising her. He wasn't railway staff, he wasn't traveling, but was standing still, his gaze fixed upon her. She had narrowed her eyes as if trying to make sure this person existed, that he'd not been an apparition. As Sweeney had come alongside her window, a platform width between them, her eyes widened again, but she didn't pull down the blind. Instead, she'd smiled shyly, likely aware he'd witnessed her initial confusion and shared the intimacy of her uncertainty. He'd smiled back and, thinking it insufficient, given an equally shy wave of greeting. The young woman had pushed aside the fabric a little further and waved back more confidently. He could see she was lying prone on a bunk bed, but had no idea if she was travelling alone or not. It hadn't mattered anyway, for only he and the woman seemed alive at that moment. They'd held each other's gaze, naturally and without embarrassment, an intense connection, for how long he couldn't say.

There'd been a jolting of carriages as the locomotive engaged, a metallic grinding as the brakes released and the train began to move on once more. If he'd been a true romantic Sweeney would have run beside the face at the window, to show what an impression she'd made on him. But he wasn't that sort of romantic. Instead he'd stood where he was and kept his eyes fixed on hers as she waved again, this time a wave of farewell. The curtain had fallen back into place and the express had been swallowed by the night, a single red light on the rear carriage marking its disappearance. Was it in such brief encounters, in such tentative recognitions, in such passing kindnesses to and recognition of strangers, a life is made? Did the woman recall the encounter as he did and did she ever think about the person alone on the platform as the Mostar-Dalmacija had made its scheduled stop in Villach? Had she held on, like he had done, to a fleeting moment, cherishing the bright fool's gold of the past? And there his memory failed. He had no recollection of walking back to Perau, of going into the house or of where he'd slept, all of those things having faded from his mind. He'd never mentioned anything to Sonja, considering she might think him guilty of betrayal.

Proust had written of the girls he saw, all of one essence. He didn't love any of them in particular, loving them all in general. The most exclusive love for a person, Proust wrote, is usually the love of something else. Sweeney had been impressed by the idea when he'd read it. He supposed at first sight these lines could be taken as a description of undifferentiated desire or a libertine's charter. That's not how he understood it. For him it revealed the affection – perhaps the affectation – of innocence. It was exclusive love indeed because it belonged only to the imagination and to no reality. And it was the love of something else too, the melancholy of possibility unfulfilled and, sweetest of all, the uncomplicated fantasy of a romance which never had been nor ever could be. The other's absence contained every possibility, and every desire, imaginable. The puritan would deem the thought a sin and Sweeney's unwillingness to mention the girl on the train to Sonja was almost an admission of its truth. Almost – for to think that way would be to feel guilty about life itself and why carry a burden for sins never committed? To question the unfulfilled temptations of his younger self seemed absurd, all the more so since he would be equally tempted today and even less likely to respond. He wasn't sure if there could be any joy without poignancy and he was haunted by these idle speculations which often came late at night accompanied by remorse for real wrongs he had committed. Such laments sounded like the song of a wandering Sweeney grown old, a self-pitying Sweeney, and he decided he was too tired to make sense of such things tonight, if he ever could.

He finished his cigarette and added the butt to those in the ashcan. When he went by the reception desk the young woman was busy on the telephone and she didn't bother to look up. Tomorrow he would meet Sonja and he needed to rest.

The Second Day

The Second Day

S weeney awoke and looked at his watch on the bedside table. It was six a.m. He would give it another hour. He'd dreamt he was on a train travelling through the night. A conductor, young, female, with a fresh round face and soft eyes, had asked for his ticket. He'd handed it to her and, as she looked it over, he'd said, 'I am going to Villach'. When she'd told him he'd taken the wrong connection, he'd jumped onto an empty platform as the train stopped in the middle of no-where. When it pulled away again, the face of another woman appeared at a carriage window, smiling at him. She'd waved and he'd run after the train with a mixture of joy and panic, waving back. The panic had awakened him with a momentary sense of emptiness. Sweeney had no need of someone to interpret his dreams. He wasn't very interested in dreams, considering them all too obvious replays of things he'd experienced or thought the day before, in this regard definitely a Frank Bascombe. It was his reality which he thought needed interpretation for reality confused him more.

Normally he was restless in bed but he'd slept solidly on his back for about eight hours, hands folded over his chest, the way he imagined they would lay him out in the coffin. It was a vision which instinctively made him turn onto his side. The faint beams of early morning were filtering through a small gap where the heavy curtains met and the room began to take shape – the desk, the chair, the lamp, the television on the wall. He noticed for the first time a framed picture hanging on the wall opposite. It was a stylised map of Villach, the townscape as dreamscape, its streets and alleys patterned like an enchanted network of pathways. A good depiction of Villach, *his* Villach, a place he had imagined for so long.

. . . .

A few years before he had become, earlier than expected, Emeritus Professor of English, a polite term to describe being surplus to university requirements. When asked at first by the curious, 'What does Emeritus mean?', his answer had been 'retired' but he'd come to think his response too abrupt and too simple. As a student he'd enjoyed Disraeli's novels, their fantastic flamboyance and cynical wit and, like most academics, once found, Sweeney could never let a good line go to waste. He'd amended his answer accordingly. 'Emeritus', he'd say, 'is a bit like Disraeli's description of being elevated to the House of Lords. After a lifetime in politics, he said it was like finding himself in the Elysian Fields.' If his questioner had given a knowing laugh, he would leave things there, both of them sharing a pleasantry confirming their common erudition. If there was a look of puzzlement, he'd explain after an appropriate pause for effect, 'In other words, people assume you're dead.' At this point there would normally be a polite laugh which Sweeney hoped was an acknowledgement of his cleverness, not his too-clever-by-half-ness. After a while he got tired of the witticism and reverted to saying, 'retired'. He'd decided his Disraelian explanation appeared overly defensive, the mark of an old pedant perhaps, hinting at disappointment and resentment when actually he felt the opposite, positive and grateful.

The university had treated him well and allowed him to keep most of his former privileges. He simply no longer had any of the old responsibilities. And when people asked him if he missed his colleagues he could give an honest answer, 'No. I don't.' He saw no reason to indulge any myth others might have about academic life. He'd never fooled himself that the accidental collection of colleagues constituting 'school' or 'faculty' had ever equated with friendship, even if most of them had been congenial enough. And though academics liked to talk of collegiality, in truth he'd rarely experienced it. Others hadn't been as a rule inconsiderate or unhelpful, it was merely they'd been happier doing their own thing – as had he. Collegiality for Sweeney had meant a respectful and aloof *modus vivendi*, one not demanding of others in case he might be demanded of. He liked to think colleagues took it for granted that as a Philip Larkin scholar he had adopted the poet's discrete, if polite, detachment and assumed his preference for privacy had become second nature, artifice as well as nature. He expected many of his non-university acquaintances looked upon his career as one of leisure as well as good fortune (a view Sweeney happened to share) and suspected they wished a little *Schadenfreude* at his expense. But in his case there'd been no existential crisis. It may have been true of others but not of him. Actually, he'd been astonished to find his world of work – no, the term was insufficient, his way of life – could be dispensed with so swiftly and so easily. Yet when he was replying honestly, his expressions of equanimity didn't seem to persuade those he told. He could detect scepticism in their surprised (or was it disappointed) response of, 'Really?'

It was true, nonetheless. He'd discovered no need for Larkin's 'old toad' of work to avoid thinking about total extinction (at worst) or how to fill in time (at best) on his way down 'Cemetery

Road'. Once Sweeney had stepped outside his academic circle, whatever spell it may have cast before, whatever magic it may once have possessed, had been broken. He was good at stepping away and not only from things but also from people. He'd joked in the past about how academics were best trained for redundancy since the distinction between work and leisure was often notional. In his case, the joke was truer than he had expected. Actually, he been made aware of the signals he should recognise when his time came by a conversation which had taken place some years before.

· · · · · · · · · ·

It had been during another literary conference in London. Sweeney had been able to spend some time with an old friend, another Professor of English and another Larkin scholar, Alan Brown, who taught at a university in the north of England. They'd known each other from their graduate days, kept in touch regularly over the years and had shared more than professional interests. His friend bore a striking resemblance to Larkin, tall, angular, domed bald head, large thick glasses which accentuated his shrewd eyes. But he was unlike Larkin in voice and accent; not soft spoken, but booming; and not middle class and middle England, but working class and Cockney. Their humble backgrounds had originally cemented camaraderie amongst a graduate body which, in those days, had been generally more affluent and privileged than they. It hadn't been inverted snobbery more a case of shared experiences and common references promoting unspoken mutual support. Unlike most relationships in Sweeney's life this friendship had endured, albeit they rarely met outside conferences and the occasional public lecture, since both preferred a light touch of association. At the conference in London, after a day of papers, discussions, and what is politely known as 'networking', they'd escaped to a pub nearby, noisy at that hour, very matey and loud in an unmistakeably English fashion, but out of the way and, most importantly, one which hadn't been discovered by other academics. Having had enough of fool research, they were glad to stand easy at the bar, letting the currents of the city's energy flow around them. Their second pint had been ordered, a ritual which normally indicated a transition from immediate satisfaction to a more ruminative state. Brown had taken a healthy mouthful and swallowed appreciatively. He'd tilted his glass slightly to inspect the colour of the beer, appearing about to deliver a comment on its quality. What he'd said was, 'You know, Eddie, I'm thinking seriously of retiring.'

At first Sweeney thought he'd misheard because a heavy set man in a pin stripe suit standing close beside them had shouted his order across the bar. He'd asked, 'Did you say retire? *You* are going to retire, you mean?'

'Yes', Brown had replied, setting the glass on his beer mat, slowly, deliberately, as if the precise location had been essential to its stability.

Sweeney had looked at him but couldn't determine if his friend was being serious or not. At first he'd imagined the re- mark to be an act colleagues often performed – threatening to leave, without being serious, something the universities' union attributed to 'low morale'. Sweeney's own name for it was 'ir- ritable growl syndrome', a mood, a rumbling of unspecific dis- content, a condition, but one rarely fatal – and quitting your job when you didn't have to he considered to be on a par with killing yourself to make a point. And few academics in his ex- perience were so demoralised they would consider giving up a good salary on a point of principle. Whenever the topic arose, Sweeney would mention the film *Liberal Arts*, which, it turned out, hardly anyone had ever heard of, let alone seen. The film is set in a very pleasant upstate campus and tells the story of a well-regarded history professor who resolves to retire because he's at odds with the educational values of the new Dean. He makes his announcement with firm determination but almost overnight realises he's made a mistake, has been too hasty, has to admit how much of his life and meaning are bound up with the college. He tries to withdraw the resignation but his pleading is rejected. He's become the past already and leaves the campus a broken man. Sweeney considered it a cautionary tale – don't make unnecessary dramatic gestures and, above all, never believe you are indispensable.

'Is the bureaucracy driving you mad, my friend?' Sweeney had joked, taking a quick drink of his beer, preparing himself to deliver another sermon on the moral tale in *Liberal Arts*.

'No, I've taken a leaf out of your book and don't take much notice of it.'

'But why do you want to retire? I find it hard to believe.'

'The truth is, Eddie, I've no one left to talk to.'

Sweeney hadn't expected that line. 'What do you mean? Have you fallen out with everyone? Have they finally boycotted an old reactionary like you?' The 'like you' had been an expression of solidarity, the 'and me' left unsaid.

'No, no, I manage to get on fine with most of them. You know Sally Lee is no longer with us and David Alcorn has gone to Durham?' Sweeney acknowledged another two members of their like-minded community. 'We'd developed a kind of old fogey support group. Now they're both gone it's literally true. I *don't* have anyone left to talk to. Of the traditional English Lit people, I'm the only one left. The younger ones aren't interested in my sort of thing any longer. They've no interest in me either, for that matter.' Yes, Sweeney knew all too well, if only abstractly. He'd sympathised, was going to say something supportive, something Larkinesque, perhaps one of the poet's best put downs, but his friend had got there before him. 'When

I get invited to their departmental seminars, or asked to attend a talk by one of their visiting speakers, I can hear Larkin saying, "In a pig's arse, friend". It's exactly what I feel like replying too.'

Sweeney had laughed. That was about right and he'd taken another sip of his beer. *Liberal Arts* could wait. 'Don't get me wrong,' Brown continued. 'Like Larkin, I'm too polite – no, maybe I'm too much of a coward – to ignore their invitations. I usually make an effort to go along – not that they'd show much interest in anything I would organise.' It had been clear from the way he'd mentioned 'anything I would organise' that his friend never did organise anything these days and Sweeney had detected in the tone the measure of what being demoralised really sounded like. 'I'm like the Fred MacMurray character in *Double Indemnity*. You know, when he first meets Mrs Dietrichson and begins his pitch to sell her car insurance? And she replies her husband could probably get as good or better deal with the *Automobile Club?*' *Double Indemnity* was one of Sweeney's favourite films. He knew most of the scenes and much of the dialogue by heart. As Brown had spoken he'd pictured Barbara Stanwyck in her silk dress and his imagination lingered on the long stockinged legs and silver ankle bracelet. He could see MacMurray in his suit, tie and hat, the slick representative of the *Pacific All Risk Insurance Company*. 'Do you remember what the MacMurray character says?' Brown asked.

He did. Sweeney could recount every word of the MacMurray and Stanwyck dialogue but he feigned ignorance for his friend's sake.

'He says, "I never knock the other guy's product". I've always loved that line. It says everything dismissive you need to say without having to say anything dismissive at all.'

The actual line was 'the other fellow's merchandise', but what was the point of pedantry at a time like this? Instead, Sweeney laughed, 'I like it. It's a great line.'

'So you see what I mean? It's not I don't respect their' …
Brown had searched for the appropriate word while taking another gulp of beer … 'ability or their "theory", it's only … well,
as I said before, there's no one left to talk to. I feel like I've
become invisible, as if I'm no longer there at all' and his voice
had tailed off as he drained his glass. Sweeney had forgotten
his response but he definitely hadn't resorted to *Liberal Arts*.

Brown did retire early. A few years later he'd published some
of his own poems. His work had been well-received and, remarkably, he'd become something of an overnight literary celebrity. He'd sent Sweeney signed copies of his slim volumes (it
was his friend who'd emphasised the word 'slim') and Sweeney
had been impressed, for the poems were subtle, original and
not (as he'd feared) Larkin imitations. He'd also heard Brown
late one night on a radio arts programmes and enjoyed hearing
him use again the line from *Double Indemnity*, still incorrectly
quoted. Both of them had kept in touch and only recently he'd
told Sweeney his former colleagues never invited him back to
give a talk or a reading, saying if they ever did ask him, he'd write
back in capital letters, 'In a pig's arse, friend'. If the invitation
ever did arrive, Sweeney knew his friend (like Larkin) would
never do such a thing.

The conversation in the pub that afternoon had stayed with
him. How would he recognise when it was time to go? He trusted recognising the signs – when he had no one left to talk to and
when he felt as if he was no longer there. He wasn't looking for
those signs but when they came, he would be ready for them.
He called this moment *The Omen*. He had been forewarned.

· · · · · · · · · ·

A few years later, Sweeney had been sitting in a meeting of
faculty board. It was the first such meeting he'd attended after

a long sabbatical dedicated to writing yet another book (he'd been good at securing research funding). There was never any reason for him to contribute in these committees unless he had a compelling point to make and he rarely had compelling points to make, or un-compelling ones either. That *was* the point. The trick he'd discovered early in his career was to remain sufficiently alert for the relevant 'peak sound' – in other words, when a matter was raised which would affect him personally. That day, nothing should have disturbed his composure. As the Dean spoke to the tedious issues on the agenda, Sweeney had looked around the room and it struck him that he didn't recognise some of the staff. Things had moved on during his time away.

He'd flicked casually through his papers checking the research profiles of the newcomers and discovered no correspondence between his interests and theirs. Here was an emerging new identity, he'd thought, of personnel and of subject matter, a first sign, and the words 'no one left to talk to' sounded in his head. But when he'd looked around the room again a fatal truth dawned on him. He'd realised he wasn't interested in finding someone to talk to and, rather than feeling worried about becoming marginalised, he'd experienced a feeling of sweet serenity, the contentment of not having to try any longer, an emotion he'd never expected to feel. He recalled the old revolutionary in Joseph Roth's *The Silent Prophet*, enjoying the prospect of life all the more because he'd come to terms with the fact that the world of political intrigue would continue beyond his time and he had ceased already to be a 'contemporary'. It gave him a delicious sense of release, a permission no longer to bother since none of what was being discussed, these details of faculty business, would ever become his concern.

There was a second sign. Towards the end of the meeting, the Dean had come to the normally tricky business of recruiting volunteers for various tiresome administrative duties, at which point people would normally glance at their feet or appear to find something fascinating in their notes. Not on this occasion, for those same new faces willingly had offered their services. The sign hadn't been their unexpected enthusiasm. No, it had been when the Dean's gaze went around the table, Sweeney had his first intimation of Disraeli's Elysian Fields. Her eyes had blanked him as if he wasn't there at all. Sweeney was certain it hadn't been a snub. There had never been any unpleasantness between himself and the Dean, only mutual respect, their dealings marked by exquisite good manners and chivalrous decorum. And there had been a further blanking for she'd looked around the table once more, again with no acknowledgement of his presence. When the meeting was over, he hadn't been sure what his invisibility implied but he was sure it had meant something. Its meaning soon became clear.

Shortly afterwards, the university had circulated across faculties an offer of early retirement. Sweeney was only too happy to accept and, thinking of his old friend Alan Brown, but more importantly thinking of himself, he'd considered the scheme, with its generous pension provisions, to be gifting him three years of life. He'd expressed 'an interest', discussed details with a pleasant woman from Human Resources, made a formal application, the Dean had supported it and the university's Finance Department had done the rest. Within six months, at the end of the second semester, he'd become Emeritus Professor. Sweeney had been in and now he was out. Thereafter he'd talked to no one in the faculty and no one in the faculty had talked to him. No invitations had been sent to him either. Like his old friend, he'd become confined to his own company. Unlike his old friend, he had no cache of poems to publish in order to prove he still existed.

His daughter had been happy when he told her of the university's offer. She'd said to him, 'You can do what the saying

on your office wall has been telling you to do.' She was refer-
ring to a framed postcard with black lettering on a plain white
background. He could never remember where he'd bought it
or where he'd found it. In capitals, in German, was a saying of
Arthur Schopenhauer's. The original saying had been modified
to read, *'Die ersten vierzig Jahre des Lebens sind TEXT der Rest
ist Kommentar'*. The literal translation he'd made for his daughter was, 'The first forty years of your life provide the text and
the rest of your life is commentary on it'. As a child, Sara had
spent many hours in Sweeney's office after crèche and later after
school, and Schopenhauer's words had intrigued her. His translation had made her sob at first because to her it implied he'd
only a few years to live and she hadn't been entirely convinced
by his subsequent reassuring elaboration. Later Sara would ask
Sweeney to tell her stories of those first forty years and she'd
enjoyed adding her own humorous commentary to them. Those
had been good days – she'd been part of his adult world, he'd
appreciated her innocent confidences and he liked to believe
Schopenhauer had played his part in their sentimental bonding.

What Schopenhauer had actually written in *Counsels and
Maxims* was more interesting than the postcard's abridged and
inaccurate summary. His advice concerned how best to live.
We would not feel completely happy, he wrote, if our mental
state was not in accordance with our years. In the first age, our
powers of mind are developing and we tend to look with contempt on experience, but there comes a point when we should
look with respect on yesterday because making sense of our
past is necessary to make sense of ourselves. Sara's suggestion
he had considered a good one. He had time to reflect on his
life – especially the part in Villach about which he suffered his
greatest regrets. His only concern was turning himself into a
relic of that past, a sort of living inversion, his present pale and
shrunken, his past full of colour and fascination, yesterday's

man (for he imagined this is what Disraeli really meant about being in the Elysian Fields).

So he began to read Austrian literature more feverishly than before and in his reading he'd found a phrase of Thomas Bernhard's, one he'd heavily underlined. Bernhard had written that we become contemptible and should be ashamed when we go past the age of fifty. Border crossing weaklings, he'd called those who did. A good joke, but Sweeney had crossed Bernhard's line some time ago without any shame, and anyway, it was a brave new world these days. No longer struggling with the demands of work, people like him were constantly invited to fill their time with 'leisure activities', putting themselves under a different sort of stress. If he'd learnt anything from advertisements on daytime television – now he had time to watch if not to admit to it – here was the insistent message. It taught him a lesson if only so he knew what to avoid. They were directed at an audience of an age fearing or anticipating death and he imagined what poetry Larkin would have made of it. Doing, doing, going, going, here, there, everywhere, travel the world, get up, don't sit, leave, don't stay – you couldn't get more anti-Schopenhauer than this. O Brave New World and in it old people should have no exemption from pleasure, not a moment to sit and think, no crevice of time allowed between life's serial distractions. He wished for an alternative, living cautiously and not rushing, thinking Pascal been right to say all humanity's difficulties stem from an inability to sit quietly in a room. He didn't have a problem being on his own and didn't feel he was missing out by being here and not being there.

Sitting quietly in his room, another of those Austrian books he'd read was Stefan Zweig's novella *Journey into the Past*. Its central character, returning from abroad after many years, discovered time was helpless in the face of feelings, for 'something of me lingers here, something of those years, the whole of me is not yet at home'. Something of Sweeney had lingered in Villach and coming here again he wanted to discover, or to re-discover, feelings he once had, knowing too well it would mean drawing attention to how different he was (or believed he was). His experience with Sonja had been his profoundly intimate 'text', the script of his sentimental education, and he hoped he wouldn't make a fool of himself today when he tried to comment on it.

. . . .

He looked at his watch again. It had turned seven o'clock. He got out of bed, walked to the window and lifted the corner of the thick layered brown curtains. The Bahnhofplatz was busy. Some school kids were mustering to get onto buses, others were getting off buses and he saw lots of good natured jostling in the confusion of young bodies. Across the road at the main entrance to the railway station small knots of passengers stood by their cases, checking once more their tickets to Vienna, Salzburg, Rome or Venice. Near them a few solitary smokers hung about looking at their mobile phones before entering the concourse. The square was in shadow still, but above it was an almost perfectly blue sky and behind the station, the green forested hills beyond St Leonhard and Neulandskron were bathed in sunlight. It was that hour when morning gilds the skies, a solace for every awakening heart, and he took the good weather as a positive indication for what was to come. Certainly no need for a 'luxury overcoat with cashmere', no need to arrive for lunch with Sonja looking like an undertaker – or like Robert Musil.

After a shower, Sweeney took the back stairs to the second floor for breakfast. Large windows gave him a view over the jumble of buildings comprising the Villach Brewery, with its old brick chimney and loading yards, to the mountains in the far distance fringing Slovenia. Sweeney stopped and leaned against the sill. The window framed the view like a painting and the tints of the peaks reminded him of a phrase he'd heard years before – angel light. He'd once taken up photography as a hobby, had joined a camera club, thinking it was a way of being artistic since he had no ability as painter. Photography was so much easier, he'd convinced himself, since things had gone digital. He smiled at the memory of how he used to go around with his Nikon camera, taking shots of things from odd angles as if he was being somehow creative. But he'd soon discovered nearly every photograph turned out to be banal and flat. It hadn't only been his lack of ability which made him abandon the Nikon to the back of the hallway cupboard. It had also been photography's distraction. His obsession with image and perspective, he'd concluded, displaced imagination and perception to the focus of a narrow lens. The irony, he explained to himself, was taking pictures of objects meant him no longer seeing them. At least the explanation justified abandoning any pretence to artistic ability and had some merit in being partly true. Angel light was the only term he'd remembered from evenings at the club, a sort of Holy Grail dedicated members spent their lives searching for. They couldn't tell what angel light meant, they could only try to show it, and what they could show was only an imperfect representation, a truth they'd been honest to admit. This morning Sweeney was tempted to capture what he saw on his mobile phone, but decided to leave the image to his imagination. He believed that's where angel light should properly stay.

The breakfast room was large, open-planned and most of the tables were unoccupied. If there had been a morning rush, he'd obviously missed it. On a long rectangular self-service island was laid out a range of cheeses, cold meats, fruit, breads, and eggs. He filled a white beaker with fresh coffee, lifted a couple of boiled eggs from a large bowl of warm sand, added a few rolls to his plate and, taking a seat at a corner table, looked around at his breakfasting companions. There was a group of what looked like IT engineers eating purposefully, with concentration and deliberation, mostly in silence, exchanging off-hand remarks to each other between mouthfuls of cold ham or cheese, making a terse greeting to another colleague arriving to join them. There were also some single men like himself, not men on a holiday from life, but in Villach on business. Unlike the engineers, the food in front of them seemed a distraction, not a pleasure, as they consulted mobile phones and laptops or glanced over notebooks and files. Immediately to his right were two women. He discovered it wasn't the food he was eating or the coffee he was drinking which recovered for him something long forgotten. His Proustean sensation wasn't found in taste but in the conversational manner of these two women.

It took him a few minutes to adjust to the rhythms of their Carinthian dialect and the cadence of their voices. He'd read that Hugo von Hofmannsthal believed Austrian German was, of all its varieties, the most mixed and culturally rich, involving many complex strands, and to understand its people you needed to understand their language. Sweeney couldn't pass Hofmannsthal's linguistic test but, though his understanding of their exchange was fragmentary and limited, he could follow the pattern of speech, their distinctive gestures, their notes of emphasis, and these were sufficient to give him access to a way of life beyond words. He couldn't be entirely sure of their relationship but had the impression they were mother and daughter, the mother in her late fifties or early sixties, the daughter in her late twenties or early thirties. They were talking about men. He could understand that much. From what Sweeney could gather, there appeared to be some crisis in the daughter's relationship and he supposed the reason for these women being together in here was to talk things through without interference or distraction. It wasn't what they were discussing, it was how they conversed which recalled for him a manner he believed to be truly Carinthian. The distinctiveness lay in their gestures, a theatricality unlike the French, unlike the Italian, unlike the Slav and certainly wasn't either British or Irish.

Like actors on a stage, the women would hold a pose or emphasise a line as if everything said must be properly appreciated, like savouring good food, like sipping great wine. But unlike actors, neither of them required an audience and neither was trying to impress since their performance wasn't for show. In this human drama, the daughter explained her predicament with a clear enunciation of righteous anger. The mother listened attentively with a knowing shake of the head and slowly and carefully accentuating every word of her response, announced her view as if providing an interpretation of a difficult passage in the script. Each spoke in turn, the one unfolding her story, the other giving her response, neither of them interjecting; and there appeared no space for superfluous lines. It wasn't gossip but confrontation with life as it can't help being lived. Sweeney was sure such conversational exchanges would have exasperated Musil for whom display and naïve theatricality was the most irritating characteristic of his fellow Austrians – believing it bad faith, not charm – people speaking differently from how they thought and thinking differently from how they intended to act.

Yet for Sweeney these two women painted a picture of his past through diction and gesture, one in which he could see himself, if only on the margin. He remembered discussions like these, minor dramas of the Maier household, ones he'd heard across the kitchen table, matters discussed with the same deliberation, the same gesticulations, the same style of storytelling, only the subject matter different. Eventually, he'd been charmed and entertained, for each performance exposed the absurdity of everyday existence. But that hadn't been his view at first. He'd been uncomfortable, uncertain about what was being said and unsure of the seriousness with which things were being said. From the tone it appeared to him confrontational and full of quarrelsome point scoring. After one such incident, involving raised voices, arms waved and heads shaken, he'd asked Sonja what the argument had been about.

'There wasn't an argument,' she'd replied, surprised by his question. 'We enjoy a little scene every so often. Didn't you notice how we grinned? We complain about the way people are and why things can't be arranged as we'd like. I think you say in English "why, oh why" – why can't this be done, why is this being done, oh why do we have to put up with it?' Sweeney had remained unconvinced she had seen. 'But we are good Austrian fatalists. We like to make fun of ludicrous things – and in ourselves especially. The Maier family is good at that. Afterwards we go back to doing what we've always been doing and make the best of things. And make the best of each other.' And he remembered how she'd pushed her finger into his midriff, 'Like we do with you.' In the simple enjoyment of their own company, talking through life's disappointments as well as its pleasures, these women at their breakfast, the Maiers in their kitchen, displayed what Alois Brandstetter considered deeply Carinthian, 'cheerful indigence, the blessings of the earth, of patience and resigned suffering'. Sweeney was cheered too by what he heard and more so by the prospect of another blessing, a morning cigarette, the packet sitting on the table, the lighter beside it, beckoning him to finish breakfast, to go outside and to enjoy his holiday from life.

The young receptionist from the night before was still on duty, seemingly as fresh as when Sweeney had arrived. As he passed, he said '*Guten Morgen*', she replied, '*Guten Morgen*', and gave him the same look inviting him to say something further but, again, he could think of nothing. Outside, the smoker's table had been cleaned, the abandoned coffee cup removed and yesterday's butts had disappeared. A new day in Hotel City and a new day in Villach, cool in the shadow where he stood by the door, but there was warmth already in the air. Sweeney took out a cigarette like it was his daily routine. What pleasure there was in doing those small things you know you shouldn't do, he thought.

. . . .

The cafés on the square had been open for some time and a few customers were sitting outside enjoying the air. He watched people as they passed, struck by the manner in which they seemed to take time for themselves and for each other. In the old days Sweeney would have asked, well, what else can you expect from provincial life? What else have these people got but time? He felt differently today. He regretted his old priggishness and unwarranted superiority which only revealed his poor grasp of how people do get by. When he'd been here before, he hadn't read the lines of Claudio Magris: original sin makes time seem unbearable, making people wish it would pass quickly, like an illness. Killing time, Magris wrote, is a polite form of suicide. On the Bahnhofplatz, Sweeney's impression was of unhurried-ness, no one, old or young, feeling any need for haste. If people in Villach were dancing to the music of time it was a slow waltz and he sensed no interest in polite suicide. To rush without lingering on the pleasures of living is a tragedy, spending time in one place but dreaming of elsewhere, doing one thing but thinking of something else, in the company of one person but longing for another, having one thing but wanting something different. Sweeney understood because he'd rushed a lot of life himself (yes, killing time) and, he would admit, had missed many of its pleasures. How would a metropolitan novelist describe the same scene? He would expect to read of Villach as a town becalmed, a place of tedium, deadliness and insignificance, inhabited by the lethargic, the indolent, the ineffectual and the inconsequential. Could such things really be true? Was such reading of life more than simply a matter of literary style? There is corruption in all things, Sweeney knew, even in the Garden of Eden and Villach was no exception. How could there not be suffering and despair? But in these few days, and as far as he was able, he decided to see life with renewed wonder. He would try to take things slowly, doing his best (and it wouldn't be hard) to avoid thinking like a metropolitan novelist.

He went back into the hotel, passed through the foyer, took the lift to level five and as he entered his room, greeted the cleaning staff already at work on his corridor. He put on his white linen jacket, checked his wallet for money, put the gift he'd brought for Sonja into his shoulder bag and headed out towards the town centre. No town, he'd read somewhere, should be too large for someone to walk out of in a morning. Even if you did take things slowly, he knew Villach would never be too large.

. . . .

When he'd looked for Sonja online he didn't have any difficulty finding her. Speculatively, he'd entered 'Sonja Maier' into the search feature of *Facebook*, filtered the many names by adding 'Villach' and there she was. He'd been lucky she'd kept – or reverted to – her maiden name, a practice unusual in Austria. He'd requested 'friendship' with little expectation she would respond and for some months she hadn't. He'd been about to abandon hope when one morning he awoke to find his request accepted. They had communicated on *Messenger*, the initial exchanges wary on her part, polite though terse, unsentimental and formal. He couldn't tell if her calm meant indifference or suppressed fury, for everything she wrote had been impersonal. When he'd told Sonja of his plans to visit Villach, she'd shown no sign of enthusiasm and hadn't suggested they should meet. He had been the one to ask (using his cliché about age and sentimental journeys) and, knowing Sonja's character as he believed he did, Sweeney accepted she had required him to take the initiative. Her reply hadn't been cold, though it was hardly enthusiastic. At least she had replied, at least she hadn't refused and he considered it was the best he could expect.

Bacchus, the name of the restaurant Sonja had suggested, sounded familiar and she'd obviously expected him to recognise it. He couldn't place it from memory and had looked for it on the town map. It was on the corner of Khevenhüllergasse, behind the Rathausplatz. So he walked in that direction, turning left into Bahnhofstrasse towards the Nikolaiplatz. The bright sunshine had already attracted a few customers to sit in front of the *Brauhof Biereck*, nursing their morning beers. The bright red brewery parasols hadn't been opened yet but they would be needed later. The cool edge of earlier lingered only in shadows and it was going to be another unseasonably hot day. Passing across the Nikolaiplatz, Sweeney ran his hand for luck over the bronze statue of St Francis of Assisi. Sonja had been a lover of animals, always a dog around (he recalled again Akko's eyes following him as he'd walked out on that hot night) and maybe St Francis would look kindly on him. By the Stadtbrücke, the *Café-Konditorei* was doing good business. On its terrace groups of young people were huddled over their mobile phones, drinking coffee or mineral water, eating a pastry or having a smoke. At one table he saw a meeting in progress, business accommodating itself to the ritual of a morning espresso. Two young men, jackets over the backs of their chairs, were taking notes as a young woman in a colourful blouse, her hair, dyed red, long and flowing, was setting out the agenda for the day.

The Second Day

Everyone appeared relaxed and Sweeney slackened his pace to complement the rhythm of the morning. Slow down, he told himself, enjoy the beginning of slow.

Along the railings of the bridge, flags fluttered from masts, the black and yellow of Villach with its eagle's talon coat of arms, and the yellow, red and white of Carinthia. The only acknowledgement of Austria was the *Rot/Weiss/Rot* half blazon on the Carinthian coat of arms. Vienna seemed very far away as did all the talk about Austria being back at the heart of *Mitteleuropa*. Anyway, he'd never considered Villach as part of central Europe. Unlike Vienna, Villach did not look east to Hungary and unlike Salzburg it did not look north to Germany. In his mind anyway, Villach looked south to Italy and Slovenia. It simply felt different, and this morning, as different as he remembered it. Here was *Alpen-Adria*. He'd discovered the University of Klagenfurt where he'd first met Sonja had been re-designated the *Alpen-Adria Universität*, the prefix, he imagined, a cultural aspiration as well as a geographical location. He liked the aspiration, for it softened imaginatively the fundamentals of borders. He stopped briefly in the middle of the Stadtbrücke to look along the river. The Drau was a deep, almost a viscous turquoise, and the only movement in the water was its eddying and murmuring around the stone emplacements. The leaves of the trees along its banks were green, golden, and red. Beyond the river's curve, the mountains swept away towards Friuli.

When he crossed the bridge to the Hauptplatz, he was pleased to find one of his favourite old haunts – the cigar, cigarette and pipe shop – was still in business. He stood for a moment and looked at its range of pipes from fashionable Meerschaum to traditional Alphorns. It appeared to be the same display as twenty-five years ago but surely that couldn't be? He examined more closely in the window items once quaintly described as 'smoker's requisites' – cigarette lighters, tobacco pouches, snuff boxes, silver cigar cutters, souvenir ashtrays, assorted packets of pipe cleaners – and was dismayed to think here was a way of life which might soon disappear. As he'd lingered outside one summer's morning, Sonja had said to him, 'I think you would suit a pipe.'

'Oh, really?' he'd asked, having in his mind those old black and white holiday photographs from the 1930s you found in memoirs and travelogues, snaps of young intellectuals, writers and artists. He'd recalled their fresh smiling faces, their tousled hair, their open neck shirts, their knee length shorts, their carefree lolling on the beaches of the South of France or at chalets on Alpine slopes and he'd pictured their pipes. He'd recalled them because they were the people Sonja had been studying, the Cyril Connolly set, and he'd been flattered to think she would consider him a suitable candidate for membership. He'd made an impression of smoking a pipe and struck a pose of Connolly's he'd seen in one of her books. 'So who do you think I'd be,' he'd asked her, 'a Harold Nicolson, a Kenneth Clark or possibly an Evelyn Waugh?'

She'd put her finger to her lower lip, considered his suggestions, and taken a step back to examine him more closely. 'No, I was thinking of you more as a pipe and slippers man, sitting in front of the fire, a tartan rug over your knees, with a book on your lap.'

'I can see you've mastered the stereotypes.'

'Perhaps there'd be a hot water bottle as well, you know how cold and damp your climate is … oh, and a cup of tea, of course.'

'You may mock but I assure you a man with a pipe, slippers and tartan rug is every woman's dream.'

'Please excuse me while I laugh. In *your* dream only I think.'

Actually, he had tried smoking a pipe once but not one he'd bought here in Villach. He'd heard it was good for you (a bit like Guinness) but had never got the hang of it. He'd wasted many matches trying to keep the tobacco lit and his over-eager puffing gave him heart-burn. And he reminded himself now that he'd never possessed a tartan rug and only rarely wore slippers.

Walking further along the Hauptplatz to the Rathausplatz, he saw at the far end of the square a poster for a play at the small theatre. He recalled vividly his first visit there because the occasion had been self-revelatory. That day he had been sitting with Sonja at the kitchen table when the telephone in the hallway had rung. She had risen to answer and after a brief conversation come back, sat beside him and stroked his hair.

'Heidi has got tickets for us to see *Der Küss der Spinnenfrau*.' Sweeney had hesitated and she'd translated for him, '*The Kiss of the Spider Woman*.'

He'd heard of the novel, if not of the play, but it hadn't been the language which made him pause. It had been the mention of Heidi. She was a close friend of Sonja's and Sweeney, whose associations were almost entirely superficial, was intrigued – impressed, he would admit – by the complex interlocking gradations of relationship which constituted Sonja's world. Heidi was part of the inner circle and Sweeney could tell she deemed closeness with Sonja to be important. That Sonja's approval was a desirable commodity he'd come quickly to recognise and it was fascinating for him to observe at work the power of her personal attraction. Charisma wasn't the correct word for it implied, at least to him, an unnatural magnetism or wilful imposition by a stronger character. There was nothing unnatural or wilful about Sonja, exactly the opposite. It was her straightforwardness which drew people, her ability to accept others on their own terms, her obvious lack of narcissism. She was open to their confidences, prepared to give of her time. In the eyes of her friends, Sweeney felt he was doubly privileged – at the heart of Sonja's private life and the object of an exclusive devotion. His privilege could have led to resentment and jealousy if Sweeney had been possessive or had wished to monopolise, but he wasn't and he hadn't, having no desire to impose or disrupt. So Sonja's friends had remained respectful rather like courtiers towards a Prince Consort. In return, he managed to get on well, if casually, with them. Perhaps the most accurate description of their attitude to him was polite acceptance or amiable indifference. Sweeney had been too much of an outsider, his German too limited, to be a true intimate of anyone and he never expected it should be otherwise. He'd assumed they found him too self-contained with no wish to be unpacked, neither feeling a need to unburden himself nor keen for them to confide in him. Heidi, unlike the others, had proved incapable of registering Sweeney's reservations and sensitivities.

'*Wahnsinn*' was her favourite word, meaning either 'crazy' ('I don't believe it' or 'that's mad') or 'awesome' ('that's super' or 'I love it') for Heidi could only speak with energy, passion and exaggeration. There could be no other manner of engagement, her theatricality being instinctive, not confected. Sweeney could never understand how reality never appeared to let her down, but accepted there was something magnificent about such breathless zeal and reserve was not a word she understood. Heidi had an unmistakable aura of innocence which could easily be mistaken (by men certainly) as inexperience and, for a certain sort of man, an invitation to bestow on her their own sophistication. To assume the first was an error and to attempt the second was to misread her entirely. Heidi's innocence was not inexperience but energetic curiosity and she did not lack sophistication. Her energetic inquisitiveness simply disordered expectations of urbane cynicism and detachment which had meant there was no 'man in her life'. While Sweeney could admire these qualities, wished he himself had a larger measure of them, they were associated in his mind with work, not play, with debate, not conversation, with seriousness, not levity, with formality, not relaxation and in these associations could be found the source of his unease. First encounters with Heidi had been amusing and since she and Sonja were such good comrades, he'd taken pleasure in observing the happiness both women had in each other's company. And he'd learned something about Sonja too, her ability (unlike him) to attract, and to engage with delight, those of a different nature to her own.

One afternoon they'd met Heidi when walking in Villach and gone for a coffee together. It had been only for a short time, but that day Heidi's relentless interrogation of him in her halting English – about his work, his interests, his views – and his responses in a mix of woeful German and hesitant English, defensive, reluctant, curt, with Sonja adding interpretation and clarification, had drained him completely. Sweeney had been embarrassed, no, depressed, by his feeling of mental feebleness and linguistic incapacity. He'd decided Heidi was not only without artifice but also without boundaries of propriety (or what Sweeney considered to be tactful diplomacy), incapable of qualifying seriousness with judicious levity. Such balanced discourse was the *lingua franca* of Sweeney's intellectual life, an artfulness conveying allusions of wisdom and more often than not serving to hide his superficiality. Heidi's insensitivity to such codes of discretion had been the source of Sweeney's discomfort and confusion, threatening to pull aside the veils of academic reputation and to reveal his deep limitations, for she had not been distracted by any practised evasions. He'd considered himself on trial, been judged, resented the implied sentence, and disturbed to realise how fragile his intellectual composure really was. How different it had been from the ludic ease he enjoyed with Sonja.

Sweeney had been annoyed with himself for his supercilious tone, despite Heidi not appearing aware of it. But Sonja had noticed it, his condescension, his 'academic snobbishness' she'd called it, and there had been a row between them later, a real argument, not one of the Maier family's theatrical 'scenes'. Sweeney's self-justification had been uncharacteristically blunt if only because he hadn't wanted to admit to Sonja she was right (something he could admit today). So experience had made him wary of Heidi's company.

'Is she going to be there too?' he'd asked, his inflection alerting Sonja to his reluctance.

'Please don't let Heidi put you off! She's so full of life. I know she can be annoying sometimes but she's harmless. No, harmless is the wrong word. She's loveable. I love her. And despite your intellectual snobbery, she obviously thinks you're worth impressing. You should be pleased. Maybe I should be the one to worry?' He remembered how Sonja had winked at him, how they'd both laughed because Heidi, for all her theatricality, was no *femme fatale* and her seducing anyone, certainly the partner of her best friend, was simply impossible to contemplate.

They'd gone and here was the interesting thing which Sweeney now recalled with wonder. The shared experience in the theatre had subtly changed their relationship. It hadn't made them wish to do everything together for they had only met once or twice thereafter. But *The Kiss of the Spider Woman* had been a transformative experience. Afterwards Sweeney had been less on edge and less defensive, indeed had become protective of Heidi and sensitive to those who would misjudge her (he worried men would mistreat her). Heidi in turn had appeared less manic and less intrusive and, as a consequence, Sonja had relaxed, her circles of friendship unbroken. Sweeney hadn't given Heidi a thought for years and he couldn't conjure a clear image of her, apart from her wavy hair (had it been short or long?) and her questioning eyes (blue or grey?). He must ask Sonja what had become of her.

. . . .

The Second Day

He strolled by the Parkhotel, no longer the stylish, exclusive residence it had been but become offices with, on the ground floor, the ubiquitous café. He continued along the 10 Oktober Strasse, a street conveying former Habsburg solidity in its public buildings and bourgeois prosperity in its villas and crossed the road at Julius Raab Platz. Here the Evangelical Church dominated the approach to the Stadtpark where he sought out one of the benches for shade from the hot sun.

The park was a leafy sanctuary under light-dappled trees. Sweeney saw an old man on crutches moving with surprising agility along the fringing gravelled path, three teenagers, two boys and a girl, avoiding school sitting cross legged on the grass, at ease with each other and sharing a cigarette, a portly woman absent-mindedly walking two small dogs and two sets of grandparents on child-minding duty, gently pushing prams. A young man in a sharp suit met an older woman in a flower patterned dress and together they headed off towards town, leaning in to each other in animated conversation. A retired couple dismounted from their bicycles, hung their helmets around the handles, sat on the bench next to him and took a quick, wordless, snack before cycling off again. On the other side of the park sat a heavily-built man in a green parka jacket, reading a large, hardback book. It must have been uncomfortable to hold because he would lay the book on his thigh and glance around, as if gathering strength, physical as well as mental, to continue. Three gardeners in their bright orange overalls were chatting, resting on their rakes and brooms, before them their work of the morning, a large pile of dead leaves. In the centre of the park, a fountain gushed high and bright, the water sparkling in the sunlight and Sweeney could feel its cool in the air. A few acorns fell from a tree and bounced on the path, disappearing into the flower beds.

Sweeney had been often in the Stadtpark. He would cross it regularly on the way into town from Sonja's house, resting here on occasions when it was hot, as he was doing today. He'd sometimes taken Akko for a walk – *Gassi gehen* they called it here – and the park was a convenient spot for the dog to leave his mark on the trees, hedges and bushes. Sweeney stretched out his legs, lit a cigarette, thinking of Larkin and how he, observing a similar park in Hull, had written of palsied old step-takers, hare-eyed clerks with the jitters, characters in long coats fishing around in litter baskets, all dodging the toad work. Sweeney did not sense these things in what he saw. He didn't detect hope-lessness as Larkin had done. Yet how could he really be certain? How could he know if these people did or did not feel pushed to the side of their lives, retired, ailing, jobless, at a loss, meeting clandestinely, raking dead leaves and skipping school or, like him, alone in Villach? He couldn't. Anyway, hadn't he decided to find wonder, not melancholy, in these days? He recalled Heidi with nostalgia, hoping cynical detachment had not subdued her spirit. Just then he was disturbed by a middle-aged man, holding a small child by the hand, who asked him a question. Sweeney hadn't been expecting it and hadn't heard what the man had said. Startled out his solitary state he replied, '*Bitte?*'

The man realised from his accent Sweeney wasn't a local and repeated his question more slowly in High German. 'Do you know where the children's playground is?' It appeared he didn't expect a useful answer because he was looking around for someone else to ask. The man spotted one of the gardeners walking towards them and was clearly on the point of calling out to her. But Sweeney did know where the playground was. He stood and pointed to the far side of the church.

'Yes, it's over there.'

'*Danke, Danke.*' The man, realising he'd misjudged Sweeney's grasp of the language and knowledge of place, became effusive in his thanks.

In return, Sweeney apologised in his best German, 'I'm sorry

I didn't hear you correctly the first time.'

'It's nothing, don't worry, likely my dialect. Are you in Villach on holiday?'

'Yes,' Sweeney replied. 'I used to come here in the past. I stayed with people I knew. It's the first time I've been back in twenty-five years.' He was unhappy about using the expression 'people I knew' but a polite enquiry by the man wasn't an invitation for him to tell his life story.

The man looked genuinely surprised, 'Twenty-five years is a long time. Perhaps I should say, welcome back.' The child was pulling at his hand to go on. He began to walk away, hesitated and turned once more to Sweeney. 'You will find a lot of things have changed, but Villach' – he gestured around him – 'Villach you will find the same. The people, I mean.'

'I hope so.'

With his best wishes to Sweeney, he allowed the impatient child to drag him away. As he watched them go Sweeney heard a church bell tolling in the distance and looked at his watch. It was 11.45. When he met Sonja, he'd planned to take things casually (as far as possible) and not to let his own bad conscience unnerve him (as best he could). It was time to walk back. He wanted to find a suitable table at *Bacchus* and he didn't want any awkwardly embarrassing indecisiveness, 'shall we go there?' or 'what about here?' Above all, the thing he couldn't afford to be was late. Sonja hated lateness. Briefly panic seized him – could it be she wouldn't come at all? No, he dismissed his fear immediately. No, that was certainly not her. No, it was unimaginable she would stand him up, even if he deserved it.

. . . .

Bacchus was a large three-storey building painted salmon-pink. At one end was a covered beer garden, partially hidden from pedestrians and traffic by a trellised hedge and as he walked by, Sweeney could see diners already at lunch on its terrace, the weather hot enough to believe summer was still here. The small arched entrance was flanked on either side by chalkboards giving details of the day's menu. To the left as he entered was a compact bar behind which beer and wine glasses were stacked. On the top shelf, among select whiskeys and schnapps, were one or two bottles of alcoholic remedies for indigestion and hangover. Sweeney recognised the dark, bitter, herbal mystery of *Fernet-Branca*, the only such remedy he'd ever tried. He couldn't remember if it had worked or not.

Some regulars were standing drinking and clowning with a slim woman behind the counter, who, from what Sweeney could gather, was capable of holding her own. Since the kitchen was on the far side of the bar, waiters exchanged a running commentary with these regulars as they carried out lunch dishes, grabbing drinks the barmaid had already set out for them. The mood was one of genial inebriation and of the four men standing, two were holding forth, the others commenting intermittently. Authoritative interventions, to which they all seemed to defer, came from a man seated alone at a table partially hidden by a wooden partition. He appeared to pay no attention, as if the banter was beneath his dignity. Before him was a glass of beer on which his eyes were fixed and around which his hands were cupped. As Sweeney lingered indecisively at the doorway, uncertain where to go next, he noticed how the man's pointed comments on exchanges between regulars and barmaid were almost like those of a professor bringing back to order students who'd strayed too far from the subject. Welcome to the University of Life, Sweeney thought.

The interior of *Bacchus* was stylised rustic, the walls painted white, each with a naïve fresco beside which was printed a saying fitting the deity himself. In the room leading off from the bar, high on the wall in Gothic script, he read '*Der Herrgott hat viel leiden müssen, viel Elend, Not und Müh, doch das Schlimmste hat er nie probiert – verheiratet war er nie*'. The Lord God has suffered much misery, distress and pain, but the worst has he never tried – never did he marry, Sweeney translated and, if true, he had successfully evaded the worst. On the opposite wall was another mural of monks and saints, enjoying the fruit of the vine and other corporeal pleasures. In this room the seats and tables were mostly taken. Sweeney was looking for somewhere more intimate for his meeting. I have no mixed motives he told himself, but was it ever possible to be without mixed motives? He walked on with a soft '*Grüss Gott*' to which no one responded, for the discussion had taken a suddenly raucous tone. A doorway led to another room of equally rustic character, also decorated with frescos and maxims, the roof arched with stained wooden slats like the inside of a wine or beer barrel. Beyond he found another more spacious room with parquet flooring leading through an open passageway into the beer garden. A cushioned-bench cubicle by a latticed window was free and Sweeney slid into it, giving him a good view towards both front and rear entrances. The atmosphere he decided was *gemütlich* but the description seemed too thin. He wasn't sure where he'd come across the expression '*unendliche Wohlgemutheit*', a sense of boundless well-being, but the restaurant seemed a good example of it. It exuded lightness of spirit and good humour, from the merriment at the bar, to here with its discreet sounds of cutlery on china, its soft murmur of conversation, a different rhythm but equally *gemütlich*.

Seated across from him a middle-aged Italian couple were picking at their lunch. The man was handsome still, tanned, fit, with a full head of well-groomed silver hair, dressed in a blue checked shirt, cream chinos and a pair of tan loafers. The woman looked more care-worn, distracted, heavier, but also attractive, her grey hair tied back, wearing a cardigan with floral motifs and a patterned tweed skirt. Sweeney didn't think they were married, if only because the man was too attentive, too considerate, too willing to smile at the woman's comments and too eager to make her laugh. Was their lunch a first excursion together, perhaps clandestinely, over the border, a day out, abroad but not too far from home? Were they escaping the misery of unhappy marriages? Or was he completely wrong? Were they a devoted couple still finding pleasure in their own intimacies, a rebuke to the mural in the bar as well as to Sweeney's cynicism?

In the cubicle adjoining Sweeney's were two elderly women, dressed stylishly, both with hearty appetites and each with a large glass of white wine. They were exchanging experiences of physical ailments, tablets taken, doctors visited, lots of head shaking along with the occasional raising of the arms in supplication to the *Herrgott, der hat viel leiden müssen*. From their accounts of suffering Sweeney detected a happier subtext – if things were painful enough for them, think of poor Hans or poor Maria (or whomever it was they mentioned) dead and gone, no longer with them, their absence palpable in the here and now. And like Joseph Conrad, they would turn back to the world where 'life flows in a clear stream', at ease with their own ailments (whatever they were), neither of them prepared to let the prospect of death, or another course of treatment, spoil a good lunch. The women cheered him.

He glanced again at his watch. It was a few minutes before noon and the restaurant had quickly become busier, the empty tables filling up, mostly with individual diners, office workers he assumed. He'd already observed the headwaiter, dressed in the same white shirt and black trousers as the rest of the staff, the difference being he wasn't wearing a long black apron. While they were quietly efficient he was flamboyant, operatic, talking to those who were lunching, sharing a joke at the bar, giving instructions *sotto voce* to the waiters as they passed, and sometimes mumbling directions to himself. There was an obvious Italian inflection to his acquired German and his Italianness seemed to license melodrama. It was not an intrusive performance for he didn't loiter in a manner to disturb drinker or diner. His presence, Sweeney decided, was really a statement of reassurance, acting out the presiding spirit of Bacchus. He saw Rossini (a name Sweeney thought fit to give the man) sweeping out to the terrace and heard him greeting extravagantly a new arrival. His voice was loud enough for everyone to notice, loud enough for the Italian couple to look up from their mutual confidences, loud enough for the two women to stop talking about what their doctors had ordered. It was noon exactly and Sweeney was certain it was her, when Rossini returned beaming, one arm around the shoulder of a woman, the other gesticulating to the room. His Italian accent had become more pronounced as he expressed his *absolute* delight to welcome her again. It was Sonja.

She accepted modestly the compliments and greeting, in return making Rossini feel the object of her affection. But her eyes were searching for him and Sweeney didn't want Rossini, in operatic mode, to escort her to another part of the restaurant. He stood up awkwardly and waved. She'd seen him already, pointed over and they made their way towards him, Rossini's arm still around Sonja's shoulder. Sweeney recalled Woolf's lines about Mrs Dalloway, how she would come into a room, how she would be with others, and yet always seemed there only for you. And here she was, Sonja Maier, and it was as if he'd never been away from her.

Sonja Maier – a common enough name in Villach but what was uncommon was her keen intelligence. And if intelligence was any measure of attractiveness, she was the most attractive woman he'd ever known (he'd never fooled himself it was the only attraction). Sweeney had been drawn by her strong facial features, full lips, light green eyes ('those cool and limpid green eyes' – he could hear the line of the old song), high cheekbones and long dark hair. Today she was wearing a powder blue tailored linen jacket over a fine-striped Oxford shirt, light blue denim jeans and a pair of fashionable trainers. Time had been kind to Sonja. She had maintained a lithe elegance, one he associated with the sports she liked, swimming and cross-country skiing. Her face remained fresh too, her expression as open, her green eyes as clear and cool as ever, except her facial features seemed – well, slightly drawn was the expression which came to Sweeney's mind. How could twenty-five years not have had an effect? The one striking difference was her hair. It was dark still (he supposed Sonja must dye it) but no longer flowing. She wore it in a short-curl bob, a change which might have been discordant but looked harmonious. From where he stood, Sweeney recognised the old enchantment of her gaze and was pleased to see it was intended for him.

He extricated himself from his bench seat and came forward to meet her. Rossini bowed to him in an exaggerated way, saying with archaic emphasis, '*Ich habe die Ehre*', 'Honoured to meet you', and left to fetch the menus. Sweeney and Sonja hesitated a moment, keeping a solemn space, and touched each other's arms formally. Her eyes met his directly but only briefly and she looked away as if uncertain. They walked together to the cubicle he'd pointed out (as if it hadn't been obvious) and before sitting, she looked into his eyes once more. 'Hallo, Eddie. It's nice to see you.' She paused and he was about to say the same when she added, 'again'. A barb, a well-directed barb, but the tone wasn't hostile, and he believed he knew her well enough that she never spoke with an acid tongue, her instincts never cruel.

'Sonja! It's wonderful to see you – again.' Letting his voice fall away on the final word, he acknowledged he'd understood her point and the truth it conveyed. A softening of her expression encouraged him to believe she'd accepted his gesture. He should display some contrition, but not so much that he became unctuous, for he was certain such behaviour would irritate her. Sonja gave a shrug when they were seated and another shrug as she put her bag on an adjacent chair. She adjusted her seat, removed sunglasses from her hair and set them on the table. In the silence which followed, Sweeney was unsure of what to say next, but luckily Rossini re-appeared with the menus. He slid one across the table to Sweeney with a simple, '*Für den Herr*', but with a grand flourish he opened the other for Sonja, laying it before her like his most honoured guest, taking a short step back to avoid further intrusion. What stagecraft he has and Sweeney couldn't help admiring it. '*Zum trinken, meine Herrschaften?*' Rossini pushed back on his nose a large pair of black-framed glasses, not looking directly at either of them but somewhere above and beyond. Sweeney gestured to Sonja that she should choose first. '*Mineralwasser, bitte*' and Rossini spread his arms wide and beamed at her. Rossini returned to contemplating the middle distance, waiting for Sweeney's order. '*Ein grosses Bier, bitte,*' Sweeney said in what seemed to him a decent Carinthian accent.

'A large beer for sir, very good, very good', Rossini replied in English and his response, which should have sounded enthusiastic, was clipped and lifeless giving Sweeney an apprehension he wasn't fully approved of.

When Rossini had left them, Sweeney asked her, 'Are you a regular here?'

'I used to be. We'd come here for lunch – we, as in two or three colleagues. I would love a glass of wine but I have things to do later.' Those 'things to do' were made categorical yet left unspecified, providing her, perhaps both of them, with a convenient escape.

She'd taught English at the *Gymnasium* on Peraustrasse

around the corner and her spoken English was perfect. Her fluency had been the convenient excuse Sweeney used to justify his poor German as well as his indolence in learning it properly. And it was only because her English was so correct that you had a clue to Sonja not being a native speaker. Another clue required some familiarity with the Carinthian dialect for sometimes she would fall into the habit of saying 'a' for 'er'. It only happened infrequently but when it did, he'd found it charming. 'It doesn't matta', she might say and he would know she was right, whatever it was, it really didn't matter at all. He couldn't help smiling at the memory and because she looked at him quizzically, he was obliged to explain. 'I was only thinking how perfect your English still is.' She didn't reply to his compliment, only closing her eyelids briefly. 'I'm sorry, Sonja, but my German is as bad as ever. I have been trying hard, but most people hear me and reply in English.'

'Replying in English? Well, what do you expect? No one would ever mistake you for a *Bergbauernbuam*'

'*Bergbauernbuam* – does it mean something, other than mountain farm boys?'

'Why do you ask?'

'I heard the word in a song yesterday. It was playing on the taxi driver's radio at the airport.'

'It's a song by Melissa Naschenweng. And no, there's no double meaning, if that's what you mean. Melissa keeps falling in love with them.'

'Is she from Carinthia?'

'She's from the Lesachtal, yes. She's very good – at least I think she's good – and has made pink *Lederhosen* and the Styrian accordion sexy.'

'Pink *Lederhosen* I can understand but the Styrian accordion?' Actually, Sweeney had no idea what was distinctive about a Styrian accordion. 'She must be quite a girl.'

'I think you'd like her but you wouldn't be her type. I can't see you scything grass, bailing hay or milking cows.'

'No, it's definitely not my thing.'

'I didn't think so.' She didn't smile but her comment was spoken gently.

He was pleased to find a light-hearted path into their conversation. 'True enough, I don't have the Carinthian look. Do you remember my first visit to the *Konsum* in Thörl-Maglern?'

She was flicking through the pages of the menu. Without looking up she replied, 'Remind me' which he hoped wasn't a sign of disinterest.

'Maybe I never did say to you' (he was sure he had), 'we were visiting your aunt and uncle and stopped off to buy something. You'd gone in ahead of me while I parked the car.' She looked up from the menu but those green eyes were still blank. 'Remember the way the staff were trained to greet lorry drivers and tourists? They would sum up people by their looks, Austrian, Italian or Slovene, and greet them accordingly, *Grüss Gott, Bongiorno, Doberdan?*'

'And if he knew you, the owner, the man' – she clicked her fingers twice – 'oh, I can't remember his name' – annoyed with herself – 'he put his hands like so' – and she put her hands together like a prayer and bowed her head as the owner used to do, deepening her voice – "Frau Kopfmueller, *Grüss Gott*, Frau Andritsch, *Grüss Gott*, Fraulein Puschitz, *Grüss Gott*". He had all the old style courtesies.' It was her first real smile. 'I'm sorry, I interrupted your story.'

'The two women shop assistants – they used to wear long white coats like hospital doctors – looked me up and down. They were uncertain, I could almost see their brains working, and said simultaneously, "*Bongiorno*". I took it as a compliment!' If he had told her the story before, she did a good job of pretending otherwise and he appreciated her indulgence.

'Even when I was a familiar face, they never used the English greeting. They simply switched to "*Grüss Gott*". I took that as another compliment.'

'Likely you were a difficult case for them. Your hair was long and dark in those days, Italian you could say. It may explain why they misjudged you.'

He ran his hand over his local Turkish Barber's number two razor cut, the popular and fashionable way to make baldness unremarkable by rendering it more obvious. 'When I *had* hair, you mean?'

This time Sonja did laugh and she pointed to the grey stubble on his chin, 'It looks like your hair is growing on the bottom, not on the top.' As Sweeney ran his hand around his chin she considered his appearance once more. 'Actually, the look suits you – if you were to ask my opinion.'

'It's kind of you to say.' He rubbed his chin again and asked, 'Do you want to know how my beard came about?'

'I have a feeling you're going to tell me.' She folded her hands together on the table, tilting her head slightly.

'I was trying to improve my German by reading online news stories and I came across an interview with a celebrated Viennese intellectual.'

'Oh, who was it?'

'I can't remember his name.'

'Not celebrated to you.'

'No …' She raised her eyebrows signalling he should continue. 'What struck me was the following. The journalist used the descriptive phrase "professorial beard". I'd never heard it before. Maybe it's peculiar to Austria?' She shook her head to mean she had no idea if it was or not. 'It wasn't a heavy beard, it was only stubble' and he ran his hand over his chin once more 'but it seemed to be a distinguishing feature of intellectual eminence.'

'For men only, I hope.'

'Yes … so I thought I'd better grow one before it was too late. Maybe a professorial beard would help get me an academic honour, like being made a Fellow of the British Academy' he lifted his canvas bag to show her.

'And did it work?'

'The university got rid of me', an answer he delivered in a deadpan voice as if it had been the only possible consequence.

As she used to do, Sonja put her hand to her lips, her eyes widened, as if astonished, and laughed loudly. 'Your sense of humour, your fantastic self-irony, hasn't changed much.' She put the back of a finger to her cheek as if to wipe away an imaginary tear. 'I'm sorry, I don't mean to laugh but when you wrote you had become Emeritus, in my mind was a picture of Benedict, the Pope Emeritus. I wondered if they had locked you away somewhere in your academic Vatican.'

Sweeney considered it to be a better story than his own Disraelian one. 'They never gave me the option. Perhaps I should have asked?' He coughed. 'I see you still have your old sense of humour too.'

Sonja was sharp and perceptive, a characteristic which in another person could have been either censorious or arrogant. But she'd also inherited a Carinthian wisdom that life requires lightness, especially when dealing with vanity and pomposity. *Das Recht auf Heiterkeit*, there is a right to gaiety, and here the two of them had once found common ground. He was glad to have a brief glimpse of that territory once more. Had she glimpsed it too? Sonja pushed the menu to one side, 'Wasn't your religion the religion of the ivory tower, the kind of thing you see in an episode of *Inspector Morse?*'

'You get *Inspector Morse* in Austria?'

'We used to get it on ZDF.' Sweeney was trying to remember what ZDF meant and she interpreted his look. 'A German Channel, there's so much choice on TV these days, probably too much. *Inspector Morse* is one of my favourite shows, so very English. But all those strange college rituals, those litanies of academic life, the conclaves of plotting dons, the privileged sanctuaries, everything so superficially dignified until Morse discovers the tribulations beneath. You get the feeling it's not only Oxford but the whole country, the whole world, is like this.'

Her words impressed him. 'I've never considered it so but, yes, that's exactly how it appears. If there is a religion of the Ivory Tower, Oxford would be very High Church and I would choke on the incense. I never had the opportunity to choke for, as you're aware, I was at the other end of the scale. Our university was more like a puritan meeting house, no ritual, only functional. Actually, leaving academic life was the best thing for me.'

She might have said nothing but what she did say, softly, was, 'I'm pleased for you.'

'So am I, for I once had a premonition of what might become of me. And it wasn't pleasant at all.'

'Oh, and what premonition was that?'

'It was the night I found myself in Vienna Südbahnhof. Remember – the first time I spent Christmas and New Year with you and your parents? There'd been a forecast of heavy snow possibly disrupting the line to Vienna? I'd panicked about making my flight home and took an early train. Didn't I tell you this story either?'

'I'm sure there are lots of stories you didn't tell me.'

'As it happened there was no disruption or delay and it was shortly after midnight when I got to Vienna. I discovered the airport bus only began its run at six a.m. I suppose it would have been possible to take a taxi but I wasn't sure if I'd enough money. So there was no option but to stay in the Südbahnhof overnight. Everything was closed and shuttered. You know how you get the feeling when travelling that time has been suspended? Everything seemed eerie. Do you remember the waiting-rooms in the station?'

'Yes, they were symmetrical, box-like structures off the main hall. The walls were glass, very post-war modernism. The station has been demolished and rebuilt. It's the Hauptbahnhof today – twenty-first century modernism.'

Sweeney had read about it and was sure he would prefer the old building to the new. 'Well, I found one of the waiting-rooms and it was empty. It was warm, almost overheated and I prepared myself for a long and lonely night.'

'Is it going to be a ghost story?' Sonja asked.

'No, it was a different sort of premonition.'

Sonja folded her hands together on the table. Her look wasn't bored but, he liked to think, one of expectation and he hoped his intuition was correct. 'About an hour later the swing door burst open and a group of *Sandler* invaded the place.'

'The Viennese vagrants, you mean?'

'The very ones and they all smelled of the streets. It's still vivid in my memory, a mix of drains, damp, urine and unwashed body. Each one was carrying a plastic shopping bag.'

'Weren't you scared?'

'Initially, yes, but most of them weren't aware I existed. And the reason was in their plastic bags. One of them sat beside me. He pulled from his bag a waxed cardboard carton of *Landwein*, the sort you find on the bottom shelf of the supermarket. I remember the image on the carton, an idyllic scene of a vineyard, a bunch of grapes, farmers in traditional dress toasting, their glasses clinking – actually, a bit like the murals here in *Bacchus*.'

'And so different from the real *Sandler* existence, there's nothing idyllic about it.'

'Exactly, they hadn't noticed me because they were out of their heads from cheap wine or possibly from something far worse than alcohol. Anyway, the man asked what I did for a living. He was a rough guy, hard too, bulky figure, a boxer's face you might say, but probably harmless. But I didn't want to take any chances, didn't want him to think I was an easy touch for money, so I lied and told him I was a student.'

'Your instinct for self-preservation was legendary.'

'And I've finally got to the point of my tale. He pointed out one of the *Sandler* seated apart on a fold-away canvas chair, the kind people take on picnics. "So you're a student, are you? See him over there, he's the professor". And the one he'd pointed out did look at first glance as if he'd come from an episode of *Inspector Morse*. He was wearing a tweed jacket, but the cuffs were torn and the fabric had thinned out pitifully. His matching trousers were also academic-like, but they too were badly frayed and the bottoms were trailing. His shirt had once been white but had become a dirty grey, the inside of the collar grimy, almost black. His shoes may have been stylish Oxford brogues but they'd become split at the sides and one sole was detached, flapping at the toe.'

'If you recall the man so distinctly after all these years, he must have made a deep impression on you.'

'One thing, more than any other, made a deep impression. It was the professorial glasses. They were perched on his skeletal, beak-like nose. Or so I believed because when he turned his head, I saw the professor didn't have a *pair* of glasses at all. At some point they'd been broken in half. There was only one spectacle, not two. It was round' and Sweeney circled his eye 'and I briefly imagined an aristocratic monocle. But no, it was only one half of a broken pair of glasses. It seemed the only dignity remaining of his former existence and he was clinging to it desperately – magnificent, perhaps, but heart breaking.'

'And you believed *you* might end up like him?'

He could tell she was sceptical, so he laughed. 'Fortunately, I have got this far with two lenses.'

She pointed to his pair of spectacles on the table, 'And you wear round-framed glasses in his memory, I see.'

He'd not needed glasses when he'd been with her. He put them on, 'I never expected to spend my life on the streets or in an alcoholic daze, yet that image of failure clinging to a fragment of former respect – yes, I took it as a message you are permanently on the edge of disaster.'

'I would have remembered your story if you'd told me. I wasn't wrong when I asked you if it was a ghost story, was I? It's clearly haunted you. And do you think you are a failure?'

'I can't tell yet.'

She looked back at her menu and said, 'Ever the optimist' but once again he detected no mean inflection in her voice.

'Sorry for dragging up my old story.' He looked at the menu. 'And what about things with you, Sonja – how are you?'

She looked up at him again, 'I'm retired too, you know that, I've told you before. The job had become a bit stressful.' She paused. 'No, it wasn't the job. For a while *life* had become stressful. And financially, since I didn't need to work full time any longer, I decided to de-stress. So I did.' Her words were terse.

A waiter arrived and set their drinks on the table. Sweeney raised his glass to hers tentatively and he hoped not cravenly, 'Here's to de-stressing.'

Their glasses met.

'To de-stressing', she said softly.

'Has it worked?'

'It has so far.'

Her answer should have sounded unequivocal yet Sweeney detected some ambiguity in her answer. 'I'm glad for you too.' They both took quick sips from their glasses and, as they lowered them to the table he added, 'And thank you for meeting me.' She appeared about to say something, but went back to reading the menu and he thought back to their conference dinner in Klagenfurt.

. . . .

At the restaurant, when everyone had been seated and the first drinks ordered, Sonja had done her best to explain the dishes from *Zwiebelrostbraten* and *Fleischnudeln* to *Champignonrahmschnitzel* and *Schweinsbraten*. When he'd looked at the prices Sweeney was certain his colleagues – they were all men – were going to order the cheapest option. He would have bet his job on it. By this point in his career he considered he knew academics well enough to understand they resented having to pay for anything. So far all meals had been provided for by the conference organisers, everything else paid for by their universities and the dinner had been the first call on their own wallets. Sure enough, when the waitress arrived to take the order, one after the other had pointed to their selection and said, '*Wienerschnitzel mit Pommes Frites*'. It had been the cheapest option.

Sweeney had looked up, noticed Sonja keeping her head down as if fascinated by something she'd seen on the menu. He'd noticed her lips pursing but couldn't be sure if she'd been embarrassed by what she'd heard, shocked by such demonstration of parsimoniousness, or whether she'd been trying to stifle a laugh. When it was his turn, in his most affected German he'd ordered '*Gebratenes Rindersteak mit Petersilkartoffeln.*' It hadn't been the most expensive item but at least more expensive than the *Wienerschnitzel*. He hadn't been certain what he'd ordered but believed honour demanded it. He hadn't done it for himself alone for he'd wanted to demonstrate something of himself to her. Why he'd wanted to, he hadn't worked out yet. The answer had come later. When he'd handed back his menu to the waitress that evening he'd caught Sonja's eye. It had been a conspiratorial look between them, the first time they'd shared a secret understanding, something deeper than enjoying each other's company. It had been a different connection. Returning to the university in the rain, sharing the same umbrella, had turned shared confidence into something deeper, with enough mystery between them to encourage romance, enough desire to encourage longing. They'd exchanged addresses, had promised to keep in touch which in those days meant by letter. The idea of a personal as well as an intellectual correspondence had appealed to Sweeney because never before had there been anyone like Sonja to write letters to. He'd visualised all those volumes of correspondence by poets and writers he'd consulted in libraries, fondly imagining his own among them. It had flattered his ego to imagine this attractive woman reading what he had to say. Yes, he had to admit, vanity had been entangled with emotion.

On the menu today, he searched the dishes for *Gebratenes Rindersteak mit Petersilkartoffeln*. If it was there, and he ordered it, would Sonja remember? But it wasn't there. Maybe he should order *Wienerschnitzel* instead? Would she remember that? She'd seen him smirk at the memory and asked, 'What's so funny?'

'Oh nothing,' he lied, 'I'd forgotten how good Carinthian cooking really is. What you just glimpsed is the happy look of the expectant diner.'

'Yes, *Bacchus* is good, traditional, your sort of menu.' She was right about him and it was good she'd remembered but decided not to mention the conference dinner. He was on his guard, careful to avoid appearing too maudlin or too befuddled with nostalgia. Once it had been possible to say before them had stood all the promise of life. Today they were in a very different place. All former promise she had every right to remember as betrayal. Perhaps it meant nothing at all to her today? Sweeney felt a pang of despair (or was it self-pity?) but Rossini returned to distract them.

'*Haben die Herrschaften etwas ausgesucht?* Have you decided what you'd like to order?' As before, he stared into the middle distance.

'*Ich möchte die Eierschwammerl,*' Sonja said.

'*Fur mich, die Zwiebelrostbraten.*'

'*Danke, die Herrschaften.*'

The menus were removed and their order trusted to memory. A notepad and pen were clearly beneath the dignity of Rossini's status. When he'd gone, there was a silence before she said, 'I have something for you, Eddie.' She lifted her thick slouch bag from the chair beside her and took out a hardback book enclosed, as was the Austrian fashion, in fine transparent film. She handed it to him across the table, 'To help you with your Austrian German, since you can spend more time practising it.'

'I certainly need the practice.'

The title of the book was *Servas! Die Herzenwörter der Österreicher* and he translated for her – *Greetings! The best loved Austrian words.* And how was my translation?'

'Not bad or, as you used to say, not *too* bad', and it seemed to him those last three words recovered for both, if momentarily, their old familiarity.

Sweeney pulled off the wrapping, opened the book and flicked through the pages from the back, hoping to find an appropriate Carinthian dialect word. The first one he saw was '*Rotzriasel*'. He pronounced it for her and she put a hand to her eyes, laughing. As he read through the dictionary definition, Sweeney saw the German word was '*Rotznase*'. He knew both words in the compound – snot and nose – but had never encountered the compound before. He sniffed and ran the back of his hand over his nose.

'Yes, that's me'.

She laughed again. 'The English term I think is "snotty brat". Does it describe you as well?'

'Even more like me', and she didn't challenge his self-evaluation.

'Thank you. And I too come bearing gifts.' He looked in his British Academy tote bag as if it contained a multitude of interesting things and pulled out a poorly wrapped present. Its silver paper looked as if it had been taped by someone wearing boxing gloves. As he handed it across the table, he knew he should have asked Sara to do the job for him.

'Thank you too, I wonder what this can be?' though she must have recognised from its feel and shape it could be only a book.

'I hope you are still interested after all these years.'

She undid the wrapping with more care and attention than it deserved. The book was a 1945 American hardback edition of Cyril Connolly's *The Unquiet Grave*, still in its original dust jacket and it had taken him some time to find. Sonja was one of the few people he knew who'd ever read Connolly and he hoped she would appreciate a rare copy. He wished for something else too – that the book might fold over the gap of dead years between them, joining past and present, the way things had been and the way they were now. She looked surprised. 'You shouldn't have, it must have been very expensive. It's a lovely edition.' She ran her hand over the cover, judging the heft of the book and its balance like a precious object, a thing of reverence. 'I haven't read Connolly in years', she said, delicately turning the pages. 'I once spent so many hours on one book alone and I can recall so little of it.' She appeared to be genuinely shocked the passage of time could have had such effect. 'When I was a student – when we first met – I used to think Connolly was living with me.'

He noticed a slight flush on her cheek and he was tempted to say, 'I felt there was someone else in our relationship'. She had sometimes said the same thing to him about Larkin. 'I'm glad you like it.'

And she did appear genuinely delighted and Sweeney congratulated himself on his choice. How nice it would be of Cyril to do something useful for him beyond the grave. He would like one of the few Connolly phrases he knew – 'memory is re-enacted desire' – to be true. He wasn't expecting physical desire, he'd assured himself. No, what he'd imagined was some reconnection of the intellectual bonds between them. Yes, that's what he'd told himself – to recover, however fleetingly, their old conversations, talking about everyone and everything, innocently, and openly. No mixed motives … but who was he fooling?

Glancing through the pages, she found a passage and frowned. She looked at him and then back to the words. 'In the sex-war', she quoted, 'thoughtlessness is the weapon of the male, vindictiveness of the female.' She read further along the page '… a woman's desire for revenge outlasts all other emotion.' Sweeney's heart sank. Maybe Connolly wasn't going to help him after all. He was going to say something trite like Connolly 'was of his time' but what has time got to do with anything?

'Can I see?' he asked. She handed the book across the table and their fingers touched briefly at the open page. His look of dismay must have been obvious to her.

'In case you're worried, Eddie, I'm not feeling vindictive and I'm not here for revenge.'

Sweeney tried to make light of her comment but he was relieved nonetheless. At the bottom of the same page, he found Connolly citing a Buddhist mantra and Sweeney read it out, 'Sorrow is everywhere, in man is no abiding entity, in things no abiding reality'. He took the opportunity to change the subject and looked about him. 'I don't feel much sorrow here in *Bacchus*, do you? Your old friend the headwaiter wouldn't allow it.' He looked directly at her thinking those bright green eyes had seen right through him. 'I'm happy you are here, Sonja. If Connolly is right and what abide are memories, most of my best memories are of you and of Villach.' He feared he sounded ridiculous.

She only replied, 'I like "most of".' He raised his hands to accept she'd hit the target and she smiled at her victory. He was relieved to leave any answer unsaid for the arrival of their order interrupted them. Sweeney thanked St Francis, not Connolly, for a blessed coincidence.

. . . .

Since their first words they had begun to lean forwards, a force of conversational attraction pulling them closer together. They moved back again as a waiter – not Rossini – laid their plates before them and wished '*Guten Appetit*'. Once he had left, they raised and clinked glasses again. Sweeney took a good sip of his beer, she a sip of her mineral water and they started to eat.

'How are the *Eierschwammerl?*' he asked after they'd taken a few mouthfuls.

'Delicious … and how's your roast beef?'

'The phrase I recall is hearty and filling. G*ut bürgerliche Küche*, isn't it? I remember it used to be over the entrance to another restaurant in Villach.'

'It's easy to forget.' She dabbed her lower lip with the napkin, 'It's much easier to remember the way things weren't.'

'Remember the forgotten – and a whole world opens up to you.'

'That doesn't sound like Larkin'.

'No, it's Marie von Ebner-Eschenbach, from her book of aphorisms' and he hoped she might be pleased by his effort to read his way back into her culture. She stopped eating, considered the aphorism and then considered him.

'Look, I understand you well enough – at least I think I still understand you well enough. You use literature as a sort of code. It's part of what makes you interesting. You were enigmatic, leaving to me and everyone else the job of deciphering your messages. I suppose it gave you a way out, an escape.' She laid aside her knife and fork and shook her head. He noticed a vein throbbing at her temple. 'You used it as a form of evasion. Your aphorism might be another sort of message. How would I know? We haven't seen each other in so many years. I deliberated a long time about coming here to meet you and it is true' – she touched the Connolly book on the table beside her – 'on my part, there's no vindictiveness and no desire for revenge. I suppose all those years ago I invested in an illusion. I'm not sure if you ever did the same so I can't say you misled me. It was difficult for a while. I couldn't understand why you suddenly went silent and we lost contact. But I really don't want to dredge up old feelings of recrimination and disappointment. I want you to be sure of that. After a while I suspected you had become like the Larkin you talked about all the time, unable to make any commitment, keeping things back. You were decent, charming, good company. It was easy to be with you. It was a precious time.' She gave him a searching look. 'Suddenly you stepped out and were gone completely. I was hurt badly. How could I not be? Maybe you were only capable of living on your own terms. Sometimes you gave the impression of being more in love with Villach than with me and the idea hurt me too. It was as if you could only deal with people through your head' and she put a finger to her temple.

'You mean I had no heart?'

'You had a heart for dogs I remember.' She didn't smile so Sweeney didn't laugh. 'I believed you wanted to keep your distance, safe behind your manners and charm. Yes, you *had* become another Larkin. It's how I made sense of what happened.'

Sweeney mumbled, 'A Schopenhauer.'

She raised an eyebrow.

'Not a Larkin, a Schopenhauer, his fable of the porcupines.'

She shook her head which didn't mean 'don't interrupt me' but, 'Tell me.'

'Schopenhauer wrote of porcupines which in the cold of night rolled together for warmth. Their spines caused them discomfort so they rolled apart again. But the cold forced them back and with the same result – until they discovered a position where they'd warmth but no discomfort. Schopenhauer's message was the good life required you' – he hesitated, unsure if he hadn't made things worse for himself, annoyed by yet another example of the stupidity of academic cleverness – 'to keep your distance.'

'And what sort of miserable philosophy is that!' There was anger in her voice. 'Every time we parted, when you left to go, it wasn't discomfort. It was pain. Maybe you never considered it. Did you not feel it too?' He was about to assure her that, of course, it was the same for him but he couldn't be certain she would think him sincere. 'One day you rolled away altogether and everything went cold, so what could I do but roll away too?' She looked not at him but to one side. 'Your fable of the porcupines is another evasive justification.'

'I can admit you are right. I imagined I could move through life and never leave a trace.' Sweeney wasn't sure where his last sentence had come from. His voice sounded panicky, blamed nervousness and cursed himself again.

'Even if you don't mean to, you always leave a trace. *Das Glück is a Vogerl aber das Herz is der Käfig.*' She could see Sweeney didn't understand. 'It's from an old song my mother used to sing. Happiness is a little bird which can fly away and leave no trace but your heart is a cage where everything is kept. My heart is where you left your mark when you flew away.' She pushed a few mushrooms with her fork. 'What you said reminded me of the letters you used to write. I loved the sound of the English word "pellucid" and reading your letters

I would say to myself, "Eddie's letters are pellucid". They were like windows into a bright world of ideas. It was like watching swifts fly across the sky. They were hints of another place, unlike the dull routine of every day.' (Despite everything, Sweeney was flattered. She'd never told him before.) 'There's a line I remember Connolly using against himself – "a narcissus with his pool before him". I could never say the same of things you wrote to me. The only thing about them was … I could never find *you*. Your letters were so pellucid you weren't really there at all. Your transparency only made you more opaque. Explain that if you can?' His puzzled look made her soften slightly. 'Alright, perhaps it's who you really were – *are* – and perhaps it's the only way you can be. Anyway, it made me feel there was more than a geographical gap between us and when you were with me it sometimes felt you weren't entirely here either. In everything we did together you offered so much – I will give you that – but withheld so much as well.'

He had loved her. It was never in doubt. But yes, she was right, he'd been the man who wasn't (always) there, an emotional failing he knew. He would like to say he'd changed and he was no longer the same person who'd been distant and self-absorbed. But he knew it would be too easy, like Epicharmus's debtor, trying to avoid repayment of money he owed by claiming he'd changed so much he was a different man altogether. No, he mustn't use Epicharmus, she was too familiar with all his literary escape routes. And yet he knew there was another side for they had never, for the same reason, exhausted interest in each other or become bored together. There had been constantly more to discover. Don't the French believe love requires '*le mystere*'? He liked to think so but was he only fooling himself again? All he could do was to sit there like a chastened *Rotzriatzel*. She must have taken pity at how he looked for she took a deep breath and exhaled.

The Second Day

'Don't be upset. I could have ignored your original friend request. I was tempted to. I could have avoided responding to the message you sent but I didn't, for it would have been childish. I could have chosen not to meet you, but I didn't do that either, for it would have been spiteful. *I* could have kept my distance by ignoring you, not replying to you, standing you up, staying away altogether. But as you can see, I have chosen not to do any of these things.' She touched again the book he'd given her. 'Connolly, who was wise in many other ways, was a fool when it came to love. Have you ever considered the same could be said of you?'

He was on the point of saying something – exactly what he was going to say he had no idea – but she put her hand up to stop him. 'No, don't answer that question. It wasn't fair of me to ask. We are the product of the choices we make, even if at the moment of each choice our cross is veiled. "Our cross is veiled" was one of my mother's phrases. We never know what burden will fall to us. Why did I choose to meet you again? You were an important part of my life. I can't deny it. And if you are wondering, I don't think of it as wasted time and I don't regret it – well, not all of it.' She smiled at him, wistfully he judged or wished, and Sweeney, in his emotionally cowardly way, hoped the worst was over. Sonja took another sip of her mineral water and paused before she continued. 'After a while, the days which followed were good too. I married Christian, had two wonderful children, I stayed in the job I loved, I was … happy.' The last word was spoken quietly and, Sweeney imagined, with less assurance. 'I still am happy. Life is agreeable, yes.' He knew she was widowed – but 'agreeable'? He considered it a curious word for her to use, since she was always careful about language. Sonja took another sip of her drink. 'When you got in touch again, told me you were coming back to Villach and wanted to see me again, do you know what I thought?'

Four Days in Villach

He lifted his glass and pushed the beer mat around with his middle finger, 'What did you think?'

'I thought you were ill, maybe you were trying to put your conscience in order before you died. It's the sort of thing which would appeal to your literary imagination. I see you're not. Anyway, in the end I considered it far too melodramatic for you.'

Sweeney had never considered she might think of that and maybe bereavement had fostered some morbid ideas in her mind. For a second he wondered if he might play up to her concern, hinting at some personal tragedy he was manfully unwilling to burden her with. He knew the idea was absurd but because he didn't reply immediately, he saw a sudden look of anxiety as if she'd made a mistake and had guessed the truth. 'No. No, not yet', he hurried to assure her. Death wasn't around the corner – well, he didn't think it was. Certainly, there were all those small and cumulative humiliations of ageing he could mention and he looked at the two old women sitting across from them. He had tales of woe as any man had, but who in God's name would be interested in hearing them? He laughed to reassure her and she did appear genuinely relieved.

'I'm glad you're ok. Anyway, if you had told me, can you think of what I would have said?' He shook his head. 'I would have said – why don't you take Holy Orders and prepare yourself for the next life.' His look must have appeared comically crestfallen, his present discomfort manifest for she stretched her hand across the table to touch his arm. 'I didn't mean it to sound heartless but I couldn't resist.' She looked at him steadily for confirmation he'd understood, assuring him of no malicious intent and lifted her glass. Sweeney sensed she was at ease enough with her advantage over him to be gracious. They toasted again.

'Your good health,' Sonja said.

'*Zum Wohl*', he replied and she tilted her head appreciatively at his German expression. 'If you don't mind me asking, what happened to the letters I wrote?' Sweeney, hoarder that he was, had kept hers in an old box file, like a past safely curated.

She didn't hesitate, 'I burnt them. Yes, I know it is a cliché but what did you expect? I was angry. If it makes you feel any better, it wasn't like I was burning you, Professor Pellucid. Your heart and soul weren't in them, after all.'

. . . .

Sonja and Sweeney had once existed in their own common imaginative space. His poor German had been partly responsible and he knew he'd relied too much on her for protection and comfort. Speaking in English with literary references had become their private language, their companionable bubble. Together they'd concluded, since everything in life had been encountered already why not reference their own experience through the words of those who had expressed it more imaginatively, more passionately, and more perfectly? And why couldn't you live life the way you read it, with the same imagination and intensity? The affectation and pretentiousness of it all made him smile. How adolescent it seemed to him as an older man but also how innocent it had seemed then. And one of their innocent pleasures had been to drop into conversation lines from novels, poems, films and songs to see if the other recognised the reference. Sweeney remembered exactly when their game had begun. One afternoon they'd been sitting on the narrow wooden balcony of her parents' house, its striped canopy extended for shade, another of those summer days when the sun had been unforgiving. They'd been reading, she sitting on the lounger in her bikini, legs stretched out, Sweeney lying on a towel in T-shirt and shorts, struggling in the heat to keep his eyes open. She'd asked him of a sudden, 'Who wrote "if it were not for literature how many people would ever fall in love?"'

'Cyril Connolly' he'd answered.

'No, clever man, it was Aldous Huxley. But I will give you one point. He's being quoted by Connolly.'

And so had begun their small discursive intimacy which often annoyed Sonja's mother (or so Sweeney had imagined) who probably suspected their cleverness a pointed demonstration of her own ignorance (as if self-absorbed young couples are ever aware of anyone else). At the same time, Sweeney had sensed Frau Maier was also pleased by Sonja's intelligence and by how much she'd achieved, observing the way she could get the better of the strange 'professor' (though he wasn't one at the time). For their lunch today, he'd practised a line, not sure if it would be appropriate, but hoping it might be. '*Glücklich ist, wer vergisst / Was nicht zu ändern ist*', a peace offering of sorts because she was bound to get it.

'Ha! Johann Strauss, *Die Fledermaus!* Fortunate are they who forget those things which cannot be changed. *You* can't change the fact that I'm better at our old game! There are some things we don't forget.' Sweeney made a sign of concession and years of silence, disconnection and emptiness fell away, for him and he hoped her. Time and experience had altered them, certainly, yet the ease they'd once enjoyed allowed them to speak without embarrassment, their conversation retaining an entitlement which former love permitted. Observing her pleasure at such a minor victory alone had made the journey worthwhile. 'We were good companions, you and I, despite everything', she said. 'It's the same old story, it's probably been said a million times but it's not *any* old story, is it? It is – was – *our* story. Do you see what I mean? It's a bit like *Casablanca*. Only you're the one who has walked back into my gin joint.' She gestured around the room and the movement of her arm, the screech of her chair leg on the wooden floor as she did so, distracted one of the old women from an account of yet another ailment and produced a covert glance from the Italian couple. 'No, it's ridiculous of me to say, for I'm no Bogart and you aren't Ingrid Bergman! I don't have his twitching upper lip and you don't have her soft glistening eyes – or her hair.' They both laughed at the image. 'But there was a story ... you do see what I mean, don't you?'

'I do,' and was pleased to imagine they looked like any other couple, in relaxed conversation, enjoying a pleasant lunch, their world as cosily familiar as the blossoms you see on the window ledge of nearly every Austrian home. 'I understand exactly what you mean.' And he did understand. She had emphasised the past, not the present, tense and maybe that *was* her point – as in *Casablanca*, things change as time goes by and their companionship couldn't be recreated as if nothing had happened in between. But he held on to one possibility. *Still* to believe in something gone is foolish. *Again*, to believe in something is not impossible. His eye caught the Italian couple and thought, *Se non è vero, è ben trovato*. And who is to say what might happen? Perhaps their former companionship was no longer true but what if they conceived for themselves another good story? Maybe they could ... but here Sweeney ran out of inspiration. He hadn't eaten much of his roast beef, his hunger returned and he attacked his plate. Sonja did the same, as if she couldn't put into words any longer what she wanted to say. They ate silently for a while.

'I met a man in the Stadtpark this morning. When I told him I hadn't been here in a long time he told me Villach had changed but not its people. The whole of Europe has changed since I was last here, Austria too, and for the better it seems.' He'd spoken light heartedly, and he hadn't expected, as he now saw, her eyes should film over and feared he had misjudged her mood, underestimating Sonja's emotional fragility. After all, he knew nothing of her mental state, assuming she'd remained strong and composed like the Sonja of old. He feared he'd touched the nerve of her husband's death but he was wrong. It was her father's.

'In the 1990s my father's world fell apart He remained a true believer, still had faith in communism. He lost hope. He couldn't understand the world any more. He wasn't bitter – he was never a bitter person – it wasn't in his nature. But he became depressed. Not depressed, depressed is the wrong word, resigned is probably correct. He was resigned, as if his life hadn't much purpose any longer. You loved Joseph Roth's novels so you appreciate what I'm talking about, don't you?'

Yes, Sweeney did grasp her meaning and tried to show as much understanding as he could by the sympathetic look he gave her. He recalled Franz Tunda in Roth's *Flight without End* who, after everything he knew and loved had been lost after the First World War, ends up a disillusioned relic, no one more superfluous in history than he. Sweeney had never shared Herr Maier's politics, or anyone's politics for that matter, but he'd admired the man and for him it was enough. He was genuinely sorrowful for he considered, at times of self-pity, becoming superfluous in history was a fate hanging over him as well.

. . . .

He hadn't heard of her father's death. But when they were together, Sonja's mother had died after a long struggle with cancer and Sweeney had flown over to attend the funeral. Everything about that day had a powerful impact on him – the ornate black coffin, the abundance of flowers, the baroque Catholicism of the service, the slow progress of the hearse at the cemetery, the solemn ringing of a bell, but above all the deep grief of her father mixed with his evident distaste for all

things priestly. Sweeney had once marvelled at how her parents'
marriage worked, the mother so pious in her Catholicism, the
father so dogmatic in his Communism and yet their family life
remaining so harmonious. One day he'd mentioned the enigma
of their relationship to Sonja.

'Is it because they love each other?' she'd replied, yet it wasn't
a question but a statement, as if it was no mystery at all. If there
had been a question it was for him. How, it implied, could you
have been so unobservant not to notice the obvious? 'They don't
need to share every interest and opinion. They understand and
accept each other. My mother has her Catholicism, my father has
his Communism, but they need each other, if they also ridicule
one another. They admit their differences but they're content
their lives should be woven together. It's what gives them personal
strength as well as mutual consideration.' He'd been taken aback
by her explanation and its simple truth. It had made him worry
about his failure to know anything at all. Hadn't she told him
again today he only understood people through their heads and
not their hearts? Maybe it was still the case.

Sweeney hadn't shared Frau Maier's churchly piety nor had
he taken Herr Maier's political opinions seriously. He had never
taken any politics seriously but respected Herr Maier as an hon-
ourable man, leaving the ideology aside. On the few occasions
when her father came along for a drive to the former Yugoslavia
and they passed through small mining towns close to the border, he would look with satisfaction at the yellow clouds of gas
belching from factory chimneys, casting a fantastic sulphurous
glow into the sky like the dull sodium street lighting Sweeney
remembered from his youth. Seeing knots of factory workers
in soiled overalls, either going on or coming off shift, Sweeney
had sensed Herr Maier feeling amongst his own. The smoke, the
factories, the workers, here was communion with the incense,
congregation and daily devotions of socialism and Sweeney had

believed him more at home in the grimy landscape of industrial labour than in the pretty packaged world of tourist-friendly Carinthia. If Heaven was Frau Maier's transcendence then collectivism was Herr Maier's.

One day he'd asked Sweeney to drive him across the Italian border to a bar beyond the town of Tarvisio. It had been an old communist haunt, cramped, smoky, and filled with artefacts from mines at one time worked around there – helmets, pick-axes, lanterns – with black and white photographs of workers, strong men in their Sunday best, standing self-consciously or self-importantly, arms folded, jaws thrust out. Arranged along the walls were party and trade union banners, once bright and colourful but become faded and tired. The reason for the visit had nothing to do with party business. Its purpose had been for Sweeney to hear a local celebrity which turned out to be a large cockatoo called Gecko and whose claim to fame was the ability to recite the opening lines of the marching anthem, 'Avanti Popolo'. He could still hear Gecko, sitting on his wooden perch by the bar, giving a rendition of *alla riscossa/bandiera rossa, bandiera rossa* delivered exactly, as Sweeney imagined, in the voice of the bird's teacher, a heavy-smoking, hard living, Friulani miner. At the end of the performance the few customers in the bar, all old men, faces deeply lined, had given Gecko a resounding cheer, fists thrust into the air in salute. It had been an experience for which Sweeney was totally unprepared. But he'd also felt that in bringing him Herr Maier had disclosed something personal, something revealing, to this stranger, this comrade of his daughter's. What else could Sweeney have done, after the initial hesitation, but to clap and cheer in solidarity with everyone else? The occasion had been bizarre and yet also a privilege. Sweeney believed her father was making him aware he had been accepted and he'd bought Herr Maier another glass of red wine to toast Gecko's performance, a sufficient sealing of the bond between them. Recalling Gecko, remembering the joy on her father's face, he stretched his hand across the table and touched Sonja's arm. 'I'm sorry to hear about your father.'

'Thank you' she whispered, 'I still miss him. He was very fond of you – but I don't think he ever believed you to be revolutionary material.'

'How right he was.' She nodded and he decided to keep the story of Gecko for another time – if there was to be another time.

She ran her hand softly over her hair. 'You are right, yes. A lot has changed – in Austria, in Carinthia and also in Villach.' She patted the Connolly book again. 'Sometimes you need to let things rest in a quiet grave. There are things you shouldn't disturb. It's also best not to go chasing after ghosts. You've heard of Ingeborg Bachmann, haven't you?' Sweeney nodded, visualising her face on the side of the *Musil Haus* yesterday evening. 'She wrote you should make sure your *Wanderkarte* – your imaginative route map – isn't out of date. *You* need to make sure *your Wanderkarte* isn't out of date too. Yes, things have changed. All the old paths and all the old landmarks are probably no longer there – or not as you once imagined them. Some may be only dead ends.'

He could accept her point. The paths on his mental map didn't seem remote or indistinct to him but he accepted they could be dead ends. Sonja's tone wasn't challenging and he detected a tolerance of him which, in the circumstances, was better than he could have hoped for. Sweeney recalled another phrase he'd picked up recently from the novels of Thomas Bernhard – 'annihilating stare'. Sonja's look had not been an 'annihilating stare'. She hadn't wanted to destroy him and it was a great mercy. His *Wanderkarte* (or was it their *Wanderkarte?*) may be out of date but if so, it didn't stop him making a new one.

. . . .

They finished eating and began discussing people they'd met, places they'd been, both of them sailing calmly as if they'd successfully negotiated dangerous waters. Sweeney remembered to ask about Heidi.

'Heidi Schojer, you mean?' Sonja looked surprised.

'Yes, your friend who loved the arts so much.'

'I haven't spoken to her for a long time. It's something I really must do. She changed career about ten years ago and works as an administrator at the *Stadttheater* in Klagenfurt. As far as I am aware, she couldn't be happier. Why do you ask?'

'I remembered her as I walked past the theatre. The three of us went there one night.'

'We saw *Der Küss der Spinnenfrau*.'

She'd remembered. '*Wahnsinn*', he said and Sonja wagged her finger at him.

He sensed the tempo and mood in the restaurant changing. The busy lunchtime trade was over. The diners at the neighbouring tables had settled their bills and departed, the old women supporting each other arm in arm out of the room, the Italian couple vanishing as unobtrusively and discreetly as they'd eaten. A lethargic rhythm resumed and the waiters' pace slowed, their presently vacant attention focussed on adjusting and cleaning the empty tables, flicking off crumbs with their cloths, re-arranging napkins and replacing cutlery. In the background animated discussion could still be heard, as one or two regulars continued to draw out the early afternoon in loud, argumentative, though sociable, exchanges. Yet the voices sounded more forced, the humour more strained. Sweeney and Sonja, unsure of what to say or how to say it, hid their momentary confusion by pretending to listen to the exclamations and the jokes coming from the adjoining room.

'Carinthians certainly know how to enjoy themselves. What is it you say? *A Gaudi* something – I've forgotten the expression.'

'*A Gaudi muss sein.* Life should also be merry is probably the best translation. It's an old Viennese song. As you are aware, people outside Austria seem to think only Vienna and the Viennese exist – as do the Viennese. When I think of Vienna I think of another line – how lovely it would be without the Viennese. You'll find it's a common sentiment in Carinthia. I'm sure those at the bar would agree. And I would too.'

'You are exaggerating surely?'

'Yes I am. But I am only exaggerating what is true for me. I could give you more to say about Vienna but I'm afraid repeating it would put you outside polite society.'

'You are exaggerating again, I take it?'

'Exaggeration helps to make life endurable … I don't think you'll know the quote. They aren't my words, they are Thomas Bernhard's.'

'Ha! Quoting Bernhard certainly would put me outside polite society. I've been reading a lot of his work, actually. Have you heard of the English singer, Billy Bragg?'

She mumbled, 'I've heard of him,' a reply Sweeney considered unconvincing.

'Well, he has a song where he says of Gilbert and George, the painters – you've heard of Gilbert and George?'

'Of course I have,' said in a way which was convincing.

'Well, Bragg wonders if Gilbert and George are taking the piss. I think Bernhard is taking the piss … in a very Austrian way.'

'You mean he's not being funny at all?'

'No, I laugh out loud at some of his lines.'

She clapped her hands, 'I do too.' She looked at him playfully, 'Have you ever considered I might be "taking the piss" as well.'

'Well then, I'm in very good company,' and they both laughed.

Rossini, no longer busy with the demands of his lunchtime performance, returned to their table, expressing once more his joy at seeing Sonja but ignoring Sweeney. Instead of annoyance, Sweeney was relieved by his interruption and sat back to consider what should happen next. Would one meeting be enough, would they be satisfied to leave things here, a civilised encounter, a pleasant lunch and an amicable parting? Hadn't he achieved as much as he could have hoped for? Had she not already shown him forgiveness? Or had she only excused him? He wasn't sure. Forgiving and excusing were different things and he considered there remained additional debts for him to pay. How they were to be paid or if they could ever be paid, he wasn't sure either. If his meeting was to be only a brief encounter, he would have no problem passing the next few days, drifting around between past and present, meeting ghosts perhaps, charting as best he could a new map. Yet observing her ease with Rossini, above all her ease with *him* in Rossini's presence, he hoped it would not be the end.

When Rossini left them, Sonja looked at her watch. 'I'm really sorry. I will have to go soon. As I told you, I have something to do this afternoon.' Again, she left the something unspecified but she'd spoken the excuse (if such it was) more reluctantly than before. 'Thanks for lunch. And thanks again for the book. It was very kind of you. I love it.'

'My pleasure – and thanks for your present too. I've learnt something from it already … *Rotzriazel*.'

'Oh, don't be so hard on yourself.'

'Sonja, please say no if you are absolutely pressed for time but would you like to have a quick coffee? Not here, maybe in a café somewhere?'

She looked at her watch again, looked at him, appeared to be calculating commitments, and then accepted. 'It really will have to be quick. We can go to the *Rathaus Café*. It's only a few steps away from here.'

The Second Day

Sweeney was delighted and said so and was happier still when he saw how Sonja appeared to appreciate his delight. He called for the bill and paid. As they walked past the remaining regulars, Sweeney could sense that the high spirits of earlier had dulled into last rites. Good humour and amiability seemed in abeyance. The waiters ignored the jokes and the barmaid looked tired by the comments. The fun had run out, probably as it did at this time every day and the melancholy of the hour was palpable. Sweeney, superstitious as ever, hoped the mood would not accompany them to the *Rathaus Café*.

. . . .

They made their way across the road towards the town hall. Sweeney followed Sonja up a set of steps and through an archway onto the Rathausplatz. The bright golden light reflecting off the smooth, sandy façade of the buildings made him flinch. He felt awkward, the melancholy he'd sensed amongst those at the bar accompanying him and he was suddenly plagued by an ill omen. In the open square, the *Rathaus Café* had set out tables and wicker chairs under wide parasols and only a few were occupied. Running along one side of the square were wooden benches shaded by trees. On one bench sat an elderly man reading a newspaper, on another a woman was speaking on her mobile phone, gesticulating with her arm. On the far side of the square a young mother was patiently helping her child negotiate the steps from the main street. This wasn't the shimmering stillness, the motionless heat, of mid-summer which keeps people indoors, yet lassitude had descended on Villach.

Sonja called over the waitress, ordered a coffee, and Sweeney asked for a small beer. The town's somnolent mood appeared infectious for Sonja sighed, stretched out her legs, laid both arms along the sides of the padded chair, closed her eyes and let her head fall back slightly. Sweeney recalled those moments of voluptuous simplicity they'd once shared, silent, as now, in each other's company. From somewhere and faintly he could hear the sultry voice of Billie Holiday singing 'The Very Thought of You' and the line '*I'm living in a kind of daydream*'.

He continued looking at Sonja. Was she oblivious of his gaze or was she inviting his furtive attention? Did she consider how she looked for him or did she think how she disclosed herself no longer any concern of his? Finally, he said to her, 'I like that song.'

The words broke her fleeting trance. She opened her eyes and sat straight. 'Sorry, I didn't mean to be rude. I needed a quiet moment. Forgive me. Which song are you talking about?'

'The Billie Holiday song someone is playing.'

She angled her head to listen, looked at him knowingly. He could tell she'd judged the song's title to be an invitation to sentimentality and his question a prompt to indulge it. Sweeney hadn't intended it to be, but if he had, discovered she wasn't going to take the bait. 'I'm glad it isn't "As Time Goes By"', Sonja replied, humming the lines as Ingrid Bergman had done in *Casablanca*. 'It's still the same old story.'

'I won't make it a case of do or die.'

'The songs they play in bars and shops are about making you feel you're anywhere *but* Villach. They like a bit of jazz and blues, a bit of style and who can blame them? Don't we all?'

'Right now I wouldn't want to be anywhere else but Villach.'

'Villach isn't a good place to be sad in. Its beauty only seems to mock your unhappiness. I've remembered another line of Connolly's. I can't recall the words exactly but it was something like you should indulge your sadness in appropriate surroundings. If the surroundings are dismal, you have licence to feel depressed. It's almost comforting he believed, like the whole world shares your mood. You can understand how his advice doesn't fit with Villach. Look around you. Your spirits should be uplifted, the sky, the mountains, the forests, the lakes.' She raised her arms. 'When they aren't, your sadness is compounded by a feeling of inadequacy.' She let her arms fall heavily by her side.

It was a conversational turn which Sweeney took to be a sign of vulnerability and a warning he should be cautious, sensitive. 'And did Connolly suggest a cure other than recommending a suitable place to be sad in – for you, Vienna maybe?'

Sonja shrugged off the reference to Vienna. 'If I remember correctly he advised focusing on the small picture, not the big picture. Shift your attention from the vast beauty of mountains, lakes and sky to immediate things, like the young mother on the steps over there with her child. Don't indulge what can overwhelm you but attend to everyday things. Find a small patch of wild flowers and it might cancel estrangement and loss. Oh, and avoid people trying to be nice to you.'

'Did you ever need to take his advice?'

She looked away from him. 'I'm not cut out to be a *donna triste*. If I need solace I have my dogs. For them, every day is the best day of their lives.'

Sweeney accepted she wasn't going to confide in him if she needed solace or not and tried to lighten the mood. 'So, you're saying the answer is … a dog a day keeps the psychiatrist away?'

'Only *you* could say that!' She shook her head, but he could tell she found the absurdity amusing.

'I can see what you mean about depression and surroundings. But I was never sad in Villach.'

'Aren't you the lucky one …'

His glib remark appeared to irritate her as if he'd made light of unhappiness or despair she'd only hinted at. He saw her body stiffen but coincidental timing was on his side again for the waitress arrived with their coffee and beer, fussing as she arranged the glass and cup on the table. Sonja was obliged to deal in brief pleasantries with her and as she did so he sensed her anger ebbing. But he knew he'd touched a nerve and was annoyed at his bungling tactlessness. Sweeney asked the waitress if he could pay the bill immediately and searched in his wallet for the appropriate note. He waved away the woman's fumbling attempt in the leather purse on her hip to find change. 'Sometimes it's difficult to pay when you want to,' he explained after she'd gone. 'You are free to leave whenever you want now.' It was his way of providing an apology she hadn't asked for.

'That's very considerate of you. You've accommodated smoothly to our Carinthian ways.'

They fell silent again and he reflected on their lunch. They had discussed very little about their lives. She hadn't talked about her late husband and he hadn't asked her. She'd mentioned her children in passing but he hadn't pressed her further. She knew of his daughter but hadn't shown any curiosity about either her or the mother. It wasn't that they'd danced around those points. They'd both chosen to ignore them, ironically keeping their distance from potentially uncomfortable matters. Her words had been without acrimony, those of someone who seemed able to meet disappointments in life, negotiating gracefully the ways of the world. And he'd always been uncomfortable with what people choose to call opening up, glad that she hadn't for he couldn't. Not yet.

'Such a beautiful day, is it normally so hot in October?'

'It's becoming more common,' she replied. 'Is it global warming? I'm not sure, but I fear it is.'

Sweeney couldn't believe he'd started talking about the weather. Sonja took a sip of her coffee. He took a sip of his beer. There was another silence. There had been a part of the *Sandler* story he hadn't mentioned for fear it would confirm his character to her all too clearly. When Sweeney had pushed through the door of the waiting-room and stepped into the main hall of the Südbahnhof, he'd glanced back. Not one of the Sandler had bothered to follow his exit. For those few hours he'd been in their world but had returned to his own. It had been easy for him to step out and to walk away. Exiting – from old places, old friends, old lovers, and from his work – had it not been the pattern of his life, something or someone once left, never returned to? And wasn't it also the case he liked others better when they were leaving or when he was going, his relief at parting making him feel tender, wistful and considerate? Maybe he preferred absence to presence? Yet he knew leaving Sonja hadn't been comparable at all. He had been a real presence for her and her family, and they for him. They had welcomed him, embraced him, he had been a part of their life and they of his. It was true what she'd told him. You always leave a trace, even when you don't think you do. Happiness is fleeting but the heart is a cage.

'This is really pleasant.'

'It is. I needed a coffee, something to help me gather myself. I was tired after lunch, I had to rest my eyes briefly – and no, it's not you. I would take it as a compliment I'm able to relax in your company' she nursed her cup in both hands and looked at him teasingly, 'once I had recovered from the shock of your professorial beard.'

'It does take some getting used to.' He brushed the stubble under his chin. 'And I'm not sure I've got used to it.'

She looked away again towards the Hauptplatz, 'Sometimes it's good to sit quietly and simply watch the day pass by and only focus on Connolly's small things.'

The passing day was a commonplace scene of nothing and everything. Across the square Sweeney saw a group of construction workers in orange high-visibility overalls strolling leisurely back to work, their progress punctuated by loud guffaws.

Four Days in Villach

Dawdling in front of a shop were two middle-aged couples, the men in traditional Carinthian hats and jackets, the women wearing colourful scarves and dirndls, obviously visitors from the country. Slowly, deliberately, they moved from shop to shop, periodically turning back to discuss something they'd noticed in a window. An elderly couple, heads lowered, one in front of the other, carrying heavy plastic bags filled with shopping, marched doggedly, still a distance to go before they could rest. Two policewomen in blue uniforms were heading at pace back to their station, hats off, faces of public authority at ease, their light-heartedness marking the end of a working shift, anticipating the prospect of leisure. On the Hauptplatz some Italian tourists in black puffer jackets, the pitch and rhythm of their voices unmistakable, wandered aimlessly towards the river. What he'd observed – the tightly braided hair of the old women from the country, the soft hats of their husbands and the buttons on their waistcoats, the carefree step of the police women, the bent stride of the old couple – none of them seemed without meaning. He knew a person would probably go crazy if the brain was burdened by every detail of existence but right now such apparent insignificances seemed important to him, as if his well-being depended on them being just so.

When he was younger, after intense mental concentration on a difficult book or poem, searching for the precise words to convey an image or an idea, he would emerge onto the street from library or study, momentarily struck by how unusual the everyday seemed, by how strange people's behaviour appeared. Then he believed himself a superior intellect dazzled by the sunlight of knowledge, temporarily unable to make sense of everyone else's shadowy activities. It was a view he held no longer for the commonplace astonished him in a different way. All these private and purposeful comings and goings in Villach, or anywhere, had a grace of their own which required not intellectual transcendence but imaginative benevolence. He supposed writers forever tear at polite social veils to uncover horrors lurking behind. How seductive it was to adopt the pose of melancholy and fatalism, but weren't cynics only romantics whose disappointments trapped them with nowhere else to go? Sweeney could understand the lure of that literary *persona* but would find it impossible to sustain. He liked to think his common sense would always break through and rescue him, a sign of his superficiality perhaps. If so, his ability to skim over life's problems set limits to disaffection and made existence more bearable.

Here in Villach, these people, every one of them, had lives as complex, intense, beautiful, melancholy, joyful and tragic as any character in a novel soon to languish in a second-hand bookshop, their routines just as interesting as the life of any writer, however imaginative. He couldn't remember sitting here before but, if he had done, would the behaviour of people have been any different twenty-five years ago? If he continued to sit here every day for another twenty-five would anything change at all? Sweeney remembered what the man in the park had told him – the town may have changed, but the people hadn't.

'I don't think I've ever sat here before.'

Sonja set her cup sharply in its saucer, 'Oh you have. You used to come here to escape going shopping with me.'

He shook his head, 'Really? And how did I manage my escape?'

'You tried to be clever – or should I say selfish? There used to be a bookshop in the lane on the other side of the church', and she pointed towards St Jakob dominating the Hauptplatz. 'You would look through the box in front where they put out books for sale, all the discounts and the special offers. You'd buy the oddest things, old storybooks for children, out of date tourist guides, recipe books, such weird things. Afterwards you'd come here to the square, sit on one of the benches and go through them while I went shopping.' Sweeney shook his head. All she'd related was a blank. 'You really don't remember? I can tell you the excuse you used.'

'Which excuse?'

'You used the phrase you picked up from little Anna, "*Deutsch ist eine schwere Sprache*". You would say something like, "I'd better try to improve my German. Anna tells me it's a difficult language" and come here to sit by the fountain.' Anna was one of Sonja's nieces.

'There was a fountain in the square?'

'Yes, almost where we're sitting.'

'And did my stratagem work?'

She laughed, 'Only when I knew you'd be a pest.'

'I understand – it worked only when you wanted it to work. Who was the selfish one? And those books I bought, whatever happened to them?'

'You left them at my parent's. They were untouched for a while. My mother and father had too much respect for your academic standing to do anything with them. They imagined you would put them to some great literary purpose and stacked them in the spare room. I dumped them one day. I take it you never did read any of them?' He shook his head, not as confirmation of her question, but to indicate he had no recollection of her story. He was sorry for those old books and sorrier for himself, for she'd spoken the words 'I dumped them' with more relish than he would have liked.

'I'm sure what you say is true. And your story may help to explain something.' He reached into his bag and pulled out a glossy but tattered visitor's guide to Villach. He handed it to her across the table. 'It may be one of the old tourist guides you were talking about, my out of date *Wanderkarte*.'

She began to flick through the pages. 'Oh, my God, Villach

in the 1980s! Look at the women with their big hair! Oh no, the terrible fashion, the clothes all seem too big, like people have bought the wrong sizes.' She turned the page to another photograph and put a hand to her forehead. 'These are worse! Ugh, those garish shell suits, they should have been banned! Did I ever look as bad in those days?'

'Let me answer your question about how you looked.' Sweeney gestured for the return of the guidebook, sought out the picture he wanted and leaned across the table, holding the book open for her. It was a double-page photo of the Hauptplatz on a high summer's day, people strolling, sitting outside cafés, window shopping. He tapped his middle finger on the page, 'Who do you think they might be?'

She took the travel guide again and raised it closer to her eyes. She scanned the page for a moment and looked at him over the top of the book, 'Who do you mean?'

Sweeney left his seat and crouched beside her, conscious of their closeness, almost cheek to cheek. In the photo he pointed to a man and a woman walking away from the camera, partially hidden by other pedestrians. The man's left arm was slanted across the woman's back, his hand touching her hip and the woman's right arm was angled along the man's back towards his shoulder. Her hair was dark and arranged in a long pony tail. She wore a short-sleeve white blouse and a pair of blue jeans. The man's hair was dark too and he wore a grey polo shirt. Sonja narrowed her focus to the couple Sweeney had indicated.

'No, no, it can't be us!' looking to him and checking the photograph a second time, 'I don't see you, the man's not slim enough … and I don't see myself either.'

'I forgot I had the guide and only came across it by accident.' When he'd been clearing out his old office, Sweeney found it lying on one of the shelves, hidden behind some dusty copies of a defunct literary journal. 'I saw a resemblance and it reminded me of one of those spooky movies, you know, the sort such as *The Shining* where characters end up in old photos?'

Sonja took a further glance, her face slightly flushed, and closed the guide book. She tapped it against the palm of her hand and placed it on the table. Sweeney, sensing her discomfort and thinking it was because he was too close, rose from beside her and returned to his chair. His facetiousness seemed out of place, but he had no idea why she'd been disconcerted. By closing the book, he knew she'd closed the subject. She looked at her watch.

'I have to go. Sorry to run off. Thanks for lunch and for the coffee'. Handing him the travel guide, she pushed back her chair and lifted her bag.

'Can I walk you to your car?' he asked.

'It's not far, only a few steps away.' Her car, a silver Volkswagen Touareg, was parked at the Standesamtsplatz behind the Rathaus.

'Nice car.'

'It is. The children live in Vienna – trying not to become Viennese, in order to please their mother. I decided to buy something safe and comfortable to visit them. You can understand why we provincials find it hard to love the national capital. It steals our children.' She opened the door, tossed her bag onto the passenger's seat, turned back towards him and gave him a quick embrace. A chaste contact he knew, but it was a little closer and more affectionate than their arms' length greeting in *Bacchus*. 'I enjoyed seeing you again. To be honest, I didn't think I would – after everything,' two words said in haste as if she regretted having to utter them, 'but I did', the final three words more emphatic.

He looked at his feet, 'It really was good of you to see me – well, as you say, after everything. It was a pleasure.' Those last words sounded foolish, but the sentiment was true. He glanced at her again hoping those green eyes would be fixed kindly on him. But she was looking over his right shoulder, the way people do when they are uncertain of what they are about to say.

'If you really want to do some ghost-hunting, I'm happy to drive you … if you would like to.'

Normally Sweeney would have danced around such an offer with the usual politeness – 'only if you have the time' or 'only if it's no bother' or some other such phrase – but he didn't. He knew she found the habit irksome and would expect a direct answer to a simple question. 'Thank you, Sonja. Yes, it's very kind of you. Thank you.'

'Look, we'll be here all day thanking each other and I must dash. You are staying at Hotel City, right? What if I collect you around ten tomorrow morning?'

He knew she meant ten o'clock precisely. 'I look forward to it,' Sweeney said and she closed her eyes briefly as a sign of an agreement sealed. He wondered if the offer had been a spur of the moment courtesy or had she decided on it before coming to meet him? She got into the car, he closed the door for her (it made a satisfyingly heavy clunk) and stepped aside to let her reverse. She waved as she drove to the top of Freihausgasse, turning right onto Moritschstrasse and accelerating quickly from view.

. . . .

They'd spent only a short time together and yet it seemed like days had passed. Sweeney experienced the sort of tiredness you feel on the release of tension and maybe it was how Sonja had been at the *Rathaus Café*. She'd shown him mercy, had acted with grace, there was another day and he looked forward to what tomorrow would bring. He stood for a while mulling over these things, but the sun was too strong. He decided to go back to the Rathausplatz and find some shade. He considered he deserved a cigarette.

He sat on a tree-shaded bench by the entrance to the theatre where he, Sonja and Heidi had gone to see *The Kiss of the Spider Woman*. He took a deep drag on his cigarette and sat forward, hunched over, elbows on his thighs. Those days with Sonja – Sweeney could only wish he'd lived them better. Betraying her, he felt he'd betrayed himself. No, life, it was life he'd betrayed. It was clear to him today. George Santayana had written of those who fail to embrace the fertile principles of life by not stripping off and plunging into adventures and who, when challenged to live better, are willing to die, stubborn and negligent, 'with a retrospective smile upon their countenance'. How easy it had been for him to avoid stripping off and plunging in while indulging the ordered daydreaming of reading – life as fertile as flowers pressed between pages of a book it seemed to him. And the image of stripping off and plunging in evoked a particular memory which still shamed him.

A Carinthian summer meant going to the lakes, locals as well as tourists flocking to the waters, spending their days splashing, swimming, diving, sailing, floating on rafts, sunbathing. Colourful wind breakers would be pitched, music played, picnics eaten, and beers drunk, a carnival of jostling display, alive with vibrant pleasures, innocent and possibly not so innocent. Sweeney had gone once with Sonja to the Ossiachersee and his first impression of it had been cinematic, as if he'd stumbled by mistake onto the set of one of those feel-good German holiday films popular in the 1950s, films he'd seen on Austrian television, manic comedies of manners and mishaps, every one of them with a joyful resolution.

Sonja had plunged straight into the lake, swimming and splashing, delighting in the good-natured pleasure of the water, intoxicated by the playful atmosphere. Sweeney had held back, uncertain of the tepid water, wary of the waving reeds at the lake edge, fearing an attack of horseflies, suspecting the attentions of mosquitoes, worrying about sunburn and his heart hadn't been in it. As the old man remembered the young one, the only word which came to mind was 'pathetic'. He could see Sonja bobbing in the water, laughing at his timidity, calling for him to come out further and deeper, shouting he should let himself go and he'd made a feeble attempt to please her. He'd swum around close to the shore a few times, floated about for a bit, splashed water back at her, given a few amorous hugs when she'd come near, but what he'd really wanted to do was to get his clothes back on and escape from nature, like some latter day Huysmans, especially from the threat of mosquitoes. No one else had seemed to worry about them, Sonja hadn't been bitten and Sweeney couldn't recall being bitten either. At the time he'd recognised he was being ridiculous, but was powerless to resist the affected absurdity he was indulging, the role of aesthete he feigned to play. He'd been annoyed with himself and he'd understood it would soon make Sonja angry as well. She'd wanted both of them to swim out to one of the anchored rafts to sunbathe and Sweeney could tell she was becoming irritated by his childishness.

Luckily for him the day at the lake had been cut short. The muggy heat had turned into the threat of a thunderstorm, heavy black clouds reaching over the mountains and blackening the horizon. A speed boat with a loud hailer had appeared, giving warning for everyone to evacuate the lake. Bathers had waded grudgingly to the shore, windsurfers had lowered sails and paddled in frantically, rowing boats and dinghies had returned to jetties. Families, playing or sitting on the bank, had scampered with their things, gathering picnics, mothers and fathers calling to their children, kids screaming in either despair or excitement. Sonja unwillingly, he gratefully, had grabbed their towels, dried themselves quickly, put on clothes as best they could, scampering at pace towards the car, she bemoaning with disappointment and he laughing with relief.

And what a storm it had been. Great rolls of thunder, fierce gusts of wind, stunning spears of lightning cracking at the summits, hail such as he had never witnessed before, the size of large ball bearings sheeting from the heavens, covering the earth white, and on the hot tarmac melting into a rushing tide. Sweeney had been captivated by the display, astonished to witness it, as they'd sat together in a café, looking out and drinking tea (for they had become quickly chilled by the sudden drop in temperature). But he'd been remorseful for his behaviour, if Sonja had shown little sign of her earlier exasperation. Had she liked being the adventurous one, enticing the reserved intellectual to forget himself, to do something instinctive and spontaneous? Had she appreciated the reversal of conventional gender roles? Or had she believed he was putting on an act only to amuse her? Still, he considered he'd owed her something and taken her hand, thanked her for bringing him to the lake, hoped the thunderstorm hadn't spoilt her day, apologised for being silly, leaned over the table, kissed her and she'd said, 'I forgive you', as the thunder struck and the lightning flashed. Yet she must have detected something more in his conduct that day for afterwards she'd never suggested they go together to the lakes. She would arrange to go with friends, leaving him to his own devices. Sitting here on a bench on the Rathausplatz, he could only imagine and lament what he'd missed.

His own devices often meant dreamy indolence. To begin with, Sonja's mother had fretted, puffing more anxiously than normal on an ever-present cigarette. She'd been afraid he would be bored lounging about the house, though he never was. His self-sufficiency and undemanding nature seemed to make greater demands on Frau Maier's peace of mind than if he'd solicited constant attention. But after a while she'd got used to him and she'd come to appreciate his independence because it respected her domestic authority. Sonja's father, he believed, had assumed idleness to characterise the intelligentsia and treated Sweeney accordingly. Rarely did he request assistance on jobs around the house for his assessment of Sweeney's practical skills was well judged. Both parents treated him like a *Luftmensch*, impractical and contemplative, and he was as happy to live up to the role as they were to humour him. Sonja had often been busy with school matters, even during the summer vacation, and glad of an opportunity to get on with her own work. Sweeney had enjoyed what the Austrians call '*süsses Nichtstun*' and what the Italians call '*dolce far niente*', such sweet idleness he never considered objectionable.

Occasionally his 'own devices' meant cycling to the ruined castle at Finkenstein. He'd bought for fun a cheap bicycle – it was called a 'city bike' – and told Sonja he was going to do 'a Carinthian Larkin', pedalling about, being creative, and seeking inspiration. Once he'd discovered the ruins at Finkenstein, his conservative instinct took him back there every time. To Sonja he'd explained it, again after Larkin, as 'Castle Going' not 'Church Going'. She'd rolled her eyes and replied, 'You will turn into Larkin one of these days and I'm not sure if I like that.' The ruins had been within easy cycling distance. Sweeney would never stay very long, but he'd preferred its quiet to the raucous life at the lakes and at Finkenstein he could experience idleness at its sweetest. Every reader desires a place of solitude if, when they find it, their books remain unread and so it was with him. He would take a book, a notepad, a beer or two, find a secluded spot, secure his bike, and spend part of a morning or afternoon sitting against a wall, browsing for a while, making a few notes, jotting some random ideas and envisaging the learned publications he would write in the future. After a short time, the book, the pad, the pen as well as his envisaging would be set aside and he'd look over the lush green of the valley, watching tree branches wave in the breeze as shadow and light played across the far mountains. As he sat on his bench at the Rathausplatz, how undemanding time seemed when he'd chosen sweet idleness. Possibly those days had been as close to heavenly peace as he could imagine. One day he'd announced he might be turning into a Connolly. 'I'm not sure if I like that either,' Sonja had said. 'Isn't it enough to be you?' He'd replied, 'It's what I'm afraid of.'

One afternoon daydreaming at the ruins, he'd heard some schoolchildren loud with collective, excited clamour. He'd cursed them, annoyed at the disturbance of his reverie. He'd shifted to a more secluded spot in the hope these intruders wouldn't find him. But they did find him. They had been English teenagers without an interest in the place, but with an interest in each other; boys pushing girls, girls pushing back, a few of them partnered off already and holding aloof from the pack. Sonja was with them. She'd mentioned something about taking charge of a visiting party, some exchange programme organised by her school, but as usual he hadn't taken proper notice. When she had caught sight of him, she'd put a hand to her lips in slow motion, exaggerating the dramatic effect of contrived astonishment. All of his bloodless, bookish abstractions had vanished. Her living flesh before him and her 'limpid green eyes' – here was a fertile principle which made sense. He'd stood uncomfortably, clutching his notepad, kicking over an empty bottle of *Villacher Bier*. She'd walked over to him, abandoning her charges.

'I saw your bike against the wall so knew you'd be here somewhere. I'm glad I haven't interrupted a tryst.' Tryst she'd said in an amused tone, letting him know she was aware how quaint the word sounded. 'I'm glad to find how innocent your pleasures really are.'

He'd replied, 'You are my only guilty pleasure.'

'Glad to hear it.'

The teenagers had become impatient, noisier, and she'd returned to calm things, preparing to give them, in English, a potted history of the castle. She'd arranged them into a semi-circle and before she'd begun, turned towards Sweeney, inclined her head seductively, and called over to him in German, 'We'll see each other later.' Sweeney had made a deep bow, waved and went to get his bike, not wanting to hang about on the edge of things, his quiet disrupted in any case. But he recalled how the school kids had looked at one another, dumbstruck for a moment and he'd imagined them thinking, was this how people in Villach behaved? Was that how easy it was to get a date in Carinthia? Whatever conclusions they'd come to, Sweeney was certain Sonja's standing with them would have grown immensely. How vivid those memories were, like fragments of a novel never finished, lines from a poem never completed. But he knew old eyes see the world differently from young eyes and ageing passions should never be mistaken for youthful ones, unless you really were a fool.

The hot afternoon had settled on him like a mild narcotic as it seemed to have done on the town. It was tempting to sit and let the afternoon pass idly yet the prospect provoked him into movement. He put out his cigarette and strolled across the square to the Stadtkino, interested to discover what films were showing tonight. As he reached the entrance, a line of teenagers emerged, followed by a man and a woman whom Sweeney took to be teachers. For a short while the teenagers, bored and restless, lounged outside the cinema, but when the adults, after a moment of indecision, told them they could go home, became animated, loud, and, exactly as the English teenagers had done at Finkenstein; the boys began to jostle girls, the girls to jostle boys, a few others departing together quickly, arms around shoulders. The teachers followed them with their eyes and once satisfied all had disappeared from view, walked across the square to the *Rathaus Café*.

Curious to discover what they'd been watching, Sweeney went into the foyer. He saw a large poster advertising Ruth Beckermann's film *Waldheims Walzer*, a documentary about the former President of Austria. The matinee, he noticed, was free for schoolchildren and supposed the film had been part of a history or civics course. He could remember the international outcry at the time of Waldheim's candidature in 1986 and the accusations he'd been implicated in war crimes in Yugoslavia. But Sweeney's interest in politics had been minimal and he found Austrian politics particularly unfathomable. The Waldheim affair had been big news, but it had been his *Metroland*. Like the character in Julian Barnes's novel – who'd been close to exciting political events in the Paris of 1968, but never noticed because his attention was focussed on his girlfriend – there had been other things on Sweeney's mind at the time. Anyway, Waldheim hadn't been a subject the Maier family had discussed or, if they had done, it had not been in front of him. And since Sweeney was a guest of the Austrian nation as well as of the Maiers, he'd considered it unseemly to express an opinion on matters not his own. To be more honest, it had been an excuse not to bother, a conveniently self-denying ordinance. And wasn't it the irresponsible pleasure of the outsider *not* to feel obliged to 'take a position', *not* to feel a requirement to 'judge', *not* to allow moral outrage to disturb relaxed composure? Sweeney doubted if he'd asked himself those questions and equally doubted, if he had asked them, he would have behaved differently. Sonja's father had been right – he would have made a hopeless revolutionary. If Sweeney had firm convictions about anything, one was firm enough – to have no opinion whatsoever about politics was the condition of being happy. He thought it would be interesting to see the film, to revisit the past, and to make an effort to understand it for the first time. He checked the next showing. It was at seven o'clock. The timing would allow him to return to the hotel and have a short rest.

. . . .

He couldn't convince himself he'd purged the stain of his treatment of Sonja and could walk blamelessly, but he did feel his step was lighter. There was something else was on his mind. It was the words of Ernie Coote, whose brother Bobby had been the subject of an Irish documentary, *The Man Who Wanted to Fly*, a film Sweeney had watched only the week before. The two brothers were old bachelors, living together in a dilapidated farmhouse. If Bobby sustained himself on dreams of becoming a pilot, Ernie's obsession was amateur radio and his days were spent logging contacts across the world. Ernie's view on foreign travel had been unequivocally dismissive. Traveling abroad meant walking around strange places, looking at buildings and coming home again. 'And what was the point of that?' he'd asked. It was easy to dismiss Ernie's words, easy to ignore the view of a man whose world was circumscribed by a few rooms, a few fields, a few roads and fewer people, a man who stayed at home content to speak with disembodied voices. Sweeney had dismissed them at the time and yet Ernie's words continued to nag at him. After all of his walking in Villach, he'd have to come home again too and what would be the point of that? He supposed he would find out in the next two days.

He passed the Church of St Jakob, Villach's most famous landmark. But his attention wasn't long captured by the building, for he could smell the aroma of freshly baked pastry from the *Konditorei* opposite and could hear spoons tapping coffee cups, glimpse the women seated at the pavement tables as others, out strolling after lunch, paused at the window display. There was laughter and conversation, the midday quiet of the town beginning to shake itself off. He turned right along the cobbled Widmanngasse which descended steeply towards the river. At the corner of Kaiser Josef Platz stood another cluster of teenagers, their eyes bright, strong opinions shouted, happy as they should be when another school day ended. How great it was to believe you have eternal life. And yet, if you believed joy could last forever, you'd think the same about sorrow. Youthful innocence was also a curse, a sweet rose with a very painful thorn. Their liveliness together, their obliviousness of his presence, their self-absorption, their self-assertion, demonstrated possession of such intensity of living – its fertile principles – which is the energy of each generation. Yet they were also possessed by it – and because everything which appears possible can never be, disappointment would shadow promise. Here were restless spirits striving to be something, to be someone, observed by one old enough to recognise the emptiness of all such striving.

He could only wish these young people well, knowing it was no longer a choice for him to keep his distance from this restless life force. *It* would keep its distance from *him*, revealing its presence in the latest trends, indifferent to his opinion, unsympathetic to his wishes, unapologetic to his judgement, his age making him suspect, and rightly so. And when he considered the prospect, he felt not sadness, but serenity once more, for the noise and clamour of the times wouldn't be able to disturb his composure – or so he hoped. He considered it wasn't irresponsible to think like that, but the essential condition of a life well-lived. Sweeney was convinced Larkin had been wrong to believe only the young can be alone freely. Passing by these teenagers, he imagined for them being alone would be like a fear of losing out by stepping inside and closing the door.

The Second Day

It meant possible exclusion, a suspicion others were having a better time, that life was elsewhere and leaving you behind. Those anxieties were surely not freedom at all. It was only now Sweeney could for the first time be 'alone, freely', conscious he was not missing out on anything. Walking in Villach, there was freedom in anonymity because it demanded nothing of him and he could accept the lives of others more sympathetically by getting on with his own. The primal quality of youth, its unlimited desire for happy endings, is a desire which fades but, he had to admit, is never entirely lost. Sweeney hadn't lost it entirely either, but he'd reached an age where the endings are more sharply etched with disappointment and where nothing pleases more than rare accidents.

At the bottom of Widmangasse, he turned into Lederergasse, the narrowness of the street providing some welcome shade and complementing the louche aspect of small bars on either side. Most were closed, but some were open; he saw only a few customers, all big men, sitting high on bar stools or leaning over diminutive counters in subdued conversation with staff wiping glasses, adjusting music systems or re-arranging bottles. Sonja was right about the choice of music in Villach for he could hear a recording of Chet Baker's 'I get along without you very well'. There was about the Lederergasse a sense of the day after the night before, as if such a gentle rhythm was the necessary consequence of the energy and excitement of what had taken place in the early hours, the erotic charge of men seeking women, women seeking men, or any variation on this theme. Sweeney wasn't interested to return and confirm his impression, but he suspected other men and women, alone in Villach like him, later as darkness fell, would find their way here in hope and expectation.

At the intersection with the Hauptplatz, he crossed and went through an archway on the corner. Where once had stood the old tollgate was the hotel-restaurant *Goldenes Lamm* and one of its waiters in his long black apron lounged at the entrance smoking, distracted as if listening to an inner voice. Sweeney continued by the pastel-coloured houses of Gerbergasse and climbed the steps of the pedestrian bridge arching over the Drau towards the glass-fronted Congress Centre, imposing its unrepentant modernism along the opposite bank. On the towpath, pedestrians wandered, youths lay on sculptured, brightly coloured moulded loungers, either reading or chatting, while cyclists carefully navigated a passage around them. Only the tourists were missing.

Thirsty again, he made his way to the riverside café. A young woman in blue jeans and T-shirt carried drinks on a metal tray, re-arranging empty tables and chairs with her hip as she did so. He took a seat, ordered a *Villacher* and lit another cigarette, letting the cold beer soften the heat of the tobacco. He recalled a line of Rousseau's about the pleasurable sensation of mere existence stripped of every other feeling. It was the sensation he experienced, a precious instance of contentment, peace without complication and he didn't want to register anything which would disturb his tranquillity. He considered life could be no better than sitting by the Drau on such an autumnal afternoon. Ernie Coote, he imagined, might see the point of being in Villach, of walking around, looking at the buildings, sitting at ease and having a beer. When he'd finished and paid, he ascended the steep steps leading from the river bank, re-joined the Bahnhofstrasse, arriving at the Bahnhofplatz and Hotel City.

In his room, Sweeney pulled the curtains, lay on the bed, switched on the TV, and began surfing the channels. One programme caught his attention. It was called *Sturm der Liebe*, a soap opera set in a very upmarket resort on the German/Austrian border, displaying an idea of the good life and distinctly Germanic – the pristine hotel, the perfectly clean house or apartment, these days all the colours bright, almost garish, everything neat, the tables set artfully for meals, the food exquisite. The actors were magnificent stereotypes, the doctor so much the doctor, the manager so much the manager and the *femme fatale* so very seductive and dangerous. Sweeney tried to follow their intrigues, but he quickly fell into a deep and dreamless sleep and when he awoke, the TV remote control was still in his hand. *Sturm der Liebe* had finished and in its place was a news magazine programme. A young female presenter stood in the centre of a bright studio, tall, striking, in an orange blouse, tight black jeans and high heels, holding a pack of yellow and orange prompt cards. These bright, brash colours seemed to be everywhere. The stiffness and stuffiness was gone as was middle-aged male seriousness. This vivacious presenter projected energy and informality, with the ironic inflection of youthful self-confidence. But Sweeney had a date with Austria's past. He switched off the vibrant image of Austria's present and headed for the cinema.

. . . .

At the Stadtkino, Sweeney descended a few steps from the Rathausplatz and went along a narrow corridor to the ticket kiosk. Those few queuing before him in twos and threes were 'women of a certain age', in their late fifties and early sixties. Sweeney was the only man in the line. They appeared to be regulars and well acquainted with each other, the cinema their meeting place, an escape from a difficult and, for those without family, often empty time of early evening, hours which can drag slowly between day and night. The French have a phrase, *les affaires cinq-à-sept*, amorous affairs, in discreet hotels or in borrowed apartments, stolen pleasures between the routine of work and the banality of family life. Sweeney judged these women, whatever their romantic desires had once been, were no longer concerned with such liaisons. A cinematic affair was their sedate *sept-à-neuf* and he could imagine how agreeable it would be to negotiate the difficult hyphenation of those dwindling hours with a purpose, a destination, an encounter with others, finding a mood of release heightened by the light of the screen in the darkness of the stalls. If he lived alone in Villach, here is where he would gravitate. After all, wasn't he here tonight?

Inside was a different world, inside was pleasant routine and agreeable intimacy – the familiar exclamations of greeting, the fuss of getting tickets and paying for them, the ordering of drinks, the purchase of popcorn (the one major concession to the mainstream), all the chatting and milling around in the foyer. He wasn't part of their fellowship, of course, but Sweeney appreciated the idea of it, companionable and safe. He imagined himself frequenting the Stadtkino and cultivating the persona of the solitary, self-torturing, genius. Sweeney *Agonistes* – and he wondered if he would become an intriguing character for these women who so far had ignored him absolutely. He was smiling at the idea when he reached the ticket-desk.

'*Waldheims Walzer, einmal bitt*e,' he said.

'*Acht Euro*,' a thin young man behind the kiosk window mumbled in return. His face had a pallor suggesting he rarely emerged from the gloom of the cinema and never felt the warmth of sun on his skin. He took the note Sweeney offered and pushed the ticket plus his change across the desk. He made no eye contact at all and there was no artificial corporate affability, nor the expected verbal dance of '*Danke*' and '*Bitte*'. Sweeney took his ticket and change and wandered into what was called the screening studio. He was the first one there and took an aisle seat in a row about one-third of the way down. The cushions were deep, comfortable, and he was glad he'd slept in the hotel otherwise he envisioned himself relaxing in, stretching out and dozing off. On the cinema's sound system

Scott Walker was singing 'Once upon a Summertime', more evidence of Sonja's comment about Villach's longing for style. Only when Walker's singing cut off abruptly and the lights began to dim, did the women file in and take their seats behind him, as if the projectionist had been waiting for them. Perhaps he had been, since they were certain of their possession.

The story of Waldheim's presidential campaign in 1986 unfolded before them in scenes of demonstration and counter-demonstration, allegation and counter-allegation, rumour and refutation, Beckermann presenting Waldheim as representative of a distinctive Austrian mentality and Sweeney thought again of Epicharmus. Waldheim's supporters argued Austria's debt to the past was no longer his to pay – you must understand, things were different then, you have no idea, terrible things happened, but you cannot judge them by today's standards, it's better to move on, not to look back in anger, not to seek retribution and not to blame Mr Waldheim; times have changed. Beckermann's soon-to-be-President embodied an appeal to this amnesiac victimhood. After 1945, had it not been the official narrative of the Austrian state? And Waldheim, how could he not shield himself and the nation accordingly, the personal become the political. How could he not state the traditional defence with all the ingenuity of the professional diplomat? At one point in the film, a very proper middle-class, middle-aged woman was interviewed on the street. When asked if she believed Waldheim's denial of association with war crimes, she'd replied, 'Of course he is telling the truth. Mr Waldheim is a good Catholic'. Sweeney remembered a line in a Bernhard novel that the Austrian mind thinks only in National Socialist and Catholic terms and, as ever with Bernhard's unforgiving exaggerations, he had laughed out loud. He did so again but, looking to the women behind him, realised none of them had done so. Suitably embarrassed, he sank a little deeper into his seat.

Four Days in Villach

Sweeney understood the conclusions to which the documentary was directing him and he sympathised with its moral force. In the *Confessions of Zeno*, Italo Zvevo wrote of individuals arriving at murder through love or hate, but only propagandising murder collectively through wickedness. The Nazis had propagandised murder into a policy, a wickedness which invaded every corner of life, degrading all it touched, its viciousness endowed with authority, purpose and destiny. Austrians of the war generation, whatever their private feelings, could hardly avoid being tainted by that regime, its drawing together into the monstrous shape of a murder state all those values in which Waldheim professed to believe – duty, responsibility, service, patriotism and self-sacrifice. How could these values not be corrupted by the vicious vanities, savage certainties, spiteful mediocrities and cruel opportunism of the Nazi leadership, a hate intent on destroying everything but itself? After 1938, Austrians had aligned their fate with Hitler and a winter's shadow fell across their lives. Do not consort with evil in such a way as to augment it, Simone Weil had written.

Yet had Sweeney any right to feel smug? When he considered his own attitude to life – his wish to limit the claims others made on him, his desire to keep his distance and be left alone, his lack of interest in politics, his disposition to prefer daydreaming to reality, his often invertebrate willingness to accommodate most things so long as his tranquillity was secure – how would he have behaved eighty years ago? Would he also have consorted with evil? These questions made him uncomfortable and he supposed such was Beckermann's intention.

. . . .

When the film ended Sweeney followed the women out of the cinema and he fancied they walked heavy with remembered sorrow. Making their farewells, they drifted off in fading light through the town. To where, he asked himself – to a bar, to a café, or directly home? Sweeney stopped to light another cigarette, moving to one side of the Stadtkino entrance as young couples, animated and happy, arrived to watch a different film, a post-Waldheim generation, with no experience of war, no memory of suffering, no shouldering of their families' guilt. He looked at the listings poster and checked what they had come to see. He saw *Wilde Erdbeeren*, *Wild Strawberries*, Ingmar Bergman's 'Road Movie in der Vergangenheit', a journey into the past which changes the life of ageing Professor Isak Borg. Sweeney had seen the film as a student when road movie had meant to him the energy, jazz and excitement of Kerouac's America, not a record of Swedish introspection. He hadn't been impressed back then, considered revisiting his judgement, but decided he couldn't sit through another two hours of cinema. Anyway, tomorrow with Sonja he had an opportunity to write his own script.

In the square, chairs had been set out randomly, some were sitting in peaceful conversation and rarely was a voice raised. Otherwise, the night was still. Lights blazing in the *Rathaus café* washed out across the cobbles like a soft glaze. Somewhere in the distance Sweeney heard the brakes of a locomotive and the clanking of carriages as a train approached the station. He raised his eyes to the stars, small beneath the heavens, a contemplative mood disrupted when behind him a young woman on her bicycle dismounted before stopping, ran a few awkward strides and almost lost her balance. When she'd recovered, securing her bike in the cinema's cycle stand, and lifted her shoulder bag from the rear pannier rack, she noticed Sweeney for the first time. As if recognising him, she said, 'Oh, Hallo.'

She looked familiar to Sweeney too, but he couldn't possibly know her. 'Hallo', he replied.

Four Days in Villach

It was obvious to her he wasn't from Villach but, for some reason, she wished to excuse her behaviour. 'I'm sorry,' she said in German and patted her bicycle seat, 'I hope I didn't scare you.' She smiled at him, then excused herself, and vanished into the cinema, her long cashmere coat open and flapping about her legs. Sweeney had no time to reply, but he was strangely moved by the mysterious charm of another chance meeting. Despite all he'd seen tonight, the past it evoked, the horrors it recalled, as he looked around he felt comfortable in the habitation of this place. He finished his cigarette and walked back to Hotel City.

The Third Day

The Third Day

Sweeney woke early to another sunny morning in Villach. He lifted the remote control from the desk by the window and turned on the television. *Guten Morgen Österreich* was broadcasting from a village somewhere (he didn't catch the name) and the sun was shining there as well. Groups of locals were loitering in the background, walking in and out of camera, pretending not to be curious, trying to look casual, as if it were normal for *ORF*, the state broadcaster, to arrive on their doorstep. Sweeney registered the names of the two presenters – Eva Pölzl, who was inside the trailer, whose fresh face beamed cheerfully, whose eyes sparkled readily and whose broad smile never faltered as she interviewed a succession of guests, and Marco Ventre, who was outside on the street, sharply dressed, fast talking, full of bravura, his microphone waving from face to face, doing his best at an early hour to sustain interest and enthusiasm. The presentation was bright and cheerful. He wondered if everything on Austrian television was bright and cheerful. If Sweeney lived here, he knew he would tune in to *Guten Morgen Öesterreich* each morning, expecting Eva Pölzl's good natured charm to cheer him.

Another day and, as Larkin asked, where can we live but days? Sweeney's answer for this day was living well in Hotel

City. He breakfasted on fresh rolls, honey and coffee, keeping an obsessive eye on his watch. There was plenty of time to get ready for Sonja's arrival at ten, but it was his holiday from life and he feared things could slip, especially if he returned to his room and became distracted by whatever Eva Pölzl was doing and saying. Unlikely he'd admit, but Sweeney suffered from a recurring nightmare, like those in films where the character has some significant business to attend upon which happiness, success or fortune hangs, but who becomes waylaid either by chance or choice. The needless anxiety it brought at such times as these – absurdly, he knew – meant he was always ready too early for every occasion.

Back in his room he could hear the housekeeping talking together in the hallway and bustling about their trolleys heavily stocked with replacement soaps, towels, bed linen, water bottles, tea and coffee. He wasn't confident enough to ignore signals from hard-working women, signals he took to mean he should get out of his room and let them get on with their job. He worried at the inconvenience his lingering might cause them, at the same time irritated for being so tender-minded. He put on his jacket, turned off the television – *Guten Morgen Österreich* had finished and there was nothing more to distract him, only a cookery demonstration which, at this hour, made him feel distinctly queasy – opened the door, stepped into the corridor, reversed the card on the handle from 'Do not disturb' to 'Please clean my room' and turned the lock. He needn't have worried about troubling housekeeping routine. The women were busy in two rooms further along from his and he was tempted to go back in again. But as he paused to re-insert his key, one returned to her trolley, saw him, and said a friendly *'Guten Morgen'*, to which he responded. He knew it would embarrass him to do anything else but walk on. Making a point of looking at his watch, he strode off purposefully, trying to give an impression of a serious man with serious things to do. In the lobby the young receptionist from the night of his arrival was on duty again and, as he handed over his room key, they exchanged a look of recognition, but neither spoke. Nothing said but all that is human, Sweeney thought.

The smoking area by the hotel was occupied by a collection of guests who looked like contract workers. Not wishing to hang around at the edge as if he were eavesdropping on their conversation – which was impossible, for their accents were so thick as to be impenetrable – he walked to the railway station subway and took the passageway under the road into the main concourse. As a stranger he enjoyed the impression of purpose-fulness a railway station gave, even when he hadn't a ticket, a time, a platform number or a destination. At least in the eyes of others (if they bothered to notice him at all) he would appear to be someone doing something, going somewhere, it didn't matter what or where. Stations provided reassurance, for his loitering would not be treated with suspicion, and Villach was not a station, he imagined, which attracted the sort of person to be suspicious of. He listened to a public announcement, looked at the arrivals and departures on the electronic screen – Lienz, Salzburg, Feldkirchen, Klagenfurt, Vienna – and, feign-ing urgency, took the escalator with travellers towards the outer platforms. But instead of following them, Sweeney turned back and onto the street.

Outside again he lifted one of the free tabloid newspapers – *Österreich 24* – stacked high in an open-sided metal con-tainer. He glanced at the front page. In a colour photograph he recognised the Austrian Chancellor, tieless in a sharp blue suit, his smile fixed, shaking the hand of some visiting digni-tary Sweeney couldn't identify. He flicked through the rest of the pages and found for the most part tabloid tales with a cast of unfamiliar characters. He was tempted to replace it, but he discovered a comprehensive TV guide which might be useful later. Rolling the newspaper, he put it in his shoulder bag, lit a cigarette, and smoked, watching traffic heading towards the centre of town. But feeling at a loss, he decided to walk back to the hotel and wait in the lobby.

Sitting on the couch with his back to the reception desk, Sweeney consulted his mobile phone as if he had important messages to read or send, shuffled around a couple of glossy magazines on the glass table in front of him and observed the few guests coming or going. Remembering he had a small packet of mints in his pocket, he put one on his tongue to mask the odour of tobacco. He wasn't sure if Sonja approved of smoking, though she had been an occasional social smoker in the past. Yet why should he be worried about her approval and why would she care what his habits were? He looked at his watch again. Too agitated to sit any longer, he went outside and leaned, as nonchalantly as he could, against the vacated smokers' table. He attracted a different sort of enquiring look from the receptionist, who glanced at him through the fine lace curtain, only shifting attention to her computer screen whenever their eyes met. Maybe she thought he was at a loss for something to do? Did she feel sorry for him? Maybe in her job she'd seen plenty of curious behaviour and his was only a minor distraction? It would be nice if she took an interest in his doings for he didn't want her to consider him ridiculous.

· · · · · · · · · ·

Sonja's Touareg pulled off Zeidler von Görz Strasse, drove into the square and parked in one of the places reserved for Hotel City. It was certainly an impressive car, making a statement, but a statement of what – a woman of substance, a woman of taste, a woman able to have the best? He wasn't sure and perhaps it was all three. Sonja let the Touareg idle for a moment, adjusting something on the dashboard, before switching off the engine. When she'd stepped out and walked to the rear of the car, he waved and she waved back. Today she was dressed in a pair of close-fitting jeans and a neat, finely checked blue shirt rolled to the elbow, under which she wore a long-sleeved white T shirt. A woman of taste certainly, Sweeney thought.

'*Guten Morgen, Herr Professor*', Sonia said, making an ironic bow when Sweeney reached the car.

'*Küss die Hand, genädige Frau*', he replied with matching irony. She held out her hand to him, playing the charm game, and he brushed the back of it with his lips, glad now he'd sucked the peppermint. They laughed, mildly embarrassed at their performance.

'You have brought the good weather with you.'

Sweeney raised his arms towards the sky. 'The gods are smiling on us.' There was a moment of indecisiveness as they looked at the heavens and then at each other. 'Would you like a coffee?' he asked, pointing towards the *Café Il Treno* on the corner of the square, brashly announcing itself across the bright red canopy over the entrance.

'No', she replied decisively. 'Let's wait until later. I have somewhere else in mind'. He gestured acceptance and she asked, 'Shall we go?'

'Like nomadic wanderers?'

'The Touareg you mean? Just get in, you'll see. It's no camel.'

As he opened the passenger door, he noticed the receptionist looking at them, the lace curtain making her face seem ethereal, a ghost of his present not his past. He wanted to believe she'd nodded her head in a mixture of approval and appreciation, like a daughter's positive judgment of her father's new partner. And it struck him suddenly – she reminded him of Sara.

In the passenger seat, Sweeney was in awe of the digital

dashboard, all the instrumentation around the driver and Sonja noticed how impressed he was. 'You like it?' she asked.

He pointed to the instrumentation and tapped his seat. 'It's more like a private jet than a car.'

She seemed not only pleased by his reaction but also relieved. Was she self-conscious about the car's luxury? He'd only known her to drive an old Lada saloon which her father had helped her buy. It had been the sort of solidarity with the Soviet Union which made Herr Maier choose little jars of cod roe masquerading as caviar, also from the USSR, which everyone else found foul and which Sweeney suspected not even Herr Maier really enjoyed. But everyone loved the *Sovetskoye Shampanskoye* – Soviet Champagne – he managed to get from somewhere every Christmas and New Year. If the Touareg's internal ambiance was luxurious, the old Lada had driven like a T34 tank, pretty basic but, as far as Sweeney could remember, mostly reliable. He was on the point of mentioning the Lada, but didn't get the opportunity for she said, 'It is a little different from your old Fiat 126 don't you think?'

He'd never loved any car as much as he had his old Fiat. No, he'd never loved any car *but* his old Fiat, the first he'd owned. 'My old washing machine on wheels, you mean? Go for a spin and shake, rattle and roll.' He held his arms out as if holding a steering wheel, jiggling them up and down and from side to side.

'Exactly so!' she laughed at his depiction.

'As Americans would say your Touareg is unreal. The 126 was as real as they come. It would be an antique today, a bit like its owner. But I still miss it.'

'Sorry, I didn't mean to be rude. I loved your old car too. It was a legend!'

'It was really something.' He was going to add, 'We had many good memories in that car' but assumed that is what she'd meant. Instead he asked, 'Have you ever read any of the novels by the American, Walker Percy?'

'No, I haven't.'

'He was interested in what he called "the malaise", the emptiness and lack of meaning in modern life. I remember one line about his own car which he described as a miserable vehicle without a single virtue save one. Driving it provided immunity to "the malaise". I felt I – we – were immune to the malaise in the 126.'

'Yes, it's difficult to feel the malaise when sitting in a washing machine.'

'Do you remember the name you gave it?' he asked.

'Of course I do – *Lupo*, like the lone wolf trekking across Europe. You were a bit of a lone wolf too, so the name fitted well.'

'*Lupo*, a vagabond map, questing on the roads of Europe,' Sweeney smiled. 'I'd never been so adventurous before and I've never been so adventurous since.'

'You make it sound so romantic … but also as if your life is over.'

'Never such romance again, I fear,' and immediately worried about having misspoken, thinking again of her emotional vulnerability (or was it malaise?) of yesterday. 'The romance of the road, I mean.'

'Yes, I do know what you mean.'

Basic in every way, his Fiat had done the job against all odds on those trips to Villach. Its little rear air-cooled engine, on German Autobahns without speed limits, rarely managed to get much beyond sixty MPH. As a result, it had been bullied by powerful Mercedes and BMWs, by large tourist coaches and by thundering juggernauts, drivers flashing their lights and honking their horns. Safety features there'd been none. The steering column had been like a lance permanently aimed at his chest, the bodywork had been as thin and protective as a tin can and the partly soft-top roof, when opened slightly, had made the 126 judder noisily. The luggage compartment in the bonnet, in a minor collision, would have crumpled like a piece of paper, crumpling Sweeney with it. Of course, there had been no headrests either. A miserable little vehicle without a single virtue was a good description except one. It protected him against the malaise.

'What about the air conditioning you liked so much, Sonja?'

'The plastic cover fitted over a hole in the floor? When you pulled it open you got a nice view of the road underneath.'

'I believe they called it the "dynamic through-flow cooling system". Creative thinking by the marketing department, wasn't it?'

'Yes, very …'

And yet for all its primitive frailties, *Lupo* had never failed him, night or day, when the whole of holidaying northern Europe, or so it seemed, had been on the move south towards the sun. He'd driven from Zeebrugge and around Brussels, over the border to Aachen, past Cologne to Frankfurt and Munich, into Austria at Salzburg, through mountain tunnels, finally to reach Carinthia and swing round towards Villach – and Sonja. Fantastic journeys they seemed to him and he still couldn't believe he'd attempted them. Could he only have done so because they were fantastic and dream-like? Sweeney considered his thoughts of yesterday. Maybe he'd been wrong to be dismissive of his youthful adventurism, his judgement of his timidity too partial, his lack of adventure much exaggerated. Hadn't he taken risks, hadn't he once had no thought for the future? So much could have gone wrong at any time. Old men forget (an enduring truth, he knew) and what they can forget is the courage and carefree determination of their youth. Those many things which in the present appeared to him as tiresome difficulties, unnecessary risks, avoidable burdens and worrisome challenges he had once dismissed or never considered. Sweeney couldn't tell when he'd crossed the shadow line between a world of possibilities where he'd lived on emotional credit and a world of solid shape defined by limits and boundaries, one with a diminishing credit balance. Hadn't he been carefree with no sense of his own mortality, with an illusion of invulnerability, with an expectation all adventures would end well? He was no longer that person for he could only visualise dangers and inconveniences. He couldn't, nor did he want to, be 'young again' since most of his former solipsism he considered despicable. But he did long for some poetic imagery to leaven the solid prose of his present. If he was seeking anything in Villach it was the experience of being alive to promise again.

'I used to worry about you on those journeys, thinking of the terrible things that might happen on the road. I was relieved when I saw *Lupo* puttering to our front gate.'

He couldn't remember her ever telling him or maybe it was wordlessly explicit in her delight on his arrival. He couldn't recall feeling in danger, but obviously she had worried on his behalf and he was touched to hear her say it. 'I wonder if I would have the courage today?' he asked.

'What if you were driving my car?' Sonja asked, turning on the engine. As she did so, Sweeney heard the throbbing bass chords of a song coming from the car's speakers. The music was haunting. The voice of the singer seemed to echo from a distance and the rhythm was hypnotic, trance-like.

'Who is that?' he asked.

'It's a band called Cigarettes After Sex. I've been listening to their songs a lot. I find them calming, I suppose in the way church-goers find Gregorian chants a comfort. The song is called "Sunsetz".' She looked at him and sang along to the words '"The sunlight on your face in my rear view, this always happens to me this way, recurring visions of such sweet days." Very poignant and nostalgic don't you think, rather like your old Fiat?' She turned off the sound. The lyrics and her look had thrown him off balance. She swiped her hand across the colourful interactive dashboard display, 'I've selected comfort mode for you, Eddie. The car doesn't have washing machine mode.' She looked as if expecting a wounded protest.

'Better if you can put it in Zimmer frame mode.'

She laughed, 'Maybe it does have Zimmer frame mode. I'm still finding new things the car can do. Sometimes I worry the Touareg is more intelligent than I am'.

He could understand. 'I've considered anything I've ever done, like writing a book or giving a lecture, insignificant compared to the design and precision of a car like yours. When you lift the bonnet and look at the engine, thinking of what it can do and what you expect it to do, it's like magic. No, forget anything as superior as yours. My old Fiat was a greater benefactor of mankind than anything associated with my old job.'

'Like a tennis ball on a piece of elastic.'

'What, a tennis ball on a piece of elastic?'

'Yes. It's strange what the mind retains. Yesterday I said I couldn't remember much about studying Connolly, but I remembered that line. In one of his many moments of doubt, he asked why anyone should bother writing when you could buy a *Kum Back*. I think it was called a *Kum Back*. It was an apparatus for practicing your tennis shots.' She made a few short motions, forehand and backhand. 'If writers like to think the pen is mightier than the sword and deserves the appropriate financial rewards, sadly, Connolly had to tell them, the *Kum Back* is the sort of thing people want to spend their money on. Like a good car, I suppose' and her hand caressed the dashboard. 'Perhaps people are right? Probably most of literature could be dispensed with.' She looked at him, obviously unconvinced by her own argument, 'But your life and mine would have been very different.'

He anticipated her making another comment about the *Kum Back*, but she didn't. 'I take it Connolly was being ironic?' he asked.

'I should think so, don't you? I can't imagine him wasting time with a tennis ball on a piece of string.'

'Perhaps it would be worth trying to find out?'

'I spent last night searching out a lot of stuff from my student days, chasing some other old ghosts – or blowing the dust off them.' She must have enjoyed the evening, for she appeared to be in good humour. 'You mustn't denigrate your work, by the way. You sounded very much like a self-pitying Connolly a moment ago. You should take some pride in what you've achieved.'

Sweeney didn't comment on her remark because she put the engine into gear and reversed the car, turning onto the Zeidler von Görz Strasse again, heading along Klagenfurter Strasse, shortly merging into the heavier traffic on the Ossiacher Zeile. They drove over the bridge and past the twin onion towers, pink and white, of the Heiligenkreuzkirche. Sonja nodded to her left, 'My parents' old house is over there.'

How could he ever forget? The small district of Perau had been like a second home to him, Perau a village within the town, secluded from the cares of the world – or at least secluded from the cares of his world. A confusion of melancholy, guilt and loss welled up in him. 'Do you ever go back there?' he asked.

'No. I have no reason to.'

Sweeney knew all too well. How right Larkin was to say home is so sad, bereft, withered and ultimately stolen – yes stolen. One day he'd driven Sara by his childhood home in which his mother had remained until her recent death. Despite the touches of the new occupants – front door replaced, gutters freshly painted, path newly laid, the whole place looking spic and span, loved as well as lived in – their care had meant nothing to him, for he had no heart to put aside the idea of theft. Possibly for the first time his daughter had sensed an emotional vulnerability in him, disturbing her expectations of reliability and strength, perhaps also fostering a novel sympathy for his weakness. He wanted to say something affectionate to Sonja about her parents, express gratitude for their decency and hospitality, commiserate her again on their deaths, tap into old memories and recall the good times, but he held back, unsure of her response. Hadn't he forsaken their decency and hospitality, as well as those good times? Why would anything he chose to say be convincing or comforting to her? Instead, he looked at her and bowed his head, hoping she would take his silence and gesture as sympathetic understanding.

On the Ossiacher Zeile they passed large superstores new to him and descended to the Kärntner Strasse with its signposts for Italy and Slovenia, the Dreiländereck beckoning. Sonja pointed towards trees hugging the road on the right. 'Today I live over there by Warmbad.' Sweeney mumbled appreciatively for he took Sonja to mean, 'I've moved up in the world since you knew me.'

Warmbad had been famous since Roman times for its thermal springs. Its brash modern logo proclaimed it to be an *Erlebnistherme* – literally, experience pools. That 'experience' of Warmbad he'd likened to a circle of Hell where parents, desperately seeking to amuse their children in the holidays or to recover something of their own childhood, had splashed about demonically, slid down water tubes resembling large pieces of indoor plumbing and plunged into frothing pools. The childish screaming, the waving, the manic energy had overwhelmed him and all he could think of was escaping a cauldron of noise and frantic bodies. His obvious discomfort had amused Sonja and he suspected she'd taken him there precisely to get that reaction. He'd liked her all the more for doing it, for after their day at the lake he knew he deserved it, and his dismay had become one of their in-jokes. It wasn't that but another 'experience' he loved, one he considered a distinctively Austrian marriage of conservative tradition and liberal permissiveness.

'Do you take the waters?' he asked.

'As in the diary of some Edwardian lady, you mean? No, I rarely visit these days.'

'I used to love the baths – not the kiddie pools but the real thing.'

Sonja had introduced him to another world which had seemed wonderfully Edwardian. And he'd taken the waters literally, drinking from the fountains tapped directly into the thermal springs, the taste mildly sulphurous, faintly metallic. He'd fancied the curative effects it would have, counteracting the cigarettes he'd smoked, the alcohol he'd drunk, the food he'd over-indulged, but he couldn't recall any consequence whatsoever, positive or negative. Together they had taken the waters in another sense. They'd immersed themselves in the thermal bath, letting the jets of water at the poolside play therapeutically on their bodies, the sort of exercise Sweeney appreciated most – sedate, relaxed, mentally not bodily conscious, dawdling, daydreaming and drowsy, Sonja poking him periodically to keep him moving along. Beside the water had been arranged soft padded recliners, men and women in towelled bathrobes lying slightly propped, reading and conversing, or prone and lightly dozing. And there had to be the Austrian essential, a café bar, around which bathers had sat on high stools in their trunks, swim suits or bathrobes, drinking beer, wine, coffee, sometimes tea, eating cakes, chatting and smoking. The sight had warmed Sweeney's heart for he took its cultured idleness to be a true measure of civilisation, the promise of health, wellbeing and restoration, internal and external, co-existing happily with reasons for seeking well-being in the first place – enjoying a drink, eating a pastry, smoking a cigarette.

Four Days in Villach

'I remember how much you enjoyed the mixed sauna,' Sonja said and couldn't help spluttering at the memory. Sweeney had entertained her with his prudish delicacy, his inhibition, his towel as if nonchalantly, unselfconsciously and accidently draped across his groin. Everyone else had been completely naked and relaxed, while he had tried not to stare, alert to Sonja's periodic, playful tugging at his improvised loincloth. The women had all been bronzed, fit and sporty, the men less so, often paunchy, but as ever their physical presence, their 'Carinthian-ness', had been so much more imposing than his own pale-skinned and slender physique. Miraculously, and perhaps because he was such a contrast to other men, his lean and fragile body had appealed to her.

'You were trying to uncover my manhood!'

'And you were such a stuffed shirt!' Sweeney laughed because he hadn't heard the expression 'stuffed shirt' in such a long time. It sounded very Edwardian.

'There's not much traffic', he said when they'd left Villach, surprised because he recalled the road permanently busy and frequently congested.

'Most of it has been siphoned off onto the motorway' she replied. 'It has transformed life along the old road.' In Sweeney's mind appeared an image of tranquillity, the air cleansed of exhaust fumes, butterflies drifting, deer grazing by the roadside, children playing safely, perhaps an old maid cycling to church, and he'd mumbled something clichéd to her about protecting the environment. 'Nothing is an unmixed blessing as you will see,' she replied.

They drove by Hart and passed the turn-off for the Wurzenpass, one of the mountain crossings into Slovenia. It was a route he'd driven only once because the vertiginous incline – or so it had seemed at the time – made him uneasy about the engine capacity of his Fiat, but in the end it wasn't the ascent which had been his greatest fear. The 126's 650 four valve, with a full load of himself, Sonja and her parents, had survived when others hadn't. He remembered a blue Peugeot sedan with a French licence plate blasting its horn at Sweeney's presumption of crawling slowly before it. The car overtook on a clear stretch of road, its occupants laughing derisively, pointing at the 126 as they accelerated by, recalling for Sweeney all the humiliations of the Autobahn. Two or three bends further and there was the same Peugeot, tight in by the side of the road, its engine overheated, steam billowing from its radiator, the fat driver in his shorts and vest scratching his head over the bonnet, his wife and two teenage daughters sitting disconsolately under the shade of a tree close by. 'Who's laughing now?' he'd delighted and was about to beep his own horn (it wasn't loud enough to blast) and give the Frenchman two fingers. Sonja, guessing his intention, had looked stern and whispered '*Nicht!*' putting a restraining hand on his arm. He'd understood and resisted the temptation. His gesture would have embarrassed her parents and offended their sense of propriety, but it had been a sweet moment nonetheless.

It hadn't been the ascent which made him sweat, but the descent. Sonja's father had helpfully pointed out to him gravel run offs had been laid for drivers whose brakes failed, so he shouldn't worry, information which only had the effect of making him apprehensive. As he'd negotiated the pass and its curves, the scent in his nostrils hadn't been of pine resin or mountain flowers but the pungent smell of tortured brake pads, burnt, acrid, unpleasant to the nose, bitter to the taste and intimating the danger he'd been told to ignore. He'd been relieved when the road began to level out again, the gravel run offs ended and he could take his foot off the brake. His whole body had been tensed like a spring, fists clenched around the steering wheel, chest tight like he'd held his breath the whole time in tight-lipped silence. 'The Wurzenpass was one of the scariest things I've ever done in my life.' He was exaggerating, but not too much.

'I don't remember. Was I with you?'

'Yes, you and your parents, we had lunch in a restaurant at the top. I'm guessing it was a Sunday.'

Sonja shook her head. 'No, I can't picture it at all. Are you sure?'

'Sure I'm sure.' He couldn't believe Sonja had forgotten. He was mildly irritated, irrationally he knew, and in silence looked out across the valley of the river Gail to where the Dobratsch dominated the skyline. The grey gradients of the mountainside were slashed with scree and in the morning sunlight there was a pinkish tinge to the rocks. The lower slopes were thick with pine, but only a few managed to struggle in thinning ranks towards the peak, like depleted lines of exhausted soldiers scaling an objective while their comrades clung *en masse* for safety below. They'd been driving for about twenty minutes, were beyond the villages of Lind and Pöckau, when Sonja slowed as they approached the town of Arnoldstein. '*Kaffeepause*', she declared, swinging the Touareg off the road and pulling into a car park in front of a few low buildings.

. . . .

There was a sign for *Café Central* and she saw his look of surprise. 'Not quite *Café Central* in Vienna, is it? It's our Carinthian version, much more relaxing. Here there's no queue of tourists ticking off another attraction on the to-do list.'

'I've never been to *Café Central* in Vienna. I've only read about it. I'm sure it will be my sort of place.'

They got out of the car, walked to the café and took their seats at an outside table, pulling wicker chairs closer together to be under the awning and in the shade. It was hot already and Arnoldstein quiet, as if its inhabitants were having an early siesta. He recalled stories he used to read in the local newspaper, reports of car engines catching fire, a cat trapped in a tree, a pensioner falling when getting off a bus. 'Really big news,' he would joke with Sonja and while he'd laughed, those stories had made him feel gently cocooned in peaceful fancy, stories, however commonplace, which put anxiety to sleep.

'I learnt a new word before I came to Villach.'

'And what is it?'

'*Geisterreich*. I should have mentioned it yesterday when you were talking of ghosts. I saw it translated as "shadowlands" – an abode of spirits as well as a border between states. It reminded me of your part of the world. "Dreamland Austria" sounds better I think – at least for my holiday from life.'

'Yes, the spirit world might suit you better.' She fluttered both her hands, 'Wooooo, there goes Edward Sweeney, the man who lives outside time', putting on the sepulchral tone of someone conducting a séance. 'The spirits are very strong. Is there anyone out there?' She put her hands on the table. 'Wait, I'm getting something – P…Ph…Philip, Philip Larkin. Oh no!' and she waved her hands to dismiss the poet's spectral appearance, 'What have I done to deserve it?' She laughed, and he enjoyed hearing her laugh.

A thin middle-aged woman in a floral blouse, dark skirt and open grey cardigan, a small notepad in her left hand, interrupted Sonja's joking. Unlike *Café Central* in Vienna, Sweeney supposed, the service in Arnoldstein made no pretence of the Old Monarchy, of 'carrying on a great tradition'. But neither was there the contempt he imagined waiters in Vienna must feel for tourists 'soaking up the atmosphere', taking selfies or photos of the coffee and cakes, glancing around at other tables, believing themselves to be in the company of Loos, Musil and Zweig. There was none of that here. Indeed, the waitress didn't speak at all, only leaned her head to one side, looking at them in turn with an angelic smile in response to their orders, a coffee for Sonja, a small beer for Sweeney. The waitress nodded and went back inside. Sweeney asked Sonja, 'I hope you don't mind me having a beer so early in the day?'

'Well, *Ulrich*' – she stressed the name – 'Carinthia is *Frühschoppen* country. Having a beer in the morning is no sin. I've checked with the Holy Ghost of Austria. I would have one too. If you remember, I did when you were driving me.'

Sweeney couldn't recall her drinking early in the day. In fact, he couldn't recall her drinking much at any time. The waitress returned slowly and deliberately, a metal tray carefully balanced before her. She set down Sweeney's beer, Sonja's coffee, along with a glass of water, and stood back, as if impressed nothing had fallen or been spilled. She smiled at them, again said nothing, and drifted away once more. There was something of the sleep-walker about the woman, Sweeney thought, noticing she was wearing a pair of bedroom slippers. He was about to tell her when Sonja lifted her cup, '*Prost!*'

'*Prost!*' he responded and touched his glass to her cup. He pulled out his cigarettes and asked if she would like one.

Astonished, she waved away the packet, 'I can't believe you still smoke!'

'I don't really, but I liked this brand. I associate them with being in Villach. Do you mind if I do?'

'Please, go ahead. Smoking is another traditional Austrian pastime.'

Sweeney nodded at the pack on the table, 'Holiday from life again,' he said as he lit up and pulled the ashtray towards him, aware of her looking as, self-consciously, he exhaled the smoke.

'Okay, I will have one to keep you company, if only for old time's sake.'

He fumbled around in his pocket to retrieve his lighter and clumsily eased a cigarette out of the pack for her. Sonja put it to her lips and he cupped his hand round the flame. She bent over closer to him and, looking into his eyes as he lit it, started to cough and splutter. Pulling back into her chair, she took a moment to recover her poise. 'Sorry, I couldn't help thinking we are like a pair of kids, sneaking off school to share a first cigarette.'

'Here's to us, children of another age.'

'Children of another age,' she smiled at the idea, taking another drag but not inhaling. She blew the smoke exactly like a young girl trying a cigarette for the first time and looking like the Sonja he'd known when they'd first met.

'Cigarettes after Reunion, I hope they're as good as the post coital ones,' he said.

She didn't look at him, appeared slightly flustered, blushed and laughed, 'You really have become a child of another age.' She took a sip of her coffee, placed the cup back in its saucer and absentmindedly rolled the end of her cigarette around the rim of the ashtray and asked, 'What did you do last night, anything interesting or exciting? Did you go out on the town? Were you tempted by the fleshpots of Villach?'

'They wouldn't let me into the fleshpots. I was under age.' ('Ha!' she sniffed.) 'But I did go to see *Waldheims Walzer* at the Stadtkino. It was interesting, but I couldn't say it was exciting. I'd forgotten much of what happened and the rest I didn't know.'

'I knew you would have made a first-rate Austrian, Eddie. People here have been good at forgetting what happened and better still at claiming they knew nothing.' She stubbed out her cigarette only half smoked and pushed the butt around the ashtray with her fingernail.

'The most interesting thing was the other cinemagoers. It was a seven o'clock showing, too early for the night owls. I was the only man there. The women were mostly my age – not many of them, but they seemed to know one another, as if the cinema was their regular rendezvous. Which film was showing didn't seem to matter. I think it was a case of having a purpose in those difficult evening hours, somewhere to go and something to do.' Sweeney regretted speaking so lightly for he thought it made him sound smug and patronising.

'Do you mind if I have another of your cigarettes?' she asked. 'Sorry, I wasted the first one.'

'It's nothing,' he said and offered her another. She didn't bend towards him and he had to stretch in order to light it for her.

Sonja held it from her and contemplated the tobacco as it burned. 'I could be one of those women you describe.' She put it to her lips, did inhale, grimaced, held the cigarette to one side of her head and let the smoke drift behind her. She took another sip of coffee, staring ahead and Sweeney struggled to think of a way to contradict her without appearing defensive. So he watched her as she smoked. The ash on the end of the cigarette toppled to her shoulder and fell onto the table. She hadn't noticed so he leaned across, blew what remained from her shoulder and brushed the offending ash from the table. His actions surprised her, brought her out of her introspection and when she realised what he was doing, said 'Obviously I'm not used to smoking.'

'Never mind not being Bergman and Bogart in *Casablanca*. We aren't like Bacall and Bogart in *The Big Sleep* either.' He said it softly and he hoped reassuringly. But she didn't respond to a possible escape into cinematic fantasy he'd offered. She leaned back in her chair and sighed.

'It's over a year since Christian died ... a year and a half nearly. We were married almost twenty-five years – a quarter of a century. It's hard to think of time like that, isn't it, almost like you're already history? He was going to retire and sell his business. I was about to retire too. We had plans for the future, to change things in our life, but they came to nothing. It was prostate cancer. He never suspected until it was far too late. It was a shocking time. It's a silly thing to say and I hate to think it – you remember how I can cope with most things – but it was so unfair. There was nothing the doctors could do, only palliative. And he was gone.'

Sweeney saw tears well in her eyes and he felt guilty for thinking only a while ago of their physical intimacy in the sauna, as if Sonja and he had been having an affair behind her husband's back. Yet why should he feel guilty about betraying a man he'd never known? And anyway, he hadn't betrayed him. He admired the way other people seemed to have the right words on the tip of their tongues, as if schooled in the way of comforting responses. Sometimes he found it hard to find those words Larkin had written of, words 'not untrue and not unkind'. He found it equally difficult at this moment, offering a silent prayer, not for Christian among the dead, but for himself among the living; but the spirit only moved him to keep silent. He knew nothing of their life together, nothing of their plans for the future, so what could he possibly say? Almost twenty-five years she'd mentioned. He made a quick mental calculation and realised Sonja must have married soon after they'd parted – or after he'd 'ghosted' her as his daughter would say. Was it why Sonja had told him he shouldn't be too hard on himself? Had Christian been the Bacchus to her deserted Ariadne, a welcome contrast to his disloyal Theseus? Had she chosen the restaurant yesterday to make a point – she'd been prepared to sacrifice everything for Sweeney, only for him to abandon her and leave her distraught? Only in a novel, only in a novel, he thought, but didn't rule out the possibility entirely. Surely, he should be relieved that she'd moved on so quickly? But he wasn't. He was unsettled to think there had been an almost seamless transfer from him to her late husband. He considered women more inventive in life and in love than men – well, certainly more inventive than him. Or was it they were more practical? He was wounded, almost as if he'd been the one wronged, an emotion utterly irrational, but there it was. Reason, he knew, was only a slave to passion (even when passion was merely nostalgic).

He reached out, gently squeezed her shoulder and let his hand linger for a few seconds. And it surprised him to see she did appear to be genuinely comforted by his gesture. He pulled out a fresh paper handkerchief from the packet in his pocket and handed it to her. She took it and dabbed her eyes. 'Thank you', she said and forced a smile. Sweeney squeezed her shoulder again, a different meaning, not a gesture of solace, but one of solidarity.

'Christian was different,' she went on, which Sweeney took to mean different from him, 'not only a successful entrepreneur, but a great socialiser. He was outgoing, involved with lots of groups. He loved to be on committees, to be in the public eye, considered going into politics too. He was forever at events, attending parties, arranging fundraising dinners, that sort of thing, all on top of managing his company. We first met at a charity evening at the Congress House. In English you would say he was "a pillar of the community", the sort of life you would hate' and she gave him a quick sideways glance.

He found it strange she should have described it thus. He certainly would hate it. But how had she felt about it? 'It sounds like he led a very full life' was the only banality he could find and it irked him to be so trite. Couldn't an Emeritus Professor of English do any better?

'Yes it was, very full. But it became trying – for me, any-way – especially when the children were born. And I had to cringe when we were described once in a newspaper as Villach's "celebrity couple". It was like we were in a show and our life an exhibition. It was so not me. Can you guess?' He expected she didn't want to hear whether he could guess or not, judging she was being confessional, not inviting his comment. 'We reached a *modus vivendi*. I was happier with my teaching, the kids, friends … and the dogs. And I loved our home in Warmbad.' The thought of the house deflected her momentarily, something obviously pressing on her mind. 'It's really too big for me. I think I should downsize – isn't that the English term?' and Sweeney nodded. 'Christian was happier out and about, in the world, his energy poured into schemes and projects, his own and those of others.' She knocked off the ash from her cigarette before it fell again – she'd hardly smoked any of it – and left the butt smouldering on the lip of the ashtray. She turned the coffee cup around on its saucer. 'We didn't lead completely separate lives. Rilke wrote, between those who are closest infinite distances exist' and she looked sideways again at him, almost furtively. 'It's only we could -we *should* – have spent more time together.'

In an instant he conceived a story. It was of Sonja being a trophy wife, someone to be displayed to further her husband's ambitions (whatever they had been). He pictured her growing resentment and his obliviousness to it, her challenge to his expectations and his denial of them, her criticism of his selfishness and his taking offence at her antipathy to the life he envisaged, their long silences, their *modus vivendi* unsatisfactory to the hopes of each. Just as quickly he dismissed the idea as cheap soap opera fantasy, a confection of his base desire to clean the blemish of his own bad conscience. So he asked, 'Your son and daughter, how did they cope? It must have been really hard for them too.' Was there no end to his banalities or were these were the right words he was looking for, both true and kind? At least Sweeney found they were prompts she didn't find unfeeling and showed no sign she found them lacking in sympathy.

'Christoph and Hannah were both at university. They were leading their own lives, or at least trying to. It was a shock to them as well, obviously – Christoph especially, he's very much his father's boy, outgoing like him. Hannah's more like me. Everything happened so fast for them, for me, for all of us. I suppose it was the moment when they were no longer children – sorry, another cliché – and they were forced to become adults overnight, helping to taking care of me or at least trying to do so.'

'And you see them often enough?'

'When I can and when they can.' Sonja took another sip of coffee and gazed into her cup. 'I noticed you were confused about my odd behaviour yesterday.' Sweeney looked quizzical. 'At the *Rathaus Café*, when you showed me the photograph in the old Villach guidebook?'

'I'm sorry, Sonja. I knew it really wasn't us. It was stupid of me. I never had any intention of upsetting you. I was only trying to be a smartass as usual.'

'But the thing is … it could have been us. I recognised the resemblance if I pretended not to. And it disturbed me. It seemed as if you'd never been away and we'd been frozen forever in the past. It cast over me a shadow of remorse, not for the life I didn't lead, but for the one I did. Oh, that sounds all wrong.' She tossed her head in annoyance, clearly confused. 'What I mean to say is I was upset for comparing things like that.' She continued to stare into her coffee cup. He got the impression she'd said all she wanted to say and took him by surprise by asking, 'What about your partner and your daughter? How are they?'

'Sara is fine, thank you. She has recently qualified as a schoolteacher – history, not English.'

'I hope she enjoys teaching as much as I did. My own children never wanted to do anything but play with computers.

IT is their thing, not education or business. And how is she, your daughter?'

'She's happily married, but her most important job in life is to look after me.' In case she didn't recognise it as a joke, he laughed loudly.

'And your partner, what about her?' She moved her cup around the saucer with a fingertip.

'She's okay too – well, as far as I am aware, which isn't very much these days.' Sonja appeared to be taking her time to think over his answer. Sweeney was keen to change the subject, shifted in his chair uncomfortably and tried to conceal his nervousness with a cough, looking at his cigarette as if it were responsible.

'The two of you are no longer together?'

'No, not for the last' – he did some more quick mental arithmetic – 'fifteen years or more.' It seemed much longer. 'We would have driven each other crazy. It was better for everyone, Sara in particular, to avoid all the rows and all the bad feeling. It was certainly better for me' and he couldn't resist saying, for it happened to be true, 'to keep my distance.'

Sonja still didn't look at him.

'Emily,' he said.

'Sorry?'

'Emily, Sara's mother is called Emily.'

'Eddie, you are really a hopeless case. You were a fool, a holy fool maybe, but a fool nonetheless.' It wasn't said harshly, as if the years had inoculated her against his foolishness. 'I had a look at the copy of *The Unquiet Grave* you gave me. Connolly wrote it under the pseudonym Palinurus from Virgil's *Aeneid*. Can you remember how he interpreted Palinurus?' Sweeney couldn't remember. 'He says he stands for the will-to-failure, the desire to surrender, the urge to loneliness and isolation. When I read it again I couldn't help thinking of you, more so after what you've told me.' She pushed her smouldering cigarette off the rim and into the ashtray. 'I'm sorry. I'm not judging you for what happened. I'm ignorant of how things are between you and Sara's mother. It's really none of my business. But you love your literary connections and it struck me – nothing more.'

'There's no need for you to apologise to me! I understand what you're saying. I could be a character out of *Sturm der Liebe*, predictable for making the wrong choices.'

'You watch *Sturm der Liebe?*' Her face was disbelieving.

'I saw a little bit of an episode yesterday afternoon.' He expected Sonja to dismiss the soap as television trash.

'I love *Sturm der Liebe*. But I never expected you would like it,' as if she'd discovered something about him for the first time.

. . . .

Sweeney had met Emily at a book launch. He disliked such occasions and was normally inventive of excuses to avoid them. But the book had been written by his Head of Department, someone who'd been supportive of Sweeney's career, and he'd felt obliged to go. These events were often attended by the same people, hosted by the same bookshop serving the same ghastly wine. This time everything had been different. His Head of Department was a woman of taste as well as self-regard. It was at her villa – a magnificent old house paid for not by an academic's salary but by her husband's barrister fees – in an exclusive location overlooking the sea, its extensive grounds running to the shoreline. The wine and food had been excellent, the people different too. His Head of Department liked to think she had her finger on the pulse of the local 'cultural scene' (Heidi came to Sweeney's mind again) and had invited writers, actors, artists, all of them, Sweeney felt, behaving like the stereotypical writer, actor or artist (just like an episode of *Sturm der Liebe*), behaviour which had made him suspicious of their creative pretensions. He'd wandered outside to escape the chatter, cradling in his hands a glass of best burgundy. The night was fresh, the air clear after a shower of rain and he'd been looking out to sea, observing a brilliantly lit ferry sailing towards the North Sea and Scotland. He'd been calculating when sufficient time had passed for him to go back in, make polite apologies, ask his Head of Department to sign a copy of her book, order a taxi and leave.

'Are you looking for the green light, Mr Gatsby?'

He'd turned around surprised by the voice. A woman was standing in the shadow of the doorway, smoking a cigarette. Her pose had looked carefully staged, one shoulder against the door frame, her body leaning slightly back, one foot hooked behind the other leg. 'I'm afraid you won't find what you're looking for out there.'

'No, I suppose I won't' and he was going to add 'and not inside either' but didn't want the woman to think him a snob. He'd walked towards her and when close enough, could see she was about his age, with long brown hair falling across one side of her face in a contrived rather than an accidental way. She'd been dressed in a green bomber jacket, a black polo-neck sweater, denim jeans and pair of Doc Martin boots, the alternative uniform of the day. She wasn't good-looking like Sonja, but attractive nonetheless and much of her attraction had been in her directness, a boldness intended to disorder the reserve of someone like him (or possibly any man). Her talent (he was to learn) was self-advertisement, promising much but delivering less, and because Emily believed in her own promotional material she could only attribute disappointment to the failure of others.

'I followed you out. I hope you don't mind.' Her accent was well-educated, but what Sweeney could hear was Lisa Minnelli playing Sally Bowles in *Cabaret*, an instant perception which should have put him on his guard straight away.

'No, why should I mind?' he'd replied, thinking he sounded a little too much like Michael York.

'I'm glad, for I wanted to talk to you. It's better out here than in there, more romantic don't you think?'

'Yes, I suppose it is.' He'd stood next to her, leaning his back against the wall. 'Your name wouldn't be Daisy by any chance?'

She'd laughed, 'No, Emily, my name is Emily.'

'Edward. It's a pleasure to meet you, Emily.'

'It's a pleasure to meet you, Edward,' she'd replied placing a coy emphasis on the word 'pleasure'. Sweeney had sensed immediately there was a chance this Emily could ruin his life, had an intimation of plunging against his better judgement into deep waters (waters Santayana likely would have cautioned against), but he couldn't resist, if only because he considered himself to be in control.

So it had begun. She was an actress (an aspiring one) and his first impression of Sally Bowles had proved insightful. Emily had all of Sally's doubts and insecurities as well as all of her brashness and *faux* vamp demeanour. He'd been flattered by her attention, he had to admit, attracted by her energy, seduced very quickly by her desire, but he'd soon become annoyed by her impulsive moods and exasperated by her unpredictability. What she regarded as spontaneous and creative he judged to be capricious and demanding. Very quickly he'd realised his mistake and all he could think about was being with Sonja again, wondering how he might surmount the remorse of a momentary foolishness. He'd concluded the right thing to do was simple – ask Sonja to marry him. His resolve (for which he congratulated himself) had made him confident of his moral worth once more. He'd felt liberated from error and all he needed was an opportunity to walk away from Emily. Then one night she'd announced, 'Eddie, I'm going to have a baby. What are we going to do?'

And what they'd done was to act out those scenes in *Cabaret* when Sally became pregnant. They'd become two characters rapt in each other, playing new roles, imagining how their future together would be so wonderful. A father, he'd be a father, and the idea which before had never crossed his mind, elated him. And feeling such elation and expectation, he knew he couldn't be with Sonja. So he had lost her. But too cowardly to confess the truth, he hoped time would solve problems of conscience. It never had. Unlike *Cabaret*, the baby was born, like *Cabaret* there was no happy ending.

After Sara's birth – time which had been a dreamlike mix of euphoria and exhaustion – they discovered their incompatibility. Opposites may attract, but in their case contraries didn't make for harmony, especially when there was a child involved. When Sweeney recalled Huxley's question (and sadly, he could only hear it asked in Sonja's voice) 'if it were not for literature how many people would ever fall in love?' he believed cinema was equally guilty and had never watched *Cabaret* again. Emily and he had drifted apart, his routine and habits as annoying to her as her unconventional behaviour was annoying to him, their respective fatal gifts to any possible reconciliation. Her unfulfilled ambitions as an actress she blamed on his smooth rise as an academic ('Oh yes, it's easy for you,' she'd say, 'your life runs on rubber wheels') and her exuberance became despair, her vivacity, querulousness, and her independence, neediness. He'd tried to be a comforter until he realised his diversions would never be imaginative enough and she would sulk when he ran out of inspiration. He had become a bore which for Emily was a sin beyond redemption. She judged him absurd and he had come to feel the same about himself and knew that way self-destruction lay. He couldn't deny his responsibility for what had happened, nor did he want to, and in the end he had to go astray, cursed by fate, with the usual punishment of loneliness for which she had no mercy. He'd gone to live nearby – a small apartment on the top floor of a block, perched among the treetops – and arranged to see his daughter most days. It had been a clichéd drama they'd acted out and Emily wasn't a soap opera fan. She had been compelled to hawk herself for small roles in theatre, mostly without success. Finally, she'd joined a *Commedia dell'Arte* troupe, became a Colombina, travelled a lot, and away for long periods when Sara was at school. These days, his daughter told him, she was getting by giving drama classes.

'Do you want to tell me what happened?' Sonja asked.

He was still too ashamed to tell her the full story. 'There was a baby. That's what happened and what changed everything. I don't regret my daughter. But Emily … you'll remember the line from Connolly, Larkin referred to it as well, "the pram in the hall", a child will drain your life of creativity and success?' Sonja nodded. 'It became her excuse. To be fair, she didn't resent Sara. She resented me. Things fell apart and we returned to our separate worlds. At least it was done before the cruelty began in earnest' and he gave Sonja a summary history, an admission of his failures, hesitantly, for he felt nakedly exposed. It was painful, for the truth was he'd never told anyone before. 'You may find it hard to believe.'

'What would I find hard to believe?' Sonja's voice sounded distant and disembodied.

'After we separated, I lived out the legend of the new man. I became the carer, part of the life at the school gate, was familiar with most of the mothers, enjoyed their gossip about the teachers and learned the stories of Sara's friends.' He sensed he'd gone on too long. He looked across at Sonja, 'It's another familiar story, isn't it?' He stopped and blurted out, for he detected sorrow in her eyes, 'Can you forgive me?'

She seemed astonished by his question. 'You really should have taken Holy Orders. You mustn't wallow in guilt like this.

It's self-indulgent. And you needn't beg my forgiveness. I told you yesterday, there is nothing to forgive. Forget the sins of yesterday and your transgressions in the past. *Geh hin mit Frieden.*' Had she prepared her line beforehand, like the song in the car before they left Hotel City?

'I will as long as you don't lead me into temptation.'

She scoffed, 'My days of temptation are over.'

'My story must sound pathetic to you.'

'You can only sound pathetic if you take yourself too seriously. I think you never took yourself seriously enough. I considered that a virtue, but it came with the vice of not taking seriously how others cared about you … and self-pity isn't a good look. You make it sound like you're leading a life of renunciation yet your good humour belies it. I wonder if what you lack is a witness to your days?' She took a deep breath. 'Don't answer my question. Perhaps it's not a good idea to be confessional and neither of us are religious types, are we? We can't resolve yesterday or fathom each other's failures, but at least we can enjoy today. Shall we make the most of the beautiful weather?'

'Agreed,' he nodded, hoped something had been salvaged for the future and grateful she didn't want to inhabit the past in grievance.

. . . .

The tables in front of *Café Central* had become occupied, the customers Italian as far as he could judge, about the same age as they were, but obviously regulars and not passing trade. The waitress spoke to them in Italian (so she had a voice), dawdling in conversation, exchanging views, sitting for a moment with one couple, moving on to sit with another. Her gestures had become more animated and she seemed to have awakened fully from her somnambulism. Italian pop songs from the 1980s were playing softly from an old loudspeaker on the café wall, the voices tinny and indistinct. Some tunes were familiar to Sweeney, like melodies from his past, but they were too faint for him to make out clearly. 'The Italians seem to like this place. The coffee must be good.'

'The coffee is good and it's the new Europe. Borders have become crossings.' She hesitated and qualified her comment. 'Well, they've become crossings for people like us.' She nodded towards the other customers. 'Italians are buying property on our side and we are buying property elsewhere too. Eva and Hans have bought a summer house in Hungary. They love that part of the world and spend a lot of time there. That's where they are at the moment. And I forgot to say yesterday. When I told them you were coming they asked me to pass on their best wishes.' Eva and Hans were Sonja's sister and brother-in-law and they had been good to him as well.

'Give them my best wishes too. I imagine it's idyllic. And it's great to see borders opening.'

She sniffed, 'We have the old problems back as well, like anti-immigrant feeling and right-wing politics. We go forwards, we go backwards.' Most things are never meant Larkin had written with his usual pessimism – or realism – yet Sweeney believed the lifting of the Iron Curtain (as he still called it) must be filed under the historical category of 'a good thing' (if the point wasn't naively Sellar and Yeatman). It was a judgement based entirely on the experience of a brief visit to Prague he and Sonja had taken one summer.

He'd sent off his passport months beforehand and it had returned from the Czechoslovak Embassy in London with a page-length green and red visa – *Ceskoslovenke Vizum* – granting four days in the People's Republic. Prominently displayed at the top (he hadn't paid any attention to it at the time) had been a declaration in English, 'This visa is valid only after exchange of the Czechoslovak currency'. They had travelled on the overnight train from Villach to Vienna to make a connection to Prague. It hadn't been a sleeper car, but travelling through the night was romantic whatever the circumstances. Sonja had slept soundly, her head resting on his shoulder. It had been raining heavily and Sweeney could remember tracking individual raindrops as they trembled across the window of their dimly lit carriage. As their train rushed across the liquid dark of the Austrian countryside, he'd had no wish to fall asleep for it was if he were dreaming already.

On the journey from Vienna to Prague they'd occupied a compartment in an old corridor coach, the cushion bench worn and overstuffed, but comfortable, with thick net luggage racks strung across above their heads. Sweeney had visualised the 1938 Hitchcock thriller, *The Lady Vanishes*, with Sonja as the beautiful Margaret Lockwood, himself as the debonair Michael Redgrave, giving the journey a distinctive edge of mystery and adventure (even if there had been no other passengers, malign or benign, sharing their compartment). At the border, the train had pulled slowly into an expanse of no man's land and come to a halt. When he'd looked out the window, Sweeney could see soldiers, in dull brown battle fatigues, rifles slung over their shoulders, patrolling either side of the single track. Periodically, they would crouch to inspect the underside of the train, stand upright and walk on, looking bored. Inside the train, a procession of uniformed officials began to work their way systematically through the carriages.

First had been the railway guard, who'd checked their tickets yet again, a sad faced man, whose demeanour was permanently apologetic and whose expression seemed to say, 'I'm so sorry for disturbing you, but what can I do? You've got to understand, it's the system's fault, not mine.' Second had been a couple of soldiers who'd made them stand outside the compartment while they'd shone torches under the seating and clambered above to check if anything had been hidden in the luggage racks. Third had been a border official, with a couple of armed police for company, who'd checked their passports, looked at their photographs, asked where they were going and why. When he'd been satisfied with Sweeney's answers, the man had produced a stamp from his pocket and, pressing it on the page, endorsed his visa. Finally there had appeared a squat, pleasant-faced woman, also in uniform, her blonde hair tied under a tight fitting hat, with one or two wisps awry. A tray hung around her neck, a cumbersome wooden affair which looked like the top of an old school desk. With her were another two sour-faced policemen. Only then had the declaration about Czechoslovak currency become clear. The woman had taken a look at his passport and in excellent English asked how long both of them intended to remain in Prague.

'Two nights', Sweeney had replied.

'Three days,' she'd said.

Sweeney had been told how much currency he was required to exchange. The rate had been outrageous, if not one for one, near enough. Here Sweeney was prepared to admit his memory could be wrong and in the re-telling of the story (he'd told it many times) he might have been exaggerating. But such had been his silent outrage to an offer he couldn't refuse, parting with Austrian Schilling for Czechoslovak Koruna, he could be forgiven for exaggerating. He was no anarchist, but for the first time he'd understood Proudhon's diatribe about the state as a legally sanctioned protection racket, an understanding compounded by the woman's permanent (he judged it contemptuous) smile.

Their experience in Prague had been equally unsettling. They'd stayed in a vast, cavernous hotel where there had been any number of staff, none of whom had shown any interest in being either pleasant or helpful. The uncomfortable, dismal room they had been given, with its poorly sprung bed, had looked over an alleyway filled with overflowing bins. Their bedside radio played only irritating folk music and the volume, Sweeney had discovered, could only be lowered, but not turned off. He had been tempted to disable it – there'd been no plug, the wiring going directly into the wall – but Sonja had feared damaging state property. Sweeney suspected it was a secret listening device and he may well have been right (much later when he watched the German film about Stasi surveillance, *The Lives of Others*, he was reminded of those few nights in Prague). The presence of that radio had made intimacy of any sort awkward and in the end had made it impossible. Both of them had become anxious and dispirited, their convivial togetherness displaced by the malignant force of political bureaucracy. When they'd returned to Villach he'd been ashamed of his behaviour and he knew the word for it was acting like a *Rotzriasel*.

He didn't want to remind her of Prague and of his behaviour so he said, 'When I was watching your TV, I discovered everything has become shiny and colourful, programmes fronted by young women with bright smiles to match. I have the feeling Austria is a good place to be.' He knew it sounded corny and she gave him a look as if she judged it corny as well.

'And why shouldn't it be? I love my country ...'

'Apart from Vienna, that is.'

'... apart from Vienna,' but she appeared uncertain of what she wanted to add by way of addition or qualification. She gently tapped her hands on the table, 'Shall we journey on?'

Sweeney nodded, finished the rest of his beer and attracted the attention of the waitress, who reluctantly dragged herself away from conversation at a neighbouring table. She returned to a trance-like state as she came over to them. In German he told her what they'd had, she told him what he owed, and he paid with a good tip. She didn't say thanks, only looked at him vaguely, but approvingly. A dream within the dream of life, that's as good a way to get through the day as any other, Sweeney thought. As they rose from their table Sweeney asked Sonja, 'What's the music I hear in the café? It seems familiar, but I can't make it out clearly.'

'It's a compilation of old Italian hit songs.' She stopped briefly to listen to the track currently playing. 'Appropriately for us, that's Lucio Batista singing *Si, Viaggare* – "*Con un ritmo fluente di vita nel cuore*" – and she translated – "Let's travel with the rhythm of life in our heart". You used to be fond of Italian songs. Surely you remember it?'

'I'm afraid not.'

'To think the poor misguided staff at the *Konsum* once took you for an Italian!' She shook her head. 'And you don't remember Lucio Batista? Maybe you were in a daydream the whole time?'

Back in the Touareg, when she started the engine, he said, 'Let the flowing rhythm of our journey continue.'

'It's too late for you to make amends,' she laughed, pulling out of the car park. They turned onto the main road which dipped gently towards the limits of Arnoldstein to rise again steeply. Beyond the rise, where aimless clouds floated in the blue across the mountains, was the Italian border. 'If you haven't worked it out yet, we're going back to Thörl-Maglern.'

. . . .

They drove towards jagged peaks faintly misted by the heat of the day. They would stay in Thörl-Maglern sometimes with Sonja's aunt and uncle who in the summer, like others in the village, would open their house to tourists travelling to or returning from Italian and Croatian beaches. The sign by their house – *Zimmer Frei* – was a common sight, the holiday trade supplementing family incomes. The border was only a short distance from their house and the village was the last, or the first, opportunity for drivers to make an overnight stop within Austria. When her aunt and uncle had full bookings, they'd asked Sonja to help out if she could and Sweeney would drive her, making a poor effort himself at lending a hand. She would assist with rooms and breakfasts while his job consisted of driving Sonja's aunt along the narrow back lanes familiar only to locals to buy provisions at the *Konsum*, avoiding the main road regularly choked with cars and long-distance trucks. When they returned, he would carry in purchases from the car, depositing beer in the cool earthen cellar and the rest in the kitchen. Once that job was done, he could live – as most people appeared to do in the Carinthian summer – outside in the fresh air, lounging on the wooden veranda in the back garden, going through the motion of reading, books open, pages lazily flicked, sometimes writing, but more often than not drowsing, the hum of traffic to one side of him, the buzzing of cicadas in the meadows to the other.

At the rear of an adjoining whitewashed house had been a neat cherry orchard. The old woman who lived there would often shout across from her balcony when she needed someone to carry in wood, to hammer in a nail, to adjust the TV aerial or to fetch something from the *Konsum*. In return, she would present a basket of cherries, fruit so sweet and luscious, unlike any Sweeney had ever tasted. He'd felt there was something decadent as he lay, stretching his left hand to lift a cherry, pulling it from its stalk with his lips, sucking the rich flesh and dropping the bloodied stone into a bowl on his right. Anton Wildgans wrote of time spent in an Austrian garden as evidence enough of the magic and the curse of his country. Sweeney had experienced only magic. He'd felt Roman then, most certainly.

'Apart from being mistaken for an Italian, do you remember much about Thörl-Maglern?' she asked.

'Yes, lots. I loved it there. You met all sorts at your aunt and uncle's house. With the arrival of each guest, I would think: this could be the beginning of a novel.'

'If only we'd written them, you and I.'

Most guests who took rooms only stayed overnight, Thörl-Maglern a way station between home and elsewhere, elsewhere and home. Some did stay longer and it was these few who remained memorable. 'Do you remember the German couple who transformed themselves into Carinthian natives?' he asked.

'The *Flachlandtiroler* you mean?'

'Is it a word I should have learned from the book you gave me?'

'The English term is "wannabe", city people who want to adopt for a while the Alpine lifestyle, wannabe Carinthians in our case?'

'I like it!'

These *Flachlandtiroler* were a middle-aged couple from northern Germany. They'd arrived in their sleek, beige, BMW saloon, dressed conventionally in casual, if expensive, summer clothes, the man tall, wiry and reserved, the woman smaller, full in figure and decisive. After spending a short time in their room, they'd re-appeared and Sweeney had been astonished by their transformation. The woman wore a flowing, blue cotton *Dirndl*, complete with a white apron decorated with little flowers, no hint of a stain on it, and a fresh white blouse with short puffed sleeves. The man had put on a pair of light-tanned, knee-length *Lederhosen*, a fine-checked red shirt open at the neck, heavy white woollen socks rolled low on the calf and walked heavily in soft leather boots.

'It's an innocent pleasure,' Sonja remarked. 'It's living an illusion – a holiday from life, you might say' and glanced at him.

The Third Day

'We all need our holidays from life.'

The German couple's illusion, Sweeney believed, had been of an authentic way of life – the people, the land, the culture, all three probably – despite their attempt looking entirely inauthentic. Sweeney recalled the man's sedentary office legs conspicuously thin in bulky *Lederhosen*, his knees prominent and bony. Had all their dressing up been the wife's idea, the husband feeling obliged to humour her for the sake of marital harmony? He'd thought of the couple when reading Bernhard who, as usual, had launched into a denunciation of the Alpine holiday with its Alpine paraphernalia, its Alpine intentions, its Alpine passion, its search for Alpine peace and quiet and, ultimately, its Alpine madness. All those years ago, Sweeney had been disdainful of this German couple for similarly Bernhardian reasons. He'd reconsidered his opinion and believed his derision misconceived, today only feeling indulgent towards them. They had managed to spend their time in an apparently blissful state, a routine of slow regular walks, of relaxing on the veranda (tactfully, Sweeney had vacated his usual spot for fear of disturbing them with his obvious incongruity), of eating well, of drinking moderately, of breathing deeply the mountain air and of absorbing what the woman would probably have called 'the atmosphere', unaware of their oddity. After a week, they'd returned to the city, *Dirndl* and *Lederhosen* packed away for another year, the husband probably relieved to get back to his suits and business, the wife longing to return next year to live again the romance of the mountains.

'You must remember the lads from Italy, the motor racing fans?'

'I certainly do. Wasn't the small one madly in love with you, Sonja?'

She put a hand to her forehead, 'Please don't put the image in my mind. He used to bring me a little present every year.'

'Aha, so I was right to be worried. What was his name?'

'Agostino. He was small, overweight, sweaty, his hair oily, but apart from all that …'

'He was sweet and adorable?' Sweeney interjected.

'Yes, exactly what I was going to say, sweet and adorable … and it was *almost* true.'

The Italians were from Friuli, all car mechanics and Ferrari fans, who stopped over regularly on their way to the Austrian Grand Prix at Zeltweg. They would pull up, three car loads, in various types of Fiat (but never in a 126) on the Friday evening of the race weekend. They'd got to know Sonja's aunt and uncle over the years and their loud voices, bustling presence, their mixture of shapes and sizes, seemed to fill every available space inside and outside the house. On arrival, as the heat of the day gave way to the cool of night, they'd sat out on the veranda, arranging chairs into a circle, inviting everyone to join them. One (Sweeney could picture his rich handlebar moustache, Roman nose and balding head) took the role of master of ceremonies, producing a bottle of their local wine along with a small, shallow, roughly-hewn wooden bowl. There had followed a ceremony of friendship, the bowl passed around from lip to lip, wine replenished when required, like a secular communion cup, with Sweeney included in the congregation. He never knew what they'd done most of the next day. They'd driven off, leaving behind on their breakfast plates in little balls, the soft inner bread of the rolls Sweeney had collected fresh from the bakery earlier that morning.

'They exasperated your aunt by disrespecting the *Kaiser Semmel*.'

'True, she considered it such a waste.'

'Typical Italians,' her aunt had shaken her head. 'They only want to eat the crisp bits. Can you believe it?' Sweeney had shaken his head in solidarity, but, yes, he could believe it for those bits were definitely the best.

'She loved them really. They were like part of the family to her.'

Returning that evening, they'd gone off to collect in the woods above the house wild mushrooms for dinner. Sweeney had thought it a risky enterprise but Sonja assured him, if you knew what you were doing, there was a rich harvest to be picked. Yes, but it was her 'if you know what you are doing' which worried him. Clearly they had known, returning with a couple of basketfuls, hustling Sonja's aunt out of her kitchen to cook a dinner of pasta with mushrooms in a cream sauce. The meal had been delicious and Sonja had shown her approval of Sweeney's bravery, squeezing his leg under the table as he'd forked his first mouthful. Had Agostino watched with despair this little intimacy, wishing he'd slipped a few deadly fungi into Sweeney's dish?

A sleek black Audi sports car with a Vienna number plate overtook as they crested the hill. 'There was the strange Viennese family.'

'Who were they?' she asked.

'Don't you remember the quarrelsome parents with the strange daughter?'

He pictured the care-worn, timid and solicitous daughter in her mid-thirties, whose dowdy dress sense, unkempt hair and absence of make-up, had signalled to men – certainly had signalled to Sweeney – 'don't come near me'. The mother was a small, rotund woman, her face slightly bloated, her cheeks flushed, her eyes watery, wary and suspicious. The father had been thin and frail, his face a grey pallor, slow moving but, unlike his wife, outwardly friendly and sociable. They'd arrived in a dilapidated green Opel saloon, hadn't booked ahead, 'speculative guests' who wished to stay on a day-by-day basis. Sweeney had guessed they'd reached the Italian border, been uncertain about what to do next and decided to stay on the Austrian side. It would be familiar and life more easily negotiated. In the end they'd stayed for three days and in the course of those days the reason for the daughter's anxious and troubled appearance revealed itself. Her parents were alcoholics.

'Don't you recall?' Sweeney asked. 'The parents drank all day and fought all evening.'

Sonja shook her head, 'No, I can't.'

They'd brought with them bottles of vodka and schnapps and the only purchases they'd made locally were beer, cheap cola and soda water for which they would send the daughter. They'd never gone walking, never gone for a drive, never strolled over to Italy for lunch or dinner – they'd done nothing at all but stay limpet-like around the house. The mother and father had sat in the shade from early morning, their glasses of schnapps and bottles of beer on the table, smoking constantly, glancing at a few magazines. Sometimes Sonja's aunt and uncle would chat with them which reluctantly as hosts, they'd been obliged to do, the guests' nasally melodic Viennese accent sounding thin by contrast with their rich Carinthian dialect. The daughter, for whom Sweeney had begun to feel desperately sorry, would sit for part of the morning, also reading a magazine, drinking a coffee or a juice, but would retire to her room around midday, only to re-join her parents in late afternoon. None of them ever seemed to eat.

'The parents reminded me of Jekyll and Hyde.'

'You paid them a lot of attention, obviously.'

For most of the day, the mother and father had remained well-mannered in a clichéd Viennese way. They'd been polite to the aunt and uncle, friendly enough towards Sweeney and courteous to Sonja. But Sweeney had been irritated by the way the father would call her 'Fraulein Sonja' in a show of charm, but to him it seemed phoney at best, lewd at worst, definitely vulgar, a sign he took of the man's mendacious existence and he couldn't avoid the suspicion there was something louche about him. Suddenly, about four o'clock, it had been as if a switch was flicked. The parents had become argumentative, the daughter rebuked for trying to quieten them, the language turned nasty, insulting, brutal. As they'd argued, a glass or bottle would get knocked over, drink would be spilled, the daughter left distraught. After a few hours, all three had become exhausted, turning to a sullen silence and then separately drifted off to their rooms. Sweeney had never witnessed a performance like it, one repeated each day like an evil recurrence. He'd been shocked, tempted to ascribe their behaviour to the heat wave – he called it 'heavy air' with neither escape nor relief from the weight of a sultry, sweltering stillness lying across the land, days in which the mountains seemed only to block the horizon and to imprison. He'd been wrong. It had been drink.

Luckily the weather had broken, one of those fierce storms which accumulate, the sky sullen with a brooding darkness, darker than Sweeney had ever seen, a sudden tempest thundering with dramatic flashes of lightning, the rain torrential, like a sign of heavenly disapproval. The downpour convinced the Viennese they'd had enough of the countryside. They'd made their farewells formally, soberly, said how much they'd enjoyed their stay, expressed a hope to return and had driven off. Sweeney described their behaviour again to Sonja and told her how it astonished him still.

'It shows what a sheltered life you've led. I did think you unworldly.'

Maybe she was right, even if his lack of 'worldliness' could be attributed, he knew, to a less redeeming characteristic, a lack of curiosity about how others lived. Sonja (like her aunt and uncle) was accepting of others' shortcomings. They all worked with the grain of those they knew and met, acknowledging the variety of human conduct – a demanding neighbour, *Flachlantiroler*,

Italian boys and Viennese alcoholics, such characters examples of how the world is. She and they proved capable of taking their measure and to understand people's limits, also what they might be capable of. And it dawned on Sweeney perhaps he fell within Sonja's range of understanding too. Maybe his betrayal came as no great surprise either – a bolt from the blue, yes, but had she taken it as yet another example of wayward human nature, one of the shocks you had to expect? It was not a question he could ask, not a line of enquiry he could pursue, but he sensed an emotional strength and practical resilience in her which meant she hadn't been devastated by his action. He hoped so. Was her willingness to forgive him part of the same disposition, taking people – like him – as she found them? And as he asked himself these questions, he knew he only was desperately and pitifully seeking solace.

. . . .

They passed the road sign for Thörl-Maglern.

'Recently I came across a reference to Thörl-Maglern in a novel,' he said.

'Really, which novel is it?'

'Robert Schindel's *Gebürtig - Born Where* is how the title was translated.'

'Eddie, I'm impressed. I haven't read it. What did he say?'

'He wrote Carinthia is an odd stretch of land and for some reason you couldn't depend on the mountains – whatever that meant I couldn't say.' Sonja's look told him she didn't know either. 'But also, if you had to be in Carinthia, you should live in Thörl-Maglern. And his reason was – with a leap and a bound you can be in Italy'.

'I think it's what you'd call a backhanded compliment.'

'I thought that too, a place you don't enjoy as *somewhere,* but a convenient location to go *elsewhere*, like the tourists who stayed at your aunt and uncle's.'

Sweeney could understand what Schindel meant. The pleasure he'd found here was similar, Italy only a short stroll away and Slovenia only a short drive. It was tempting to believe those escape lines more important than anything else. And yet wasn't the whole of human life here in Thörl-Maglern? There was little reason to think cosmopolitan life any different. Nothing, like something, happens anywhere Larkin had written – and everywhere.

Sonja turned off the main road and parked near the *Freiwillige Feuerwehrhaus*. Sweeney saw it had been extensively renovated and freshly painted white. The building was an impressive presence, like a place of communal reverence. As if confirming its quasi-sacred character, there was a large mural of St Florian, patron saint of the fire service, in the garments of a Roman soldier, carrying the flag of the Holy Cross and pouring water from a pitcher onto a burning house. *'Gott zur Ehr, dem Nächsten zur Wehr'*, 'To the honour of our God and the protection of our neighbours' it proudly proclaimed. Sweeney appreciated the linking of the two Great Commandments in a common social purpose, the fire brigade as secular saviour.

'We can do a tour of the village,' she said when they stepped out of the car, 'in the best nostalgic spirit … for both of us.'

On a wooden bench in front of the *Feuerwehrhaus* sat a very old man, dressed in a fine tweed suit, white shirt and red tie. He was leaning forward on his walking stick, enjoying the sun, the glory of the day all around, probably with little better to do of a morning than sit here, passing his time in rest and quietness, watching in hope for the Lord perhaps. Sonja waved and they both greeted him with a cheery *'Grüss Gott!'* The old man only raised his stick slightly, nodding his head in gracious acknowledgement.

'Do you know him?' Sweeney asked.

'No, but he looks like a real *Menschenkenner*'.

A connoisseur of human nature sounded about right to describe him and Sweeney recalled another Ebner-Eschenbach aphorism – 'Respect the commonplace. Centuries of wisdom are stored there'. To encounter any human practice, as simple as an old man's raised stick in greeting, was to encounter culture infinite in depth. Sonja's parents, her aunt and uncle, they were *Menschenkenner* too. Sweeney wasn't sure if he was, feeling more a wanderer, a sleepwalker (like the waitress at *Café Central*?). Larkin had puzzled over this matter too, wondering how we spend most of our time living on imprecisions. Here, Sweeney's lack of comprehension and fluency, made him feel acutely his own imprecisions. The old man, without the education Sweeney had received, knew so much more, his dialect deeply rooted in the wisdom of local shadings, in the truth of untranslatable words and meanings, about all of which Sweeney remained ignorant. And yet hadn't his marginality made life here so fascinating? Wasn't it congenial to his *Luftmensch* persona?

He said, 'I'm sure he would have some great stories to tell.'

'He is a son of the German language, but not a German, and counts himself lucky to be Carinthian.' From her glance he knew he'd missed some literary reference, but she didn't volunteer it and he didn't ask. As they walked, she adapted her pace to suit his own and he considered offering his arm, not with the intention of physical intimacy, but as an act of companionship. Sonja seemed happier to keep her distance and, after what they'd discussed at *Bacchus*, he could understand.

. . . .

They walked to Pessendellach, past open fields bordered by forest, before turning up the hill towards Oberthörl. Along the way Sonja spoke about how as a young girl she'd loved travelling from Villach, in winter, playing in the snow, in summer, picking flowers and berries, as if it had been her magical playground, rhythms more romantic, adventures more exciting in the meadows and woods than in the streets and parks of town. Her recovery of the happy innocence of those days, her animated description of them and the people who'd shared them with her, trailed its own melancholy and loss. How could it not be otherwise? *Sunt lacrimae rerum* – and it was a question whether those tears were *for* things lost or *in* things lost. Reflecting on the Latin phrase, the toe of Sweeney's shoe caught the edge of a small crack in the road and he stumbled forward. Sonja put her arm out to steady him and when he'd recovered his balance, she didn't remove it. 'Here, let me help you', she said. It was more than mere assistance and it wasn't amatory fancy, rather compassionate reassurance, a physical gesture confirming the words Sonja had spoken, which he had only half believed, that he had no need to carry around a burden of guilt. When they'd made it to the top of the rise, Sonja stopped and pointed to a rough track leading off the paved road, heading into the trees on higher ground. 'Do you remember we went sledding here one Christmas?' she asked.

'I do. I'd never been on a sled in my life before. And I certainly remember the cold that winter.' It was true. In Villach the temperature had fallen one day to minus twenty Celsius. He'd gone out in what he'd considered sufficiently warm clothing, with borrowed gloves and woolly hat, a scarf pulled over his chin and mouth. The deceptive thing had been the sun and the blue sky with a pinkish tinge, the air perfectly still, but when he'd returned after a short while he'd no feeling in his fingers. They'd felt dead and bloodless and as the circulation returned the agony was almost unbearable, partly because so unexpected. He'd never cried with pain before but, despite his best efforts not to, he couldn't prevent the tears flowing, an experience which taught him to respect the Carinthian winter. 'I'll never forget your mother's cure for frostbite.'

'*Tee mit Rum* I take it? It was her remedy for all winter ailments.'

'*Stroh Rum* was an acquired taste,' and Sweeney grimaced. 'At first I tried to drink it neat. The aroma was deceptive for it smelled like sweets from my childhood – rum butter toffees they were called – but it didn't taste like that. It was thin, herbal with a distinct flavour of chemicals. When I tried to pour a glass your mother snatched the bottle from me. "No! No! No!" she'd shouted.'

'Yes, I can imagine the scene. But she was absolutely right, wasn't she?'

'She was. *Stroh Rum* in a large, steaming mug of black tea was just the thing, like swallowing fire. After my second cup, and much to the amusement of your mother, I was too drunk to notice any pain.'

'Yes, I can imagine that too.'

They climbed a short distance up the path which gave onto an old oxen track snaking before them. On the descent from the woods the oxen, with their loads, must have zig-zagged for stability's sake. 'We went up and down this way, remember?' Sonja pointed to the boundary of the woodland.

'My greatest sporting achievement, if you call avoiding a broken neck an achievement' and she gave him a playful nudge. He'd enjoyed himself immensely, doing as an adult what Sonja and her friends had done from an early age. They'd travelled by train from Villach to bring Christmas presents to her aunt and uncle. It had been too tempting not to take advantage of the snow which, on the old track, had settled and hardened into a natural toboggan run. The two wooden sleds hanging in the old outhouse had belonged to Sonja, a smallish one from her childhood years and a larger one from her teenage years.

Sweeney discovered he could control and guide the smaller one better, and control and guidance meant not falling off or crashing against the banks. For brakes he'd used his feet and remembered doing terminal damage to his cheap Moon Boots, footwear which had been all the rage back then, the white synthetic insulation hanging out from tears above the rubber soles caused by friction against ice, like stuffing from a child's soft toy. They'd trudged up and tobogganed down the oxen track most of the afternoon and when they'd exhausted the fun as well as themselves, they'd gone to *Gasthaus Neuwirt* where they both ordered *Tee mit Rum*. Together on an upholstered bench, the conversation of the other customers like a lullaby in their ears, experiencing waves of comforting fatigue, they had fought the desire to sleep against each other's shoulder. 'What a great day that was,' and she seemed happy to hear him say it, slipping her arm through his once again.

'Shall we go to *Neuwirt?*' he asked.

'It's next on the tour,' as they descended towards Unterthörl, the stream beside them sparkling, racing and bubbling over loose rocks. It could have been spring not autumn.

'Autumn is the mind's true spring,' he said suddenly.

'Who wrote that?'

'I can't remember. The light on the water reminded me of it.'

'I like it. Have you ever read Colette?'

'No. Should I?'

'Yes, you should. I ask because she wrote something similar. Colette couldn't agree with those who called autumn a decline. She imagined it as a beginning, the green of spring becoming decked in gold to inspire wisdom.'

'I like it.'

'She also feared it could mean the opposite of wisdom, the ripened woman fooled into thinking there would never be another winter.'

'I don't like that line.'

But his mind wasn't on what Colette had written. He could hear the voice of Yves Montand singing the autumnal song '*Les feuilles mortes*', the line '*Mais la vie separe ceux qui s'aiment*' and the finality of '*Les pas des amants desunis*'. He hoped autumn wouldn't be a season of false promise and enduring separation.

. . . .

Gasthof/Pension Neuwirt stood directly on the main road where once trucks had crawled their way to the Italian border and where, in holiday season, cars had inched beside them in funereal column. The road was quiet and there were no trucks and precious few cars. The *Gasthof* was standard Austrian post-war design, a solid block of a building, plain fronted, painted white on the upper two stories, and brown along the ground floor. The attached pension was salmon-pink, with two rows of wooden balconies along the upper rooms. It had been once a proud statement of confidence in the prosperity of the village, occupying a strategic location, advertising itself as a dependable, welcoming place for the traveller to rest and refresh. Sweeney wasn't sure who passed by or if anyone stopped, so he asked her.

'When they completed the *Autobahn*, Thörl-Maglern was left stranded. It is one of those mixed blessings I told you. People can live without the disruption, noise and pollution – you remember how bad it used to be every summer – but the passing traffic was their livelihood too, like my aunt and uncle's. Life went elsewhere.' Sonja pointed towards the valley where, in the distance, Sweeney could glimpse the sweeping tarmac ribbon of the *Autobahn* and the large blue signage bridging its carriageways. Arranged about it were trailer parks, trucks and containers standing in organised ranks. 'The *Konsum* has gone – no one left to mistake you for an Italian – and the train doesn't stop here anymore.' The train doesn't stop here anymore! It sounded like a death sentence. Yet *Neuwirt* didn't look run down, maybe today making a different statement, one of defiance.

When they entered, everything was as Sweeney remembered it, which is not to say everything had remained the same. To the left of the entrance was the old dining room with a right-angled, cushioned bench, the one on which they'd struggled to stay awake. In the space before it was arranged four wooden tables and chairs. The room was empty and diners, if there had been any, long departed. To the right was the bar, a simple counter, behind which was shelving stacked with glasses, a few sporting trophies and, on the top, the usual array of bottled liquors, mostly unopened. Close to the door was a metal table like the one outside Hotel City. Leaning against it was an Italian couple, both with espressos, a tall woman in her early thirties, with flowing blonde hair, dressed in tight black trousers, knee-high suede boots and a denim jacket, beside her a man in his forties, smaller, more corpulent, wearing a waist length sheepskin coat, inappropriate Sweeney thought, for today's fine weather. They appeared to be acquainted with the owner, a middle-aged woman, slim but strong and, in her patterned nylon coat, looking like a hard-working farmer's wife, proud to be a host in her own kitchen. Like the waitress at *Café Central,* Sweeney noticed how she shifted conversationally between speaking Italian with the couple and speaking Carinthian dialect with the rest of her customers. The Italians finished their coffees, waved goodbye to the waitress and only engaged those at the *Stammtisch* with a parting '*Caio*'.

The *Stammtisch* ran along the wall opposite the entrance and at it sat six men all of whom, apart from one in a car mechanic's overalls, were obviously retired. Their discussion was loud, animated and one of the six appeared to be the butt of jokes for the day. Someone had to be, maybe they took it in turn and maybe it was an honour to be found interesting enough to be the laughing stock for an afternoon in a genial, if unequal, battle of wits. The owner stood at one side of the bar, leaning on it with her elbow, making curt observations on behalf of the one being mocked, if only to balance the game a little. For it clearly was a performance, one with familiar roles, like a verbal juggling act where the object was to keep the conversational plates spinning on poles of absurdity for as long as possible. When, or if, those plates were to fall, they would expect to find something else in their collective juggling box to entertain them and if not, it would be time to go home, there being no purpose to the performance other than for its own sake. Outside, problems might be waiting for each one of them, but inside there was time for amusement.

Sonja and Sweeney sat at the table directly behind the *Stammtisch* and he whispered, 'Evelyn Waugh once wrote he never knew how teetotallers got on in the world since all useful knowledge was to be found in bars.'

'Where did he write that?'

'It was in one of his travel books.'

'I haven't read any of those. Are they worth getting?'

Sweeney couldn't say whether they were worth it or not for it was the only thing he could remember, so he improvised, 'They are interesting enough, but you'd probably not call them great literature.' It was the best he could come up with and luckily Sonja didn't pursue the subject any further. The waitress came to take their order. Sweeney ordered another small beer and Sonja an orange juice. The waitress hadn't recognised her, which surprised him. 'Don't you recognise the people here?' he asked.

'One or two look familiar. I haven't been in *Neuwirt* for a long time. I think the Italians who left live in Thörl-Maglern. They were talking about going across the border to do some shopping. The owner is new to me.'

'There was a story I read a long time ago', he said. 'I can't think of the author or the title of the book, I don't remember whether it was fact or fiction or where exactly it was set. So let's make it Austria. It's after the last war, after all the destruction, after everything which had taken place. A writer returns to a town where he'd lived – let's make it Villach – and hasn't seen it for many years. Streets he knew have been bombed, buildings he loved destroyed and in the chaos he recognises no one. Everything appears other than what it was. He turns a corner and there, standing where he'd always stood, is the hot chestnut man – only there are no chestnuts and his brazier is cold and empty. The writer is astonished at first and then angry. What on earth is the man doing? Doesn't he understand the whole world around him has changed utterly? Doesn't he realise what he's doing is pointless? Doesn't he understand how absurd he looks? He's about to confront the hot chestnut man but stops, for it suddenly dawns on him how magnificent such stubborn endurance is. In a world of madness, maybe the old man is the only one who'd stayed sane.' Sweeney wasn't too sure why he'd mentioned the story.

'I see what you mean. You're thinking of the people in here, how things change but stay the same, like the still point of the turning world? Do not call it fixity, there is only the *Stammtisch*. Eliot could have written those lines in Thörl Maglern.'

'Yes, that's exactly what I mean. Thank you.'

'You're welcome – and there is still a hot chestnut man in Villach, you know.'

'Is that so? Well, I'm glad to hear it,' and he was.

They sipped their drinks, content to be observers and listeners, to catch each other's eye like conspirators, when a burst of laughter broke out or someone slammed a palm on the table to make a point. Sweeney didn't understand most of what they were talking about (the dialect was too rich), but he didn't need to. Sonja whispered to him, 'There's a line in *Der Rosenkavalier* – do you recognise it – *"leicht muss man sein mit leichtem Herz und leichten Handen"?'* Sweeney shook his head. 'You have to take life easy with a light heart and light hands or God won't have mercy on you.' She nodded towards the *Stammtisch* and Sweeney decided it was a good commandment to heed.

When they'd finished their drinks, he asked, 'Sonja, can you do something for me? Can you ask the owner to give the *Stammtisch* a round of drinks? I don't want them to feel obliged to me and I don't think I could explain to her clearly enough in German.'

'Why?'

He couldn't really explain it properly in English either. 'I like their determination, in a world where everything changes, to carry on regardless – especially in Thörl Maglern where the train doesn't stop anymore. Please, here's fifty Euros' and he pushed a note into her hand.

'There's really no need.' She held the note between finger and thumb and flipped it against the palm of her other hand. 'But alright, yes, I'll do it for you.'

As Sonja went to the bar to pay, Sweeney left, saying '*Auf Wiedersehen*', but he didn't think anyone had heard or noticed (maybe he should have said 'Caio' like an Italian in honour of the old *Konsum?*). Outside, he smoked a cigarette and considered he might have been over-sentimental. What if they felt his gesture patronising? He could hear loud exclamations from inside. He leaned against the wall and watched a bus pull in across the street. A few school children got off with those familiar brightly coloured, box-like, Austrian schoolbags high on their backs and he was gratified to see the village was not only a place for the aged. The bus, empty of passengers, headed towards the border. Sonja took some time to come out.

'I had a bit of a chat, sorry. There was some back and forth about my aunt and uncle when they realised who I am.' She handed Sweeney his change, which he stuffed clumsily into his pocket.

'Was everything okay?'

'Well, the owner said it was generous of you. The old boys were grateful, of course. They asked me why you'd done it. I told them you are a famous writer and they had given you an idea for your next novel. Don't look so surprised! They will feel immortalised and you can be sure they will be talking about it for weeks.'

'So long as you didn't say I was T S Eliot ... or Evelyn Waugh.'

'No, neither of them ... and I didn't mention Robert Schindel either.' They laughed at a good deed done. Sonja sighed, 'Do you mind if we don't go by my aunt's old house? It makes me so sad to see it.'

'Not if it makes you sad.'

'Lately it has become a bit run down. It's been unsold for some time and has a terrible air of vacancy. I think it's best for you too to remember the place as it was.' He sympathised. Selling your past is not for the faint-hearted. 'Let's walk to the churchyard instead,' she said and, taking his arm once more, they went under the road and railway bridge, making their way towards the church of St Andreas.

. . . .

Sweeney was saddened to find out the train no longer stopped here. It seemed yet another metaphor for an era (his era) gone forever. Even in former days most trains didn't stop and only a limited number of connections to and from Villach were scheduled. However, he'd been fascinated to observe how, when passenger trains passed, the station master would button his tunic, put on his hat, and make his way onto the platform to wave through expresses headed for Venice, Trieste or Rome. It was a practice Sweeney liked to think lingered from the days of the Habsburg Empire, like the romance in Roth's *Stationmaster Fallmerayer*. Yet it wasn't tradition alone which made the station memorable for him. It had been an epiphany on the day of their sledding trip when returning to Villach.

The waiting-room had been cosy and warm that bitterly cold night, a comforting, almost somnolent atmosphere of polished wood and old railway sleepers. In the station-master's office, the phone had rung intermittently, or there'd been a dull metallic clanging, which Sweeney took to be the alert for an approaching goods train. They'd been the only passengers there because, with her ordered approach to life, Sonja had made sure they'd arrived with plenty of time to spare. He hadn't minded, for rushing was something he hated too, only her margins of safety were larger than his. As she'd sat on a bench reading, he'd wandered over to consult the large Austrian Railways timetable, looking closely to check the timing of the Villach train, as if their departure depended on his confirmation of it.

He'd turned his head, said something inane like, 'Yes, the train is at 19.15' and Sonja had ignored him. Sweeney had taken a step back and, taking in the schedules of all trains, discovered that with only one or two connections from this little halt he could reach most parts of Europe. The 19.15 from Thörl-Maglern would open for him a whole continent, north, south, east and west – so long as he had the right visas and had brought enough money. For an island dweller, it had been a pleasing vision, and he'd imagined taking the Romulus to Rome, the San Marco to Venice, the Adria to Ancona, the Blauer Enzian to Munich, the Lehar to Budapest, the Chopin to Warsaw, the Avela to Belgrade, the Austria to Amsterdam, the names alone conveying exotic promise. As he'd stood in the small waiting-room, he imagined an opening out to all sorts of adventures, his location no longer peripheral, no longer isolated, no longer provincial, but part of a vast network of possibilities (as Schindel had imagined too). But suddenly there'd come to him like a dark backlash another revelation. Yes, he could go there … but they could come here with armies bent on destruction, occupation and conquest. And as he'd stood before the timetable, Sweeney imagined the violent ebb and flow of Europe's military fortunes – the hubris and arrogance of nations, the suffering and survival of peoples, the joy and heartache of families, the disorder and anarchy in politics, the civilisation and barbarism, the successes and failures, the advances and retreats. History had suddenly made sense to him. Schindel's appreciation of Thörl Maglern as a sort of cultural, national and linguistic crossroad, was only one truth. Another was its vulnerability and insecurity. How easy it appeared to slip from the fantasy of freedom into the nightmare of terror. He'd walked over and sat beside Sonja – she still hadn't raised her head from the book – and told her of his grand revelation. She'd looked up slowly, concentrating neither on the book nor on him, recovering something from her mental library. Her eyes had narrowed, 'The lines you're seeking are "Who are those hooded hordes swarming, Over endless plains, stumbling in cracked earth … something, something … Falling towers, Jerusalem Athens Alexandria, Vienna London". Eliot, *The Waste Land*' and she'd returned to her reading. If those lines had meant little to him before, they had right then.

As they walked past the turn off to the station, Sweeney gave the building a wave and she looked at him with surprise. 'Are you greeting another ghost?'

'No, I'm waving farewell to the train that used to stop here.'

She squeezed his arm affectionately, 'You *have* become an old romantic.'

They continued along the earthen track beneath the steep railway embankment, dry and dusty still in October. Their path to the church took them across open fallow ground which, he remembered, had been planted with corn. When passing, Sweeney could never resist breaking off a cob, peeling back the stiff leafed covering and running his fingers over the silky silver strands layering the golden corns beneath. He would hear the rustle of the crop as the warm breeze played through the stalks, believing it to be the gentle sound of life's rhythm, but the whistle of a locomotive would announce the heavy beat of modernity as an inter-city express had flashed by or an endless goods train had clattered metallically over the bridge.

The red steeple of St Andreas was one of the most recognisable landmarks in the *Dreilandereck* and sacred ground for almost 900 years. Sweeney had never gone inside, one of those people who linger at the door of religion rather than stepping across. He liked Larkin's conclusion to 'Church Going', about gravitating to ground where it was proper to grow wise in if 'only that so many dead lie around.' He'd enjoyed gravitating to the peace of St Andreas for here were many dead lying around, not only parishioners, but also soldiers from the First World War, men from all over the old Habsburg Empire, Bosnians, Slovenes, Czechs, amongst them, whose simple graves and metal crosses stood outside the church walls.

He followed Sonja into the graveyard, their shoes crunching the fresh gravel, leaves of overhanging trees rustling in a southerly breeze. She stopped at a plot with a rectangular black polished granite headstone. In silver lettering was written *Familie Koller* beneath which was chiselled the dates of her relatives' birth and death. The grave was well-kept, the grass cut neatly around it, any weeds plucked from its borders as well as the bed of tiny white stones covering its length. A bunch of flowers, still reasonably fresh and tied together with a ribbon in Carinthian colours, had fallen sideways before the headstone. Sonja laid her shoulder bag on the grass and crouched to set the flowers aright, brushing with her fingers around the headstone where a few dead leaves had fallen. Speaking as much to herself as to him, she said, 'Eva and Hans come regularly to tend the grave. I do when I can. The children would also when they lived at home.' Without standing she reached behind into her bag and took out a small candle holder, a red cylinder with a golden lid. She placed it in front of the flowers, removed the top and looked to him, 'Do you mind if I use your lighter?' He fished it from his pocket, bending to hand it to her. Sonja straightened out the wick, lit the candle, and replaced the top. The flame flickered brightly in the shadow of the headstone. 'They say it should burn for sixty hours,' but there was a sceptical edge to her voice. It should last until the third day and he wondered if the time was deliberate.

Sonja stood and moved back from the grave, coming to stand close beside him. There was no bowing of the head, no saying of a prayer, but if the act was not formally religious, it was holy in respect. Small ceremonies allow you to mourn and to celebrate together – Sweeney had read something like that in *Murder in the Cathedral* and he understood it for the first time, sensing there was more here than cold earth and death. He considered putting his arm around her, but feared she might think the gesture inappropriate. So he put his hand at the small of her back, letting it rest there as they stood in silence. A light hand it was and she didn't seem to mind, leaning more firmly against his palm as if consoled by his touch. After a short period of silence she sighed and turned to face him. 'Are you hungry?' He knew it wasn't a question.

'Yes, shall we go and have some lunch?'

'Good idea,' she answered and Sweeney respected the transition from dignified sorrow to anticipated pleasure.

They left the graveyard, took the tarmac lane rising to the main road back to the *Feuerwehrhaus*. They didn't speak much to each other as they walked side-by-side, not arm-in-arm, enjoying the quiet of the countryside. Their silence wasn't lifeless, but easeful, saying nothing, yet conscious they still had much to say and it appeared enough. Once, life together seemed as simple as their companionship did to Sweeney now. With Sonja there had been none of the fickleness of Emily, no demands made upon him impossible to satisfy. Had it been they'd anticipated each other's needs before they became demands, or had they never made a demand considered unreasonable? As they reached the Touareg he told himself to stop idealising what once was, for no one is without complexity and no relationship without tension.

. . . .

Moments later as the car rounded the corner to Italy Sonja said, 'There's the border. You'll find it very different than before.'

The old frontier post was desolate, abandoned, and they passed through without check. If he had really been searching for ghosts, here was the place to come. To the feel of encroaching physical dereliction was added an atmosphere of absent energy. Here he remembered permanent busy-ness – documents being prepared or finalised by clerks in import/export offices, heavily-laden trucks queuing, cars sitting in long lines, garage attendants pumping fuel, motor repair and body shops with mechanics attending to cars lifted high on hydraulic jacks, police and customs officers milling around, on and off duty. The bars had been busy, tourist shops displaying souvenirs, toys and sports gear hanging outside their doors, restaurants and cafes serving the passing trade, always noise, bustle and, above all, life. All had vanished and the border post was deathly quiet. Sweeney was disheartened but didn't want to dwell on the bleakness he experienced.

'Do you remember how the Italians wore their hats?' Italian police and customs officials seemed to have them perched at an angle on their heads, not tightly fitting. When he'd remarked on their behaviour, Sonja had told him it was because of male vanity and insecurity, young Italians fearing hats worn too neatly would make them go bald.

She brushed her hand through her hair and sang, '*Macho Machos bleiben in Mode, Macho Machos sterben net aus*'. It was an old hit song from the 1980s by Rainhard Fendrich.

'Was it true? What you told me about hats and baldness? Was there ever any evidence to prove it?'

'Everything I told you was true. How can you doubt me?' Sweeney was about to say, '*Se non è vero, è ben trovato*' for it certainly was. But she interrupted him, touching the side of her nose. 'Let's keep it our secret, shall we?' and parked outside the *Pizzeria Bar Italia*. She pointed to the sign, '*Pizza, Herr Professor?*'

'*Mit vergnügen, gnädige Frau.*'

Getting out of the car, Sweeney noticed an embedded metallic line in the road designating the Italian/Austrian frontier. As he walked towards it, Sonja called to him, 'Where are you going? It's over here.'

Standing astride the line, Sweeney raised his arm in the air, 'Do you remember me doing this?' and hopped from one leg to the other, shouting, 'Austria, Italy. Italy, Austria. Austria, Italy.'

She responded by moving her front foot back and forth, singing, '*Avanti e indre, avanti e indre, che bel divertimento.*'

He jogged over to her and asked, 'What was the song you were singing?'

'*Avanti e indre*' and she sang a few lines of the chorus and translated for him. 'It means "forward and back, what great fun, come and go, all life is here". It was a song my mother used to sing when I was a child. She told me she sang it as I took my first baby steps and the memory makes me happy. It was a fifties hit for Nina Pizzi – appropriate don't you think?'

Sweeney wasn't sure if Sonja meant appropriate to what they were going to eat for lunch or as a description of life's ups and downs and answered to cover both possibilities, 'It certainly is.'

From the outside the *Pizzeria Bar Italia* looked oddly makeshift. Painted lime green, the top floor was fronted with dark stained wood and to its right a one-story extension had been added with the same combination of paint and stain. Above the entrance was a large sign promising *Tabacchi* while over the front of the building ran a transparent heavy-duty polythene awning protecting a veranda cluttered with curious odds and ends – a few plastic tables and chairs, a table football game, earthen pots, some empty, some containing withered plants, a disused vending machine, an old sideboard, a wheelbarrow and, at the far end, an enormous pile of chopped wood which formed a barrier with the adjoining property. Sweeney liked the clutter, as if the tide of change had washed outside the remnants of the old place, but the owners hadn't the heart to dump it all, wanting to retain some sentimental connection with the past, however fragmented (at least he wanted to believe that story).

Sonja noticed his glance at the jumble, 'The place doesn't look great, but the pizzas are excellent.'

'I'm not worried. Everything you tell me is true, Sonja.'

'See, you're finally getting the hang of it.'

The Pizzeria wasn't busy and after entering through a little tiled archway, they found a table in a corner. The room was flooded with sunlight, but the heat wasn't oppressive despite the wood-fired oven. And the pizzas were very good indeed. Sweeney had been hungry, but the size of his order almost defeated him. He also enjoyed the carafe of red wine – *vino nero* they called it here – which was served slightly chilled.

'What do you think?' she asked after a while.

The Third Day

He gave a thumbs up, trying to avoid the stringy cheese on the pizza slice he was eating sticking to his professorial beard. 'Best pizza I've had in years' which was nothing other than the truth. 'Everything you say really *is* true,' and Sonja accepted his compliment with a smile. On the wall above them was a large framed photograph of Monte Lussari taken on a mid-winter's evening, the snow deep, light from the church windows shining diamond-like across the mountainside, a beacon of hope and safety. He drew Sonja's attention to the photograph, 'Do you remember the day we went with Eva and Hans to Monte Lussari?'

'Yes, I have fond memories of that day.'

. . . .

It had been another lazy summer's morning. They'd been sitting in the kitchen, enjoying comforting morning rituals in the sanctity of the room in which – or so it seemed to Sweeney – Carinthian families spent most of their day. Sonja's mother had been busying herself around the stove, preparing something for lunch (it never seemed too early to think about lunch). Frau Maier had short dark hair, bright green eyes like Sonja's, her pose independent, her manner direct, though her independence and directness conveyed an unmistakable hint of insecurity. As Sweeney was to find out, her self-confidence could be a delicate thing and her performance of it much less convincing than she imagined. It was a vulnerability he found endearing, but one which could lend itself to self-pity. Only Frau Maier's religious faith was unwavering and so long as Sweeney remained quietly within the walls of her confession, he could appear a comrade in the mother's struggle against life's un-Godliness. And when he didn't share her opinions, Sweeney was astute enough to conceal any dissent. And why wouldn't he? He was a guest, not a heretical adversary. Frau Maier was an energetic woman

189

but busy, it seemed to Sweeney, mainly within the home, rarely going out except to the local shops, sometimes to the supermarket, but frequently to church. The house was her domain and Sweeney had adapted very easily to her sovereign authority – easily, because he kept a respectful distance, intruding into her space as little as possible, lending a hand when he was asked, but never presuming to do so. In return, she accorded him respect, if often unwarranted, for his intelligence, regardless of what the evidence obliged her to believe about his indolence, linguistic ineptitude and incompetence in most practical things. Her English was also excellent, a facility perfected after the war in dealings with the British occupation force stationed in Villach. Her conversation, theatrically Carinthian in every way, included anachronistic English idioms, like 'fuddy duddy' or 'gone for a Burton', which Sweeney had enjoyed immensely.

Frau Maier would have a cigarette in her hand and somewhere about the house would be others burning in ashtrays, to be smoked when she moved from room to room, one of her peculiarities being an aversion to carrying one around. Smoking was a pleasure to be enjoyed stationary, whether sitting or standing, but never moving. Sonja was constantly warning about her mother's habit, calling her Mathilde, after the Habsburg archduchess who burned to death in 1867 when hiding a cigarette under her clothes. She would say, 'one of these days you'll set fire to the house leaving cigarettes around … and the rest of us with it,' but these warnings never had any effect. That morning, like every other, Frau Maier had been smoking and humming softly to a song playing on *Radio Kärnten*, the channel which provided the musical background to her day. She loved the old hits, Peter Alexander and Udo Jurgens, and Sweeney was certain the song that day had been Roy Black's *Du bist nicht allein* (as Sonja said, it is strange how some things stick in your mind). Elfriede Jelinek called Austrian radio stations busy little rodents, gnawing away at your day from the moment you wake, directed at 'petty people tied in apron strings'. But Frau Maier was no petty person, quite the opposite.

Herr Maier had left earlier, dressed formally and respectably in jacket, shirt and tie, soft hat firmly set unlike those Italian border officials (and he still had a full head of hair), small briefcase in hand, on one of his frequent, time-consuming, Kafkaesque engagements with Austrian officialdom. Sonja used to refer to him as 'K', at the same time intimating her father enjoyed these occasions, almost as if it were part of his personal struggle against the state. On his return he would express frustration about further complications and yet more official forms would be extracted from a folder, spread on the kitchen table, Herr Maier attempting to explain to his wife new developments in the matter. Sonja would be called in aid to confirm some obscure technicality or to decipher some byzantine bureaucratic formulation. Then it would be lunch and thereafter Herr Maier would occupy himself with his various domestic tasks until the next ritual encounter with malevolent officialdom.

Sweeney had been drinking a cup of coffee and leafing through a few illustrated weekly magazines Sonja's mother would buy – *Echo der Frau* and *Bunte Illustrierte* were her favourites – mainly for the crossword puzzles. These puzzles had been neatly completed by the time Sweeney got to look at the magazines, an achievement which impressed him greatly. The titles covered stories of German celebrities, very few of whom he could recognise, and he'd realised for the first time how specific to place was any claim to fame. Yet these personalities had exerted a strange fascination with their perfect tans, perfect smiles, perfect homes and apparently perfect family lives. A few editions later (or so it had seemed) those same celebrities would return to confess their pain at separation or to reveal some secret tragedy. The line between the look of perfect happiness and the look of perfect sadness seemed to be a thin one. Here was the stuff people loved to read and Sweeney loved to read it too, for these articles seemed to offer truths about life everyone could understand and from which they could derive comfort. Was it voyeurism combined with *Schadenfreude?* No, he didn't think so. Perhaps it was the comfort of enjoying a cup of coffee in a modest kitchen and feeling, for the present at least, fate had been kind to the reader in a way it hadn't been to someone with a perfect smile who recently seemed to have had it all. Sweeney thought of Larkin's poem 'Sunny Prestatyn', the smiling girl on the defaced poster being 'too good for this world'. Yes, some people did appear too good for this world and their fall into life's complications allowed everyone else to feel at home.

Sonja had been sitting across from him, shuffling official papers taken from a nondescript box file. She'd been promoted already to Deputy Head of English and with the post had come the invasion of work into her vacation. He'd caught her eye, held up a magazine and pointed to a story he'd come across about some entertainer, someone Sweeney had recognised because he never seemed to be off the television and knew she disliked him. 'One for you, he will be presenting a new show in the autumn.' She'd made a face and in return held up some memo written in dense official German. 'Here's one for you, another teaching regulation to commit to memory.' Sweeney had made a face as well.

The doorbell had chimed. It had been Eva and Hans. Eva was about eight years older than Sonja, about the same height, looking much like her, but was more care-worn – two young children more care-worn – and more stressed by her work as an accountant. Hans was tall, well-built and with a full beard, someone who had real presence, of character as well as physique. Like Sonja he was a schoolteacher, not a native of Villach but of Klagenfurt, the great rival. However, Hans had such a strong and energetic personality, wilful yet benign, it was impossible even for Villach people not to like him and at least he wasn't Viennese. Eva spoke excellent English with, Sweeney noted, a slight American inflection. She'd believed it her duty of hospitality not to make him struggle with his imperfect German, but Hans, who could speak English competently, had confined himself to Carinthian dialect, expecting Sweeney to understand, only speaking English to him when he'd needed to avoid any confusion (which was irritatingly frequent). He was also, like Frau Maier, keen on certain English phrases and would say, at appropriate and inappropriate moments, things like 'time is money' and 'don't worry, be happy'. But his defining characteristic was an impatient streak, his most common expression being '*Zack, Zack*', like the English 'chop, chop', let's get a move on.

The reason for their visit that morning had been to ask if they wanted to come to Santa Maria in Excelsis, the church at Monte Lussari. 'Pilgrimage' had been the word Eva used. Sweeney had never been on a pilgrimage, but a day trip to Italy, well, why not? He'd looked at Sonja, who'd already put her papers into the box which he took as the cue to say yes. Hans, who'd remained standing in the kitchen doorway, half in, half out, gestured for everyone to move, '*Zack, Zack!*'

He had owned a black Mercedes saloon, formerly a Vienna taxi. He drove as he lived life, handling the car like a racing driver, his impatience made clear by his frequently pumping the horn, blasting annoyance at other drivers, even when overtaking. Sweeney had found such road craft alarming, but when he'd glanced uneasily over his shoulder to the women in the back, they'd shown no concern whatsoever, happily chatting, oblivious to horn and overtaking. They'd crossed the Italian border, negotiated the streets of Tarvisio and made their way to a large car park at Camporosso. Though there was a cable car to the top of the mountain, they'd agreed to walk the *Sentiero del Pellegrino*, the pilgrim's way, which wound around forested slopes to the summit. Most 'pilgrims', Sweeney had noticed, chose the cable car. Why not take the waiting (and effort) out of salvation?

Along the lower slope, sunlight had fallen like arrows through the pine trees scenting the air, their shade keeping them pleasantly cool. Sonja, the fittest, had kept company at the rear with Eva, for whom exercise was only incidental to life. Like her mother, cigarettes were central. Initially, Hans's pace had been '*Zack, Zack*' and Sweeney had done his best to stay with him. After a while, '*Zack, Zack*' had relented (his own smoking taking a toll) and a few of cigarette breaks later, the four had re-joined as the forest gave way to alpine meadow. The full heat of the sun at this elevation had come as a shock to Sweeney. Everything had been still, the only sound being the soft rhythmical, metallic jangle of alpine cow bells. Clear of the forest and looking to the summit, Sweeney had expected to find a primitive church. He'd imagined Monte Lussari as a bleak sanctuary, but had been astonished by what he saw, the house of the Lord on the top of the mountain, exalted above the hills, surrounded by a small village, a cluster of solid whitewashed buildings which seemed to cling precariously to the edge. At their destination was a collection of bars and restaurants providing a cuisine catering for three peoples, Slovene, Italian and Austrian. And these nations, walking peacefully in the name of their God, Alpenstocks rather than spears in their hands, had jostled together on narrow streets with gift shops selling holy bric-a-brac, postcards and souvenirs. When he'd mentioned to Sonja how surprised he was, she'd replied, 'Pilgrims need their comforts too. Don't forget we're not puritans in Carinthia. The wisdom in our part of the world is simple. You've got to love yourself before you can love others.' Sweeney remembered thinking it was another excellent rule of thumb.

The Third Day

They'd parted company. Eva and Hans had gone to seek spiritual guidance in Santa Maria in Excelsis for whatever troubled them and Sonja and Sweeney had strolled off to enjoy the view. The vertiginous location and the purity of the air had made him feel light-headed. Tired from the climb, he'd lit a cigarette and, inhaling, became dizzy. Sonja had put her arm around his shoulder, squeezing in close against him. They'd looked across the sharp peaks to the valley shimmering in summer haze and where, he fancied, valley dwellers lived endlessly at ease under their vines and trees. '*Schön, ga?*' she'd asked. He'd hesitated before replying, as if registering everything properly, 'Yes, it is incredibly beautiful,' he'd replied.

But it hadn't been the view which made him hesitate. Sweeney had experienced what he could only describe as a mystical vision. He'd shifted his gaze from valley to mountain to sky, noticed the slowly flowing white clouds and sensed all time in him, every possible moment. Rather than feeling a fleeting inconsequence in the immensity of it all, it was life eternal he'd felt part of, as if seeing himself differently, from another, disembodied perspective, not helplessly adrift in a hostile and meaningless universe, but embraced by an infinite compassion. He remembered clearly what he'd done. He'd put his hands on Sonja's face, turned her shoulders so they were face to face, and had kissed her softly on the lips. He'd imagined elderly pilgrims smiling indulgently as they'd passed, thinking 'What a delightful young couple, look at them in the beauty of love.' Sonja's sister and brother-in-law had joined them soon afterwards and together they'd gone to lunch. Sweeney remembered nothing else, not what they'd eaten, not how they'd got back down the mountain, not the return journey to Villach, not what he'd done thereafter, not a thing. And if that vision had been a sign for him to live differently, he hadn't read it correctly and very soon he'd fallen back into fundamental Sweeney, confined by his old limitations and hesitations. At times of self-pity he considered himself still blighted by ignoring his sign and the subsequent fall from grace.

Sweeney push away his plate and said, 'There's something I never told you about Monte Lussari.'

'Oh, what is it?'

'I had a vision.'

'Maybe I was right about you taking Holy orders. And what was your vision?'

'It wasn't of the Virgin Mary – I hadn't given her a thought. It had nothing to do with Santa Maria in Excelsis – we never went in. There was no voice from above either – for I heard nothing. Afterwards, all I could think of was a revelation of "eternity now". I felt at once completely out of myself – a mystic harmony with all things – but also more deeply within myself than ever before – a sweet communion with life.' He stopped, embarrassed by his confession, and laughed. 'As you can tell, I found it hard to make sense of it.' She seemed taken aback, didn't reply, and he was obliged to continue. 'I still do. I can't describe it for I could only experience it. What I am going to say will sound ridiculous, but it was like seeing myself through the eyes of God. And of course, despite what you say, I'm not holy enough to see anything through the eyes of God. There was no spiritual transfiguration and I stayed the same old person … unfortunately.' Sonja still said nothing. 'I didn't think of it at the time – but you've heard of Larkin's poem "An Arundel Tomb"?' She nodded. 'There's the famous last line, "What will survive of us is love"?' She nodded again. 'Larkin was sceptical as usual, wrote it was an "almost-instinct, almost true". But I knew it was truer than Larkin believed possible … well for me anyway … that day at least.'

'Your own life illuminated by eternity? I would rather say to look through the eyes of love than through the eyes of God.

Maybe it's the same thing – and perhaps Larkin was right after all. I'm not talking about romantic love – well, not exclusively. I'm talking about children, family, neighbours and strangers. I'm talking about the old man at the *Feuerwehrhaus*, those women you saw at the *Stadtkino*, the old boys at *Neuwirt*. You do seem to see those people differently today. Maybe you aren't the same old person?'

He asked her in a tone as blithe as he could make it sound, 'If I'm not the same old person, what's new about me, what's changed then?'

She considered him for a moment, 'At first glance, I'd say you've lost some of your indifference towards those things, those small things, other people think are important. To me you *do* seem more compassionate than before. Don't misunderstand me. You were courteous, respectful, civil, and always pleasant. You still are. I can't think of anyone who didn't like you, even when you gave them good cause. I suppose what I'm trying to say is … you never showed much interest in other people's lives. Like your letters, you sometimes showed little interest in the details of your own.' She touched the corner of her mouth with a paper napkin and delicately set it on her plate. 'And I'm definitely not saying you were "high-minded"' – and her fingers made quotation marks – 'only you never seemed to find great value in the commonplace, maybe losing sight of what makes life worth living. No, maybe even more basic than that – what makes life tolerable. Anyway, I felt it was a "loving" gesture' – she made the quotation marks once more – 'you made back there in *Neuwirt*. It isn't what I would have expected in the past. You probably would have called them a bunch of bores, though you were never cruel or at least never meant to be.' She cleared her throat. 'So what's new about you? I think your indifference has shaded into compassion toward others – or if compassion also sounds too high-minded for you, what about sympathy?'

No, compassion sounded good. At least he wanted it to be right, and was about to say so when Sonja asked, 'Your vision' (he was pleased she didn't make quotation marks again) 'why did you never say anything to me at the time? I still remember you kissing me. Was it the same moment?'

'Yes it was. You remember?'

'Of course I do. I'm glad you've finally told me. I'm only sorry you didn't tell at the time. It makes my own memory more precious. I like your phrase "sweet communion" for that's exactly how it was for me too.'

They were interrupted by the waitress (she looked to Sweeney like a young Anna Magnani) who said something to them as she passed by, setting their bill on the table. He hadn't understood. Sonja explained the woman was going off shift and wanted to settle everything before she did so. 'Her words were "*Non c'e fretta, davvero*", there's really no rush, but she's clearly keen to go home.'

Sonja wanted to pay, but Sweeney objected, 'No, no, don't forget where we are. *Macho, Macho* is the rule.'

When the bill was settled, Sweeney gestured to the waitress to take a photograph of them both. He handed her his mobile phone and the woman tried to get a decent angle, moving *avanti e indre*, finally shaking her head and motioning them to sit together. Sweeney moved around the table and slid close beside Sonja on the bench, their thighs touching briefly. '*Alora, si, va bene, va bene.*' The waitress waved for them to put their heads together. When he leaned in, Sweeney was aware for the first time of Sonja's scent and its subtle fragrance stirred him. The waitress took a number of shots, handed back his phone and they thanked her. He showed the images to Sonja, thinking they didn't look uncomfortable together, for which blessing he thanked the image of Monte Lussari on the wall. 'Can you send the photos to me?' she asked. 'Of course', he said.

The Third Day

As they left the pizzeria, Sweeney lingered amongst the clutter on the veranda, inspecting the odds and ends abandoned
there. 'Do you mind if I have another cigarette?' he asked when
they were finally outside. As he smoked, lamenting again the
absence of life on the border, Sonja walked off a short distance,
checking messages on her phone. Shortly he expected her to say
there was something in Villach for which she must return, some
business she must attend to. He stubbed out his half-smoked
cigarette, not wishing to detain her any longer.

Instead of suggesting they return immediately she asked him,
'How do you feel about completing the grand tour through
Italy to Slovenia and back by the Wurzenpass?'

'*Andiamo, geh ma, gremo* – let's go!'

. . . .

The road to Tarvisio curved beyond the tunnel at Coccau,
the valley floor partly concealed by bordering trees which cast
long shadows across the road. The Valcanale, or Kanaltal, was
once Austrian, but had been ceded to Italy after the First World
War. Every so often traces of its former possession could be
read in flaking or faded German signage, still faintly visible on
roadside buildings, not everything of the old Habsburg Empire
having vanished into thin air. If vestiges of its Austrian past,
like ghostly apparitions, survived in those peeling residues, an
enduring geographical truth was obvious – in architectural style,
agricultural practice and Alpine culture, if not in language –
crossing the border made little difference. Sweeney looked across
at Sonja, driving casually, her right hand on the steering wheel,
left elbow against the window, head resting on her hand. She
seemed to be enjoying, in the words of Nina Pizzi's song, all
the comings and goings of their journey. He found it hard to
understand why she was so benevolent, for she really owed

him nothing, surprised to detect no reserve of resentment to be tapped in anger against him. When she put her left hand back on the steering wheel again approaching Tarvisio he said, 'Thanks again for taking me on my sentimental journey.'

'Don't you think it is a sentimental journey for me as well?'

He had no good answer to her question so said, 'I liked visiting Tarvisio. Italian disorder was a respite from your Austrian orderliness. Don't get me wrong, I preferred Villach, but it was good once and a while to feel some things weren't so under control.'

'Nice of you to think we have things under control. You've been away a long time, haven't you, *Signore Avanti e Indre?*' He was certain she was enjoying herself.

Sometimes the formal orderliness of Austria had felt irritating. Sweeney had some affinity with life this side of the border where drivers parked on footpaths ignoring bye-laws and where pedestrians crossed streets ignoring traffic lights. It had seemed to him a civilised anarchy and different from the Austrian way (as well as more like home). He remembered standing at a pedestrian crossing in Villach, everyone around him waiting for the lights to change. Sweeney had looked along the street to his left – not a car in sight – and along to his right – not a car in sight either. It hadn't been a major highway, only a narrow street, a few steps across, and he had sauntered out nonchalantly. It had been a big mistake. He could hear behind him an elderly couple tutting and on the other side as he approached, dark looks and mutterings of 'Doesn't he think of the example he's setting the children?' – it is what he'd imagined hearing anyway. For the first time in his life he'd experienced the meaning of the term 'public opprobrium'. In Villach, he never did it again – at any rate when there were others about to shame his conduct.

'I was thinking about your protocols for crossing the road and how pedestrians wait for the traffic lights to change.'

'You mean like not getting run over if at all possible?'

He laughed and conceded her point. 'Today it's my daughter who tells me off for taking risks when crossing the road.'

'Wise girl – she sounds like a sensible Austrian to me.'

He looked out at life as they drove along the main street. There were still cars parked on pavements, still pedestrians willing to dodge traffic. 'Did I ever tell you I'd come across Tarvisio before coming to Villach?

'No, I don't think you did.'

'It was in a novel by Eric Ambler called *Cause for Alarm*. It was written in the late 1930s and most of the action takes place in Mussolini's Italy. It's one of those Englishman abroad tales.' She nodded, recognising the genre and grimaced, but had to brake suddenly to allow a woman, marooned half way across the street, to reach the safety of the pavement on the far side.

'To be fair to Ambler, it isn't a formulaic story full of awful foreigners and a plucky chap. It's about an Italian Fascist conspiracy to steal British armament secrets. The interesting thing about the story is this – the Communists are the good guys. It's only with the help of a Soviet agent and a bit of derring-do that the English hero saves the day. They are chased across Italy by the bad guys and pass through Tarvisio to reach safety.'

'They weren't headed for Austria I take it. There'd be no hope for them in 1938.'

'No, they were trying to get to Yugoslavia.'

'And what did Ambler have to say about Tarvisio?'

Sweeney chuckled, 'Nothing much and the little he did say wasn't complimentary. He described it as an overgrown village where everything was shut by ten o'clock because everyone went to bed early. The Englishman in *Cause for Alarm* asks if, by any chance, there'd be a Turkish bath. The hard-nosed Soviet agent replies, "Is that meant to be funny?" Obviously, Ambler, like the agent, considered the place a backwater. There's much more to Tarvisio today than in Ambler's depiction of it in 1938. Can I suggest why?'

'Please tell me.'

'Snow – rather the *meaning* of snow – is the difference I think.'

'And your reasoning is?'

'For the characters in Ambler's book, snow is why good citizens go to bed early. It's portrayed as a seasonal curse. It's a cause of illness. It's an obstacle. It's a threat to life and livelihood. Everyone is forced to struggle against it. Snow means the opposite these days, the opportunity to make money, to attract tourists, to build apartments, to provide jobs, to put Tarvisio "on the map", and why not? Overgrown village it may still be, but it seems a prosperous one. Maybe it has a Turkish bath these days too.'

Sweeney thought he could tell what Sonja was thinking and expected praise for his great historical and economic insight. What she said was 'I think my father would have told you, "First time as tragedy, second time as tourism".'

'That's very good' and she accepted his praise. 'I told your father once about the Ambler story, about how the communists were the good guys, not the bad guys, how Yugoslavia was on the good side, not the bad side. He'd liked that.'

'I'm sure he did.'

Only now did something occur to Sweeney. Maybe it was because of a casual remark about Ambler's novel that Sonja's father had taken him to hear Gecko squawk '*Avanti Popolo*'. He couldn't be sure but he liked to think it was true. 'Did your father ever mention a large cockatoo from around here called Gecko?'

Sonja sang the lines, '*Avanti popolo, alla riscossa/Bandiera rossa, bandiera rossa*' and had to brake suddenly to allow a car to reverse off the pavement into the street. 'My father loved old Gecko. He would have had it in the house if he could ... and if mother would have let him. Did he take you to see it?'

Sweeney told her about the trip and Sonja was surprised he'd never mentioned it before. 'I can imagine you both. The *Odd Couple* comes to mind.'

. . . .

They had reached the end of the main thoroughfare and Sonja turned sharply to the left in the direction of the Slovenian border, manoeuvring cautiously along the narrowing and steeply descending street. They drove by the covered market where Sweeney had bought his first and only leather jacket. It had been a soft brown blouson, buttoned not zipped, which he'd worn until it had fallen apart many years later, its elbows worn thin, its fabric lining frayed into shreds in one or two places. It was the only thing he'd purchased there and it had been one of the best buys he'd ever made. The stalls specialised in leathers of all kinds, not only jackets, but also waistcoats, hats, skirts, purses, wallets, bags and trousers, the last popular with Germans and Austrians, women as well as men. As far as Sweeney could remember, he'd never seen an Italian, man or woman, wearing leather trousers. The market had been a wet day option for tourists at the Austrian lakes who needed an alternative to sitting in their hotels, camper vans or tents and looking out at the rain or at each other. It was close, a long queue at the border notwithstanding, but a good way to pass a damp morning or afternoon. Day trippers might buy some fancy leather gear, a pair of those trousers perhaps. And in other shops they would find Italian wines, cheeses and meats, freshly baked bread, not forgetting pastries and ice cream. There would be time for a coffee, perhaps an *apertivo* and certainly lunch. It was most definitely Schindel country.

'Do you want me to stop at the market?' she asked. 'You could get a pair of those leather trousers you wanted but hadn't the courage to buy.' Sweeney put one hand to his thigh and made a face suggesting, as best he could, the discomfort of a constricted groin.

'No, I didn't think they were your thing', and she eyed his loose, creased, dark blue linen trousers. 'Whatever happened to the nice leather jacket you bought?'

'I wore it for years, but it finally fell apart. I was a bit superstitious about getting rid of it. I feared disposing of it might bring me bad luck.'

'For an intellectual you were always so superstitious. Or did you justify your habits by affecting superstition?'

'That's the sort of question you shouldn't ask because I couldn't give you an honest answer. I could be habitually superstitious or superstitiously habitual.'

'Or is it part of the persona of an absent-minded professor with the beard to match?'

'Not *macho, macho*, I'm afraid.'

'No definitely not *macho*.'

He recognised a nondescript shop front and pointed out to her a row of houses on their right. 'I went there with your father a few times to have my hair cut. Is the barber still in business?' It was too late to stop for the traffic had thickened as the street narrowed further and Sonja could only let the flow of cars take them on past.

'I really can't say. Franco was his name. He was another of father's old party comrades. I'm sure he must have retired years ago. Was there anyone, a son or daughter, to take over the business? I have no idea.'

Sweeney hadn't been aware of the party connection. He'd only assumed Sonja's father wanted to go there because the hair cutting was old school. Franco had been a traditionalist, a razor and hot towels man – no 'unisex', no 'hair salon', no 'fashion styles' – simply 'barber', but one who took pride in his trade. The red and white pole outside the one-room shop had been all you needed to know. And there'd been only the one Franco too, no assistant and only the one chair, so if you didn't like waiting it was best to get there early. Most of his Italian customers didn't seem to mind waiting. They were happy to spend a morning or afternoon, talking together and with Franco, as if the shop was their gentlemen's club. Now Sonja had told him of the Communist connection, had it been a meeting place for old party members? From what he could recall, politics was unlikely to have been the currency of conversation for the exchanges had been far too good-humoured.

'Your father wanted to be here immediately after lunch to make sure we were first in line. We'd wait at the door for Franco to re-open at two o'clock – could have been later – two-thirty perhaps, but certainly no earlier.'

'Father was typically Austrian for sure. And Franco was typically Italian. Nothing would interrupt his lunch.'

At midday Franco had pulled the shutters, walked home to join his wife, took time to enjoy his food, for Franco was a Sicilian and proud of it. Sweeney could picture a small, wiry, sharp-featured man, swarthy, dressed in jacket, shirt, tie, and slacks, strolling casually up the street to re-open for the afternoon, Sweeney and Herr Maier the only ones waiting by the door. Over his arm he'd carried his long, brown knee-length jacket with its top pocket for combs and razors, large hip pockets for brushes and oils. He would greet Herr Maier with a shake of the hand, nod politely to Sweeney, unlock the releases on the window and door, gently raise the metal shutter, open up the shop, stand back, thrust out an arm, and say '*Prego*', ushering both of them inside. As they'd taken their seats on the bench against the wall, Franco put on his coat of office, arranged his implements neatly, stacked the fresh towels, turned on the steriliser and washed his hands, everything done calmly, with deliberation and precision. Finally, he would gesture towards the barber's chair (Sweeney always went first) and the afternoon's business would begin.

'He was a real master of his trade, an artist.'

'I remember you came home looking like a shorn lamb.' She looked him over briefly. 'Actually, you looked quite like you do today.'

'Don't forget I had hair in those days.'

'You keep reminding me.'

Since Sweeney could speak no Italian and Franco no English and very little German, he could enjoy the sensation of razor on hair and skin. Sonja's father had spoken Italian with reasonable fluency and certainly understood it very well. Had those two been talking confidentially about party matters? Sweeney would never know and, if he had, it would have been of no interest to him. When his cut was finished Franco had swept off the protective gown and brushed a few hairs from above the collar. He'd looked at Sweeney in the mirror in front of them, making him aware with a slight incline of his head everything was to his satisfaction (therefore it would certainly be to Sweeney's) and he could go. And waiting for Herr Maier, Sweeney had spent his time flicking through Italian colour magazines laid out on a low table by the door, stories about different celebrities from those in Frau Maier's German magazines and equally strange to him.

. . . .

They drove towards Ratece on the Slovenian border. The narrow sliver of Italian land between mountains he only recalled as a sort of no man's land. It was here, on these slopes, the two heroes of Ambler's thriller struggled to escape the fascist net.

The Third Day

In Sweeney's memory, it was a place of dismal and decaying mining industries, a sad landscape depopulated of its young, where tourists stopped briefly, if at all, a shadow place darkened by thick pine forest. But he discovered his mental picture was wrong, confounded by houses and buildings which seemed freshly painted and refurbished. The land looked neat and well-cultivated and there was an air of prosperity, not deprivation. 'I used to think everything around here was run down. Was I wrong or has there been a change for the better over the last few years?'

'I'm not sure if there has been a great transformation, but there's more prosperity, I suppose – Alpen-Adria prosperity. It's what they call the Dreiländereck these days – Alpen-Adria.'

'I saw your old university has changed its name too.'

'To be accurate, it's the *Alpen-Adria-Universität Klagenfurt*. We want to keep the Carinthian flag flying.'

She negotiated a few sharp twists and turns in the road, drove over a bridge, up a hilly switchback, and onto a plateau of rich, open farmland. 'The biggest change has been in Slovenia,' she said, 'getting independence, opening the border and joining the European Union. Father believed it was about money, money, money', singing the final three words to the familiar Abba melody, rubbing together the thumb and forefinger of her right hand. What did Sweeney understand of these things? Very little, he conceded. But at least there was one very special thing he'd experienced in Slovenia.

It had been July 1991. Hans had asked him if he'd like to join a cycling trip with him and his friends, Harald and Thomas. Only for a few days he'd assured him; it wasn't going to be the *Tour de France*. Sweeney had imagined '*Zack, Zack*' and not being able to keep pace, but Sonja had reassured him when he'd told her. 'Those boys train at the bar not the gym', she'd laughed and raised no objection, saying he could do with some exercise and it would give him an authentic experience of Carinthian male bonding. Sweeney had asked if she was joking, but she'd been adamant. Reluctantly he'd agreed, oiling his 'city bike' without asking where 'the boys' intended to travel, leaving the planning to what Franz had called portentously '*Das Radpräsidium*'. When Sweeney had mentioned *Radpräsidium* to Sonja her response had been dismissive. '*Radlgang* is more like it.'

'The last time I was in Slovenia was in the company of the *Radpräsidium*.'

Sonja snorted, 'Hans loves impressive titles. It's coming from Klagenfurt which does it, I suppose. Didn't I call them the *Radlgang?*'

'You did and I have to say, you were absolutely right.'

'What do I keep telling you? Italians, hats and baldness, Austrians, bikes and boozing, I am always right.'

On the day of departure he'd loaded the bicycle's panniers with spare clothing and toiletries and the gang had set off, no pretensions to fitness, no concessions to cycling fashion, not a single piece of lycra among them, only shorts and cotton T-shirts. They'd cycled along the route Sonja had driven today, but instead of going east towards Ratece, they'd pedalled further south and then climbed steeply, endlessly as it had seemed to Sweeney. He had to push his bike, his leg muscles aching, his lungs on fire, the final third of the way to the summit of Passo del Predil which, until very recently, had been the border with Yugoslavia, recently become the state of Slovenia. The flag had changed, the name of the country had changed and the symbols on the large metal sign at the border had changed, but the customs officers and guards had probably remained the same. They had been friendly, checked their passports casually, and waved them through.

'You must have had a good time. That crew certainly knew how to enjoy themselves.'

'I did, once I had mastered the Carinthian art of *saufen*. Isn't *saufen* the word for boozing?'

'It was never in doubt. You had more to fear from a hangover than from the traffic.'

'Right again, Sonja.'

If the ascent had been strenuous, the descent had been alarming. Sweeney's risk avoidance had been mocked by the willingness of the others to see how fast they could go down straights and around hairpin bends. They'd disappeared quickly from view and he only caught the *Radlgang* again on the outskirts of the town of Bovec. Later, Sweeney had discovered his tires hadn't been properly inflated – he hadn't bother to check – and the discovery provided an excuse for his lack of team spirit and cover for his timidity (despite that explanation, he was thereafter 'Speedy Gonzales' to the *Radlgang*). Entering Bovec, they'd discovered strolling through the streets in pairs, soldiers in brown battle fatigues, Kalashnikov rifles slung over their shoulders. The short war against the Yugoslav Federal Army had recently been won and these youthful warriors were victors in their own land. Beneath the peaceful surface it had been possible to detect a strong current of euphoria and no-where had it been more obvious than the bars and cafes where, outside at tables on narrow streets, young men had played the heroes with young women, basking in their sudden celebrity, the atmosphere charged with an obvious erotic energy. Few had bothered to take any notice of four sweaty, dishevelled cyclists, a motley crew in their assorted gear, but those who did had given them a wave as they freewheeled by in search of the *Pension* booked for the night. When they'd found the house and made their arrangements with the owner, a stout, middle-aged woman in a brightly patterned dress who'd greeted them with exceptional cheeriness, they'd parked their bikes against the wall and sat along a wooden bench in the bowered garden. Quite soon their laddish chatter had petered out and given way to a weary silence.

The owner of the *Pension* had reappeared, carrying a metal tray with a bottle of chilled Slovene champagne and five glass flutes. Sweeney had considered it a hospitable gesture on such a hot summer's afternoon. The *Radlgang* had expressed their appreciation and Sweeney had joined in since '*Hvala*', or thanks, was one of the few Slovenian words he knew. The woman had opened the bottle, firing the cork into the branch of a tree, not spilling a drop, to collective applause, and she'd filled their glasses with a practiced flourish. Wiping grubby hands on their shirts, one by one they'd taken a flute and afterwards, the owner had filled her own. She'd raised her glass, made a toast, and they'd cheered again. Sweeney had heard 'Slovenia' mentioned and he'd joined in the cheer, if self-consciously, for he wasn't sure what he was celebrating. They'd taken turns to shake the hand of their host and after a short while she'd retreated to the house, leaving the bottle with them.

Sweeney had wandered over to Thomas, the most fluent of *Radlgang's* Slovene speakers, 'It was nice of her.'

'It was very generous indeed.'

'What was the toast, I didn't understand all of it?'

'It was a toast to Slovenian freedom and independence … and to us boys as well' and Thomas had swept his arm around the group 'the first visitors to reach Bovec since the war ended.'

Sweeney's feeling he'd disappointed the gang by his hesitant descent had been replaced by an unwarranted feeling of bravery rewarded and he decided to make the most of it by helping himself to another glass of champagne.

'Did I tell you we were welcomed like liberating troops?' Sweeney asked her.

'Yes, you made a big deal out of it as I recall. I'm glad you didn't do it in front of my father.'

'You could say we were the advance party of tourism he feared would follow tragedy.'

'Only *you* could say that' and she patted his arm as if indulging a child given to wild imaginings.

'I still think it is one of my better stories.'

'I can see the title of your memoirs already – *Sweeney liberates the Slovenes* – a bestseller along those lines?'

'Oh, you can be cruel sometimes, Sonja.'

'Ha!' was all she said for she had to manoeuvre sharply as two motorcyclists with German registration plates overtook at speed before a corner. She swore at them, tooted the horn, and both cyclists raised their hands to give her the finger as they sped on. She swore at them again, 'Those *Piefke* bikers think they own the roads. They make me so mad,' shaking her head, swearing once more under her breath.

'I can see that.'

'Sorry!' and they both laughed. The German bikers reminded Sweeney he had another story to tell.

. . . .

'Do you remember a German we gave to a lift to once? He'd kayaked down the river and was hitchhiking back to his campsite.'

'A German kayaker? I don't think so.'

It had been during his first summer in Villach and they'd toured about most days in the 126. Sonja had been keen to show him all the sights, just as he'd been keen to see them. Leaving early one morning, they'd joked about 'doing Yugoslavia in a day'. Exactly how they'd arrived at where they met the kayaker, he couldn't remember. 'We'd been driving in Slovenia and were heading for the *Autostrada* to Villach. We saw a man dressed in a wet suit hitching a lift and took him back to his camp site.'

'I don't remember him, no. Why do you ask?'

'He was a plastic surgeon from Hamburg. He gave me his card and told me I should look him up if I ever visited.' Sweeney pulled down the sun visor, slid open the cover of the vanity mirror, poked at the bags under his eyes and pulled at the skin of his neck. 'Maybe I should find out if he'd still repay the favour.' The card lay in Sweeney's large box of Carinthian odds and ends, a Sebald-type fragment of the past.

'You shouldn't worry. Mother used to say men mature while women get old.'

'Well, you must be the exception to the rule,' he said and meant it.

'So you are the expert on women's looks too?' But he imagined there was a hint of appreciation in her dismissal.

It wasn't the kayaker's profession which mattered. It had been something he'd mentioned in passing which, at the time, had meant nothing to Sweeney and he'd only recently come to understand its significance. When the plastic surgeon had asked Sweeney about his job and discovered he taught at a university (amazed, it seemed, that a 'Don' should be driving a car as plebeian as a Fiat 126) the subject shifted from kayaking to history. He'd said 'The river you can see is called Isonzo.' Sweeney had looked at the rocks midstream and at the gravel banks, thinking the descent must have been a daunting one. The rush of the water, audible above the noise of the 126's engine, had sounded threatening to his ear. But then he wasn't a kayaker. If he had been, he would probably have taken the obstacles and dangers as an invitation, as a challenge. The German had given the impression of someone who'd accepted the invitation, had risen to the challenge and been satisfied with his achievement. 'You have heard of the Battles of the Isonzo?' he'd asked. 'No?' He'd seemed taken aback at the lacuna in Sweeney's historical knowledge. 'The Italian and Austro-Hungarian armies fought

along here and in these mountains during the First World War.'
Sonja had vacated the front seat for the German and Sweeney
had turned to see if she could help him out, but she hadn't
been listening.

'Maybe you've read Hemingway, *A Farewell to Arms?*' the
man continued.

Yes, Sweeney had read Hemingway's book as a teenager, but
it hadn't been the location which made an impression. It had
been the drinking and the *machismo*. Sweeney had turned to
Sonja once more and asked, 'Hemingway, *A Farewell to Arms?*'

She'd leaned forward, 'Hemingway? Yes, he wrote about his
experiences as an ambulance driver in the war. He was fighting
with the Italians.' When the kayaker had nodded in agreement,
she'd sunk back into her seat again and Sweeney had worried
she might be resentful of an intrusion into their time together.

It hadn't taken long to reach the site upriver. The German
had handed over his card fetched from the glove box of his
Volkswagen camper van, apologised about not offering any
hospitality, telling them he had to return immediately to collect
the kayak he'd hidden by the river bank. They'd made their
goodbyes and Sweeney had driven off, happy to have Sonja back
in the seat beside him, even happier to find her good spirits
hadn't deserted her.

Years later the *Radlgang* tour had followed the Isonzo River
from Bovec to Kobarid (in Italian, Caporetto, and the Battle
of Caporetto in 1917 was the subject of Hemingway's novel).
Having re-crossed the border into Italy near Cividale del Friuli,
they'd cycled by memorials of war – statues of soldiers, old
canons on plinths, cemeteries large and small, but Sweeney had
paid little attention. His concern had been his sore backside, his
sore legs and especially, his sore head. Each morning he would
be hung over from drinking the night before for it had been
the *Radlgang's* custom to buy a crate of local beer (twenty-four

bottles), honour demanding all of them be drunk before bedtime. In male bonding, Sweeney had also proved himself a disappointing companion, never getting beyond three bottles at most ('Hey, Speedy, what's wrong? Are we drinking too slowly for you?'). He'd also passed on the offer each morning to fill his water bottle with white wine spritzer, deciding he didn't want to be sick as well as sore.

As he sat beside Sonja in her comfortable Touareg, looking out at a perfect autumnal day, he thought of David Hume's remark that it isn't contrary to human reason to care more about scratching your little finger than to worry about the suffering of all humanity. He supposed ignorance might excuse him, but if he had been familiar with the history of the conflict, Sweeney's aching body and sore head would likely have trumped memorials to fallen soldiers. Only recently had he read about the *Isonzoschlacht* and what he'd discovered astonished him. There hadn't been one battle but twelve. Caporetto was only the most famous of them for English speakers, partly, or mainly, thanks to Hemingway's novel. Over three years, winter and summer, Italian and Austro-Hungarian troops had fought in appalling conditions. Unlike the images Sweeney carried around in his head of the Western Front – mud, flooded craters, a no-man's land of blasted trees and flat expanses of quagmire – here the campaign had been fought throughout the winter along glacial ridges, in deep drifts on precipitous mountainsides, with avalanches a constant threat. In summer they'd fought across rocks, boulders and scree which heavy shelling turned into a hail of lacerating fragments, the opposing lines sometimes only twenty metres apart. The scenery was spectacular, yet he knew, as he hadn't back then, that amidst such grandeur there'd been over one million casualties.

'I never realised so much slaughter happened here during the First World War. It's what our plastic surgeon friend was trying to tell me. You've heard the English expression "blissful ignorance"? I wandered here in blissful ignorance.'

'The graves at Andreaskirche should have been a clue.'

'I suppose, but they seemed to me like an adornment, part of the church's peaceful beauty, almost aesthetic decoration and not history.'

'Yes', she replied, 'I see what you mean.'

'The contrast between the splendour of place and the tragedy of war is heart-breaking. You made it clear you're not a fan, but it reminded me of something Schopenhauer also wrote. He considered the world as object, beautiful, but the world as subject, suffering. And he believed the suffering is so awful because the world is so beautiful.'

'Maybe I've misjudged Schopenhauer. The Slovenes have been removing the unexploded shells from the battlefields because they make the landscape unsafe for the hikers, the bikers and the climbers.'

'It's the story of our times, Sonja. As your father would have said …' and they finished the sentence simultaneously '… first time as tragedy, second time as tourism,' laughing loudly together, the suffering of mankind forgotten once more.

. . . .

They crossed the border, the old customs house and police building also standing vacant and derelict. In the meadows stood *kozolci*, hay racks topped by a slanting roof with long rows of horizontal wooden poles and draped with freshly mown grass, for Sweeney the signature of Slovenia. Sonja slowed, indicated a right turn, and accelerated across the road into the large car park of a *Kompas Shop*. They got out of the Touareg to enjoy the view. Sweeney offered Sonja a cigarette, but she shook her head and they leaned against the grille of the car. 'You must remember the old supermarket. They've rebuilt it since you were here last. Take it as another sign of the times. There's no need to smuggle any goods across the border these days.'

It was the sort of duty-free shop you'd find in any airport terminal – only here it stood in the middle of a breath-taking landscape. His passport allowed purchase of goods denied to Austrians living in the border zone. Hans had organised the trips and they had been typically *Zack, Zack*. He would grab cartons of cheap Yugoslav cigarettes while Sonja and Sweeney picked a bottle of Scotch for her father and a box of chocolates for her mother (she only smoked the Austrian brand *Dames*). Back in Villach the bounty of their run would be divided. In all those trips, not once had the boot of the Mercedes been checked, not once had customs officers asked about their purchases, and not once had Sweeney been called upon to flash his passport.

When he'd finished his cigarette, Sonja asked, 'Do you want to go inside, maybe buy a present to take home?'

'No, there's nothing I need. Do you?'

'No, but I would like a coffee. Shall we drive to Kranjska Gora and complete the grand tour?'

'Yes, a coffee would be good.' He rarely drank coffee in the afternoon, but it was a good time to make an exception.

. . . .

In Kranjska Gora they parked and walked to the *Slascicarna Café*. Sonja assured him they'd been here before, but Sweeney didn't recognise it. Maybe it too had been refurbished. The *Slascicarna Café* was a typical alpine building, the walls painted cream with a sharply sloping roof and a decorated wooden balcony draped with hanging flowers. They sat at an outside table as they'd done in Arnoldstein, the sun still warm, yet Sweeney could feel now and then a current of chilling air. They both ordered coffees and he persuaded Sonja to have a cake. The main tourist season was over, only a few hikers trekking by with packs and poles, some of them stopping briefly at the café to buy ice cream. Otherwise there was only the quiet of an off-season afternoon. He feared the same listlessness might descend on them, but he was wrong. Sonja became talkative, as if the caffeine and the sweetness of the cake had re-animated her. There was nothing revealing in her talkativeness, nothing 'heartfelt' as Frau Maier's magazines would have described it. She spoke matter-of-factly about her life, adding only a few details to what he had gathered already – about retirement, about her house in Warmbad, the children in Vienna, keeping active, the book club she helped to organise, the new dog, the continuing rhythm of her days. As Sonja spoke, he listened as attentively as he could, his mind filtering out names he didn't recognise and places he'd never been. He was pleased to detect in what she said the old Sonja Maier, self-confidently engaging with life. At least it was the impression she gave, for she wouldn't, understandably, open too wide a window into her soul. Sweeney only registered the fact she hadn't spoken again about her late husband and wondered what his absence meant.

When she'd finished her cake and was slowly sipping the rest of her coffee, Sweeney pointed to his pack of *HB* on the table and asked if she minded him smoking. 'No, I don't mind. And if you don't mind, may I have one with the rest of my coffee? I feel as if I should join you again in your bad habit.'

'It's my pleasure, *genädige Frau*.'

'Oh, do stop calling me that, you make me sound like an old granny.'

'I will … if you will stop calling me *Herr Professor*.'

'Agreed,' she said.

He shook out a cigarette for her and, leaning across to light it, cupped his hand around the flame. As their heads moved together, he was aware of her scent once more. Their eyes met, both of them conscious of their closeness. She leaned back quickly again as he lit his own. 'What about you, Eddie?' she asked 'Yesterday you never told me much about what you're up to these days.' She blew the smoke from the cigarette over her shoulder and took another sip of coffee. He deployed the same evasions he used with others, telling her he was doing what he'd always done, but having more time to do it, reading, writing, trying to limit calls on his time to do things he no longer had any wish to do. 'Above all, I'm trying to stay healthy' and when he'd said it, Sweeney looked at his cigarette and back at her.

'Up to a point, Lord Copper.'

'And I try to avoid the temptation of opening the gin bottle too early. Larkin wrote of his growing worry about "getting half drunk at night". *Rutschen* is the German word, isn't it, sliding into dependency?'

'Yes, well done, so the book I gave you yesterday has come in useful.'

'I exaggerate about the alcohol,' he felt obliged to say, but in truth he did worry about a possible 'slide' when he heard of the sound of his gin bottles dropping into the recycling bin.

They fell silent again, content to look around them. For more than two decades they had lived their lives apart. They had been on separate paths, had travelled across vast territories of experience, heading in different directions, following distinctive maps. Yet Sweeney was struck how easily their movements and thoughts coordinated in the short time they'd spent together. They had no map and maybe things should be just so between a man and a woman at their age. Sonja looked at her watch and attracted the attention of the waitress to pay the bill. 'No, I insist,' he said. She was going to argue, but conceded with a 'thank you' and asked, 'Are you ready for the Wurzenpass challenge?'

The Third Day

He made a sound of alarm and she slapped him on the arm. 'That's enough of the theatre, *Zack, Zack!*'

. . . .

It turned out the Wurzenpass wasn't terrifying at all and not as he remembered it. Sonja coped with the climb and descent like she was driving on the flat. Once they reached the main road to Villach, he said 'You've finally cured me of my fear of the Wurzenpass.' She smiled, but didn't say anything more. He anticipated an awkward parting, once more not finding the proper words, when they arrived at the Bahnhofplatz. All he could think to say when she stopped the car was, 'Thank you again for the tour, Sonja. Can I invite you to dinner tonight?'

'I'm sorry, I can't tonight. I have somewhere to be later,' and like the day before she left 'somewhere' unspecified. Why, though, should she be obliged to explain anything to him? 'You are going home the day after tomorrow?'

'Tomorrow's my last full day in Villach. I'm leaving early the following morning. It's only a flying visit.' He was going to add 'this time', but decided not to.

'What about tomorrow evening?' she asked, 'Tomorrow is the 10th October holiday. I'm with friends most of the day, but free for dinner.'

Sweeney had forgotten the significance of the date. It was the anniversary of Carinthia's vote in 1920 to remain part of Austria. He tried to hide his ignorance, implying he'd simply overlooked it. 'Tomorrow evening would be great. Where and when?'

'I will take you to my favourite place. It will be new to you, but I'm sure you'll enjoy it. I'll make a reservation and I can meet you here at the hotel. Does six-thirty suit you?'

'I look forward to it.'

Four Days in Villach

They got out of the car. She walked around to give him a quick hug and he thanked her again. 'See you tomorrow', she said, got back into the car and waved as she drove away. Sweeney waited until the Touareg had disappeared from view before walking over to the table outside the hotel, lighting another cigarette. The square was busy, people coming and going, taxis collecting fares, buses pulling in and out. The light was beginning to fade, soon night would fall and Sweeney would be alone once more in Villach. Standing at the hotel entrance, he reflected on their time together. Neither of them had crossed the good humoured, comradely boundary which seemed to chart their relationship differently. After the initial uncertainty and wariness, Sonja had seemed to relax. There hadn't been the coldness he'd feared and when she'd laughed at his terrible jokes, he didn't think it had been merely out of courtesy. And he couldn't forget the glances they'd shared, the way they'd walked arm-in-arm or how she'd been comfortable enough to touch him and, in return, had appeared genuinely comforted by his touch. Those moments recalled the contours of their former relationship, as if easy affection and flows of sympathy hadn't completely died. And there remained the playfulness, the verbal parries, like fencers energetically flicking each other's foils, a lightness of being which once had been their normal rhythm. Today in the Touareg, as in the Fiat 126 all those years before, he'd experienced none of Percy's 'malaise', no emptiness of spirit, no darkness of heart and he believed it had been the same for Sonja. Nothing in their journeying had seemed aimless or meaningless.

It hadn't only been what they'd talked about which lifted his mood. It had also been what they hadn't, their silences. No, he corrected himself, not their silences. It had been the unspoken companionship. Both of them had left things, perhaps the most important things, unexamined. On the other hand, they hadn't felt obliged to fill moments of quiet with endless chatter. He considered it a miracle that time had not erased the gift they always had – forwards, backwards, to and fro, *avanti e indre, avanti e indre, che bel divertimento*. And it is great fun. It *is* what life's all about. Backwards – it had been pleasant to revisit past times. Forwards – perhaps, before them stood the promise of new times. Yet he knew what an unreliable narrator he was. Like Billie Holiday, he could be living in a kind of daydream, but so what?

He faced the question of how to spend the rest of the day, fearing the hours might weigh heavily on him. Should he go out for dinner? He'd enjoyed the atmosphere at *Bacchus*. He could envisage sitting at the same spot and ordering the same dish, yet he hesitated. There was a passage in Elizabeth Bowen's book *A Time in Rome*, one he'd found in Keats and Chapman around the same time as *A Wayfarer in Austria*, the truth of which impressed on him the limits of his own innate conservatism. His natural inclination, no matter where he happened to be, was to find somewhere he liked, a restaurant, a café or a bar. He would follow some deep instinct which convinced him that twice makes custom, believing, with an excess of faith, in returning to a favoured place, thinking his presence there would establish a special connection, encourage a sincere welcome, or deliver a certain privilege. The evidence for this belief was limited, he had to admit.

Bowen had laid bare for him its fundamental illusion. Nobody, she wrote, in what today would be called the 'hospitality trade', really esteems people they see too often, people who appear to be sure of their welcome, people who expect their appearance to be especially appreciated. Believing it to be true, Bowen tried to avoid becoming a devoted customer of any one place, spacing out her appearances at restaurants and cafés, carefully calculating the possible advantage (more welcomed when she hadn't been seen for some time) against the potential disadvantage (a long absence making for waning interest as if she had been unfaithful in a love affair). On balance, it was wise to vary one's behaviour, Bowen believed, advice Sweeney rarely took. His habit was to re-trace a pattern, either to recover the pleasant serenity he'd experienced the first time or, if the experience had been disappointing, to seek in the same pattern something different, a moment, an atmosphere, which might make things better the second time (when custom became established). Repetition was his sedative, soothing doubts that his existence was purposeless, his wandering or loitering meaningless.

Resistance to novel possibilities involved a form of egotism, he'd admit. In the years after Sonja, his routine had irritated the women he knew – there hadn't been many – who dismissed as sophistry his argument that novelty-seeking was only a different sort of habit. For them, Sweeney's novelty soon wore off as they came to the conclusion neither he nor his routines were worth the bother and were only the excuse for selfishness. Emily especially had considered his behaviour an insult to spontaneity, for to contract a habit of any sort she considered a spiritual failure. He couldn't really blame these women. Sweeney knew if he went out tonight, he would wander about for some time indecisively, only to find himself back at *Bacchus*. He was convinced free will would be useless for he couldn't imagine being tempted off a fated path. After his pleasant day with Sonja, he didn't want to suffer the remorse of a disappointed return. He decided he would substitute his room for the town, considering he'd filled his head with enough impressions for one day. Stubbing out his cigarette, he entered the *Billa* beside Hotel City.

From outside the supermarket looked a cramped space, but inside it stretched for some distance and was impressively stocked. Sweeney picked a few *Kaiser Semmel*, chose a large bag of salted potato crisps, ordered some sliced pork from the delicatessen and a small cut of cheese as well. He browsed the Austrian wines and selected a bottle of *Blaufränkisch*. Queuing behind the locals to pay, he flattered himself he belonged. But as he fussed around with the notes in his wallet, the woman at the check-out observed him scanning her cash register to confirm the bill. She, like the *Austrian Airlines* attendant, must have noted his British Academy canvas bag and drawn the same conclusion. She repeated the sum for him in English. His appreciation of her wish to help a stranger was qualified by his mild irritation at being identified as a stranger. After Sweeney had paid and received his change, he made a point of thanking her in German to which the cashier replied in the local dialect. He left feeling honour had been served.

In his room, he drew the curtains, switched on the table lamp, spread out a few tissues from the box on the desk and arranged his purchases. He poured some *Blaufränkisch* into a toothbrush glass taken from the bathroom, made a cheese and ham roll and crunched some crisps. He'd been right to think of Room 506 as a refuge. It might have confirmed an intensity of exile, its stillness a terrible dread, but no. The pool of light from the table lamp cast soft shadows, conjuring the innocence of his student days, the old security of scholarly contemplation and Sweeney experienced pleasure in sweet solitude. The heavy silence was comforting, not oppressive, yet experience had taught him there was a danger on its edge, a lurking despair of loneliness. Life cannot be horded, he knew. Was there ever any sense in hiding from the world, recalling Sonja's comment about renunciation and lacking a witness to his days? Sipping his wine, he dismissed the question, and settled for untroubled seclusion. He looked at the TV guide in the newspaper picked up this morning, hoping to find something interesting.

The Fourth Day

The Fourth Day

Sweeney awoke from a sleep heavy with forgetting, uncertain where he was, his mind disordered like an old rummage sack. The confusion unnerved him. When oblivion was replaced by images of recent days, he questioned their truth and his judgement of them. Sonja had advised to focus on small things, he remembered, so he looked at the three quarters empty bottle of *Blaufränkisch*, the remains of a bread roll on the table, his clothes scattered across the couch and yesterday's newspaper lying on the floor. Their existence disproved the sensation his journey was a dream and their presence buoyed him with enthusiasm for the new day. Later at breakfast, Sweeney flicked through a local edition of the *Kleine Zeitung* searching for the time and place of the 10th October commemoration in Klagenfurt. He wanted to avoid Villach today and the possibility of blundering into Sonja and her friends, perhaps causing awkwardness for her and certainly embarrassment for him. He found the details he was looking for and after breakfast took the train to Klagenfurt.

The official event was being held at the *Landhaus* between Alten Platz and Heiligengeistplatz. Sweeney wasn't well acquainted with Klagenfurt and what he had known of it was mostly forgotten. When the train arrived, he decided to follow others who'd journeyed from Villach, parents with young children mostly, for he expected they had made the trip for the same reason he had. It turned out to be a mistaken assumption, for once outside the station these families headed off in different directions, the parents likely taking their kids to something more enjoyable than a public ceremony. Uncertain what to do, he chose the direct route to the city centre along the Bahnhofstrasse, expecting he couldn't go too far astray. Soon he heard a band playing, traced the source of the music and, coming around the corner of a narrow alleyway, he discovered a respectable crowd – in all senses of respectable, number, demeanour and style of dress – standing at the entrance to the courtyard of the *Landhaus*. A number of women were dressed in their *Dirndl*, over which they wore neat-fitting woollen jackets. Quite a few men were dressed in traditional Carinthian suits, brown jackets with green flashings, in the deep pockets of which, Jelinek had written, much was concealed. Today, however, these people were keen to demonstrate, not hide, their provincial patriotism yet Sweeney detected no carnival atmosphere, more an occasion of amiable harmony where dutiful motivation and festive enjoyment combined. It was an atmosphere with which an outsider like him, for whom the occasion was mere spectacle and without emotional or communal significance, could feel comfortable and unselfconscious. He managed to find a free space directly behind some Austrian Army officers in their grey-blue dress uniforms. In front of them was a detachment of armed troops wearing olive-green service fatigues and standing at ease, their faces expressionless. Along the far side of the courtyard local dignitaries sat on a temporary, steeply tiered bank of seats. Across from them was the official platform and at its edge a choir and a military band stood side by side. Above proceedings, the twin towers, gallery and balcony of the Landhaus were decked with large Carinthian flags, unmoving in the still morning air.

The Fourth Day

When the music finished, the speeches began. Sweeney didn't understand everything he heard, but he could identify a common theme. The past wasn't ignored, but each speaker was keen to talk about the present and, more passionately, about the future. Old historical claims, former cultural divisions and bloody military struggles had been transcended, the language of the speakers proclaiming constructive resolution, mutual respect and shared understanding. Carinthia and Slovenia were spoken of in borderless terms, the either/or of 1920 – Austrian or Yugoslavian – recalibrated as inclusive linkages between regions. Carinthia had become a 'hub' or a 'bridge' or a 'tunnel' linking together European states, north and south, east and west. Slovenes, Italians, Austrians, Sweeney heard, formed a 'network' of connections, a 'web' of associations, all of which secured Carinthia's place at the heart of the 'new Europe'. Identification with Austria and beyond Austria, with Europe meant no one in Carinthia should feel marginal in or excluded from the new, culturally capacious, diversity-embracing *Heimat*. These words, Sweeney imagined, were intended to be an answer to a lament he'd found in Maja Haderlap's novel *Engel des Vergessens* (Angel of Oblivion) about the fate of Carinthian Slovenes. No longer would they have to shuttle between their dark, neglected cellar and the brightly-lit upper rooms in the house of Austria, no longer would they be trapped by language, culture and history. The speeches also appeared to address Bachmann's questions as well – what had Carinthians to be proud of and why would they want to attract the world's attention? Those gathered at the *Landhaus* were told to be proud of *Alpen-Adria* and the attention of the world should be on Carinthia because it was a model for Europe's future.

Sweeney had heard such uplifting talk before. It reminded him of Raymond Chandler's line about there being two kinds of truth, the truth that lights the way and the truth that warms the heart. These speeches were classics of the heart-warming kind.

He didn't doubt the sincerity of those who spoke, sure in their belief a combination of political art and patriotic goodwill *would* light the way to a better future. It was probably sufficient that these speeches be made and be heard. When he looked about, those around him appeared calmly supportive, clapping politely, if not enthusiastically, when moved to do so.

When the speeches were over, the band struck up the Austrian national anthem and the officers in front of him stood limply to attention. No one Sweeney could see was singing, not even mouthing the words, albeit everyone remained respectful. After the national anthem, there was a short silence as the conductor recomposed himself and the choir readied themselves to sing the anthem of Carinthia, that love poem to its geography – *mein teures Heimatland, mein freundlich Heimatland, mein liebes Heimatland, mein herrlich Heimatland*, my precious, my friendly, my lovely, my glorious, homeland. At the first notes, the mood changed and people did begin to sing, not in full voice, but in muted, almost conversational, tones. Sweeney observed the officers in front of him stiffen and he assumed here was the real point of the day, celebrating Carinthia first and Austria second. When the choir stopped, there was more polite clapping and a few self-conscious cheers, while the children waved small, home-made flags. It was all quite restrained and civil, a world of difference from the hysterical scenes and morbid declamations he'd witnessed in *Waldheims Waltzer*. As the armed troops marched off in tight formation, Sweeney expected the band to play the *Radestsky March* (he was disposed to some demonstrative clapping), but it was to a tune he didn't recognise.

Once formalities were over, there followed the usual milling of spectators, the hesitations, the belated greetings, some uncertain what to do and where to go next, some lingering to make sure they hadn't missed a friend or an acquaintance, some slowly pushing through to head home, others intent to continue the celebrations elsewhere and walking off with purpose. Sweeney was clear where he wanted to go next. All his mental concentration making sense of the speeches, all the standing, all the press of spectators had made him thirsty. This midday heat was not the shimmering breathlessness of a Carinthian summer when intense sunlight destroys colour and shadow, but it was hot nonetheless. It should have been a simple task to find a bar, but he wandered around for about fifteen minutes without success, going one way, then the next, circling back, *avanti e indre*, his coming and going on the streets of Klagenfurt no fun at all, merely frustrating. At last, down a cobbled alley, he saw painted on the wall of an old two-storied building, a sign for *Bierhaus zum Augustin.* When he entered its welcome cool, he heard a loud babble of conversation and discovered every seat and table taken already by a festive crowd.

· · · · · · · · · ·

Zum Augustin turned out to be a sprawling building, its rooms linked maze-like through arched corridors and the knots, cracks and joints of the irregular wooden floorboards creaked as Sweeney made his way around. Bright, cavernous rooms were filled with diners as were smaller side rooms and annexes. The noise and bustle of a busy lunchtime enveloped him and there was little sign anyone was in a hurry to leave. And why shouldn't they linger and relax? Today was made not for his pleasure and convenience, but for theirs.

It was on his second tour he sensed he'd been here before, something about the sound of his footfall on the uneven flooring, the odour of the polish, the contrast between light and shade all brought echoes and intimations of another time. Was it here the dinner had taken place when, for the first time, he and Sonja had recognised the connection between them? He wasn't certain, but he wanted it to be true, a coincidence (not *mere* coincidence, surely?) to give meaning to the accident of his being here, as if a broken circle had been re-connected as a sign of better things to come. Finally, he found a free spot, another of those tall metal tables in one of the back bars. He ordered a beer from a passing waitress, feeling comfortably on the edge of the sociability and gregariousness in *zum Augustin*.

Standing alone in *zum Augustin*, he thought once more about Bowen's book on Rome, about how she found it remarkable the way some authors seemed able to gain access to the inner life of a foreign place by seeking out others and recording their conversations. The characters these authors discovered, Bowen noted, never failed to confide something symbolic or significant, to reveal a mystery or to pour forth ageless wisdom, all in their regional dialects. She admitted such things never happened to her. Bowen wasn't questioning the authenticity or veracity of these authors (for a good story is a good story) and accepted the deficiency probably lay with her. Yet she preferred to avoid talking to people wherever possible and, released from the burden of everyday conversation, she found the proper measure of her own holiday from life. Listening in, hearing fragments of conversation, observing others, provided insight enough for there was, she suspected, little people could disclose about themselves you wouldn't already intuit from watching them, if only for a short time. After the usual exchange of necessary words, her desire was to be left in a 'beatific trance' and happiness meant making this trance last long enough so time didn't feel oppressive or her aloneness complete.

It had been Sweeney's experience too. Here was the difficult trick, he knew. How to establish the limits of disconnection from others and yet be able to freely re-engage when required? People shun those who bear the mark of true loneliness for fear of contagion, repelled by its aura of desperate neediness. He was aware it was a human stain to be avoided at all costs. But he didn't think he bore the mark on him and was happy to stand in his own beatific trance, catching fragments of conversation, watching people, enclosed, as Bowen described it, in his own 'interesting hush'. When necessary – responding to polite requests from a waitress to squeeze by or catching someone's eye unawares – Sweeney let smiling do his talking. And his smile did comprise a wide vocabulary, as useful to him in Klagenfurt and Villach as it had been to Bowen in Rome, allowing him to be at peace with his ordinariness and, in *zum Augustin*, allowing him to be at peace with his beer.

It was *Puntigamer – Das bierige Bier* they called it. Sweeney took a long drink and, yes, *Puntigamer* was definitely '*bierig*' and he wanted another one. He caught the barmaid's eye by lifting his glass, smiling at her as she set another in front of him. Later, sweeping past on another round with a full tray of drinks, they exchanged only smiles again. The good citizens of Klagenfurt, noticing his smile, his beatific trance, his interesting hush, might think he was someone who had ordered one beer too many and Sweeney conceded they could be right. He should have had something to eat, for these *bierige Biers* were making him feel (in St Augustine's own words) 'other-worldly in the world'. Didn't he have someone to meet and somewhere to go later? And hadn't he better go back and get ready? He was cheered in his solitary state to think he did have someone to meet and did have somewhere to go. He finished his drink, paid his bill, exchanged more smiles and headed back to the railway station, his step less steady than when he'd arrived this morning.

. . . .

He returned to Villach in plenty of time for his meeting with Sonja (he didn't think the word 'date' appropriate). He swallowed two aspirins, rehydrated with bottled water, had a quick nap, showered, trimmed his professorial beard, brushed his teeth and did his best to tidy himself. He had little choice about what to wear, but a fresh shirt and a change of linen trousers could make all the difference he thought. He wasn't sure what difference it would make or why a good impression was important. He could only imagine some things between men and women just were. At least he'd done his best. He looked again in the bathroom mirror, ran his hand over his chin, pushed at the skin under his eyes, stuck out his tongue, blew against the back of his hand to smell his breath (he couldn't detect any lingering odour of stale beer) and, taking a step back, checked the shape of his jacket, brushed some fluff off his trousers and fixed the collar of his shirt. He decided he didn't look hung over, didn't look shabby, if he didn't look smart either, and concluded there were no signs about him of the 'professor' among the Südbahnhof *Sandler*, no worried old man about to die – well, not yet. Suitably reassured, Sweeney took the lift to the lobby to await Sonja's arrival.

The young receptionist was back on duty. They acknowledged each other wordlessly and Sweeney sat on the couch, looked at the clock on the wall, glanced at his watch, pretended to check his mobile phone, but mostly kept an eye on the entrance. He was glad he'd come down when he did for Sonja was ten minutes early. As she entered the lobby, he tried to read her expression – was it dutiful, courteous, obliging, a look, in other words, implying she'd prefer to be elsewhere? He didn't think so. She looked genuinely pleased to see him. For some reason, she appeared taller and younger than she had the last two days and he noticed her cheeks were slightly flushed. Tonight she was wearing a black ruched sleeve blazer, dark tapered cotton trousers, fashionably short above the ankle, a light, beige crew neck sweater and a pair of loafers. Around her neck was a fine red silk scarf. As he stood to welcome her, he noticed a glance of appreciation by the receptionist who pretended to busy herself with some papers at the desk, but whose interest in them was unmistakable. Sonja and Sweeney embraced briefly and he remarked how stylish she looked. She shrugged, dismissing the compliment and he wasn't sure if it was modesty or a self-confident statement of 'What else would you expect of me?' He began to apologise for his own appearance and she shrugged again. 'It's not the ball season,' putting her hands lightly on the lapels of his jacket to correct them slightly. 'There now, are you ready to go?'

He said yes and pointed to his clothes once more, 'As ready as I'll ever be.'

When he handed over his key at the desk, the receptionist offered him nothing more than another smile but, as Sweeney knew already, she was a girl who could say a lot without words. As the automatic door slid open, she did call after them '*Schönen Abend noch*' and in English to him, 'Have a pleasant evening.' Both of them turned and raised their hands in appreciation.

'What a lovely young woman,' Sonja remarked.

'Yes, she's great,' he replied.

'She reminds me of Hannah, my daughter.'

Sweeney was astonished by her daughterly reference which literally stopped him in his tracks. He looked around for the Touareg and she took it as the reason for his momentary confusion. 'No car tonight. I'm looking forward to a glass of wine with my meal.'

Sweeney recovered his composure, 'Shall we take a cab?'

'No. I thought we could walk and see more of the town?'

'Good idea,' he said, for the air was fresh, the sky powder blue and the outline of the mountains sharp in the glow of the setting sun.

'We can take a roundabout route. Villach is a neat little

town, so don't worry, it won't take too long. The exercise will give you an appetite.'

He was about to offer his arm, but she'd set off already. She led him along the Bahnhofstrasse, cutting through the Kaigasse, onto the Draupromenade, and crossed the river onto Steinwenderstrasse. As they went, Sonja kept up an animated monologue about what had changed and what had stayed the same in Villach – tales of *Wanderkarten*, old and knew, Sweeney thought – and he tried his best to pay full attention. What fascinated him was not Sonja's recounting of Villach's recent history, but her vivacity and he wondered, glancing at her flushed cheeks, if she had, on account of the holiday, and like him, been drinking earlier in the day. They turned onto Völkendorfer Strasse, a street he wasn't familiar with, and afterwards Sankt Johanner Strasse, somewhere he also didn't recognise. How could this possibly be? He must have walked along these streets many times.

'It's strange,' he remarked to her, 'but none of it looks familiar to me.'

'You were here many times before. And we definitely walked along these streets together.' She must have been right, but Sweeney could find no clues to his past and no prompts for his memory.

It took about forty minutes to reach their destination and he was surprised by a restaurant – *Freindal Wirtschaft* it was called – on a corner, standing at the edge of town where green fields and Villach met. 'Welcome back to Johannes Höhe,' Sonja said to him. So he must have been here too. Had she brought him to this spot for some sentimental reason and should he have grasped her purpose already?

'It all looks much the same,' for he supposed it must do, hoping his reply sufficiently vague to cover all possibilities. Luckily for him, there didn't appear to be any ulterior meaning in her remark, no special association for him to recognise, for she added nothing more. The restaurant sat at an angle to the street, fronted by a little terrace with wooden tables and chairs. There was soft light glowing from large windows on either side of the entrance. It had become noticeably cooler during their walk, but it was still comfortable enough for a few customers to sit outside over their drinks, mostly cocktails Sweeney noticed. On the tables, lights flickered in coloured glass bowls and as he passed by, Sweeney caught the aroma of cigarette smoke.

. . . .

Sonja gave her name to the waitress who led them through a narrow arch to a table at the rear. Sweeney had a natural resistance to what was 'in' and he knew immediately the restaurant to which she'd brought him was definitely 'in'. But tonight he was determined to suppress every instinct of reserve or criticism, for he could sense Sonja loved it, and recognised with surprise, if one wanted a measure of how he'd changed, that was it. He hadn't been so accepting when younger.

She leaned towards him as they sat, 'I think there is something magical about this place.'

He looked around, 'Yes, I see what you mean.' He took in the peaceful lighting and how it softened the room with a diffuse enchantment. The walls were painted green and on them hung religious images (he would love to find out if one of them came from Monte Lussari) as well as trophies of small animal skulls (real or faux, he couldn't tell, but hoped the latter). The window shelf beside them supported a collection of old books and Sweeney had to suppress the instinct to lift one or two for inspection.

'I wasn't sure if you would like it given how traditional your tastes are. I knew *Bacchus* was more your sort of place. It's one of the reasons I chose it the other day.' She paused briefly, 'Well, I like *Bacchus* too, but here is my favourite restaurant.' Sweeney assumed she intended to say more about the place, perhaps something like, 'Christian and I liked to eat here.' He could imagine it being somewhere Villach's 'celebrity couples' would be seen (and be photographed). But she didn't say anything further, and he was thankful – for himself, so he wouldn't have to deal with that part of her past tonight, for her, so she wouldn't have to regret his intrusion into a part of her married life (as he imagined it must have been).

'Did we come often up here?' Sweeney was relaxed enough to ask her.

'No, not here exactly, but we did go sometimes to the Eggerteich, the little lake nearby. On really hot days we'd come up, trying to find some fresh air.' He couldn't recall those trips either, but pretended he did, thinking only for her sake he should have remembered better. It was true. His *Wanderkarte* was out of date. 'I'm sure you're familiar with the old saying.'

'What old saying?' he asked.

'Don't you know it? '*Villach liegt am Eggerteich/Rundherum ganz Österreich*' – Villach lies on the Eggerteich and all around it, lies Austria. You believed Villach was the centre of Austria, didn't you? Maybe you still do?'

'I've never heard this saying before. But I'm glad to hear Villach, my Villach, has been officially confirmed.'

'The people of Villach have always known it.' Sonja was in a playful mood and he suspected her words were to remind him of the barbed comment she'd made in *Bacchus* – she felt he'd liked Villach as much as her. However, she didn't allow him to dwell on his suspicion and asked, 'And what did you do today?'

'I'm ashamed to say, Sonja, I went to Klagenfurt.' She merely raised an eyebrow. 'I went to see the 10th October commemoration at the *Landhaus*.' She looked confused. 'I didn't go to the one in Villach in case you felt I was trying to bump into you. I didn't want to embarrass you in front of your friends.'

She put her hand to her forehead in disbelief, 'I think you were put here on earth to make me laugh.' And she did laugh and at least she hadn't added, as she had every right to, 'and to make me cry'. She told him the commemoration in Villach had been held the night before. 'I was having lunch with friends today, nothing special.' She put her elbows on the table, her head on her hands, made a sad face, 'You poor boy, having to spend part of your holiday from life in Klagenfurt.' She looked at him mischievously, 'You mentioned him the other day, but there's something wonderful Thomas Bernhard wrote about Klagenfurt.'

'I can see by the look on your face it can't be anything good.'

'He described it as a town of fifty thousand people who know nothing about the outside world, but who think they are at its centre – when Villach is.'

'Did Bernhard really say Villach was at the centre of the world?'

She laughed at his question, 'Can you imagine Bernhard saying anything remotely positive about us? No, he didn't write it – but I say it! And what did I tell you about everything I say?'

'It's true.'

With a big smile of confirmation, Sonja spread out her arms, 'There's a clever boy. Your visit has been worthwhile for this enlightenment alone.'

Sweeney bowed his head in deference to her greater wisdom and asked, 'And do people in Villach collect every bad comment made about Klagenfurt?'

'We enjoy telling-it-like-it-is' and she drew out slowly the words of the English phrase.

'All I can say is I'm glad to be here at the centre of the world,' stopping short of saying 'with you' even if he wanted to and meant it. 'And I suppose for once – and only for today – Klagenfurt had its compensations. I managed to have a few beers in *zum Augustin*.'

'You really did go back in time! *Zum Augustin* – that's where we had the conference dinner with those English academics. Remember what a poor lot they were?'

So he'd been right. A circle had been completed. He wagged his finger at her, 'Tonight there must be no looking at the menu for the cheapest item!'

'Aren't you in luck? There is no set menu, but I can assure you, the food is delicious and so is the wine. Or is that unfortunate for your wallet?' He could tell immediately she considered her remark insensitive because she added, 'Sorry, of course we can share the bill, if you like …'

He waved away her suggestion, 'I wouldn't dream of it. Here's the deal, as the Americans say. I pay the bill, but you choose the food – and the wine too, of course.'

'It's a deal, my friend.'

'A deal made in Villach … and all around it, Austria.'

'You are a fast learner.'

'You are a good teacher.'

'And you are still a great flatterer. Let's order, shall we?' And she did, telling Sweeney after the young waitress had left, dinner would be a surprise for him. The bottle of wine arrived promptly and on the label he read *Blaufränkisch*. If it turned out to be as palatable as last night's bottle, Sonja had made a good choice.

As the waitress poured their wine, suddenly Sweeney had a fantastic sensation that the restaurant had been conjured for their visit only and imagined it disappearing once they'd left. He knew the idea was ridiculous if taken literally. But what of the emotional experience – was it not all too imaginary and transient? He recalled a novel he'd read in French class at school, Alain Fournier's *Le Grand Meaulnes*, with its tale of a

The Fourth Day

mysterious lost domain, of dream-like wanderings, of extraordinary encounters, of romantic failures, of the struggle to return and of the hero's discovery that nothing could ever be the same as it once was (or as he'd once imagined it). As a boy he'd never warmed to Meaulnes's character. And yet had he not turned out to be like him? Was his journey to Villach not as fantastic (and narcissistic) as the capricious illusions of Meaulnes? The idea came as a jolt and must have revealed itself in his expression. Sonja mistook its meaning.

'Don't you like the wine?' she asked.

'I do like it,' and he turned the bottle scrutinising the details on the label which meant nothing to him, 'it's excellent.' He took another sip. 'Hmmm, yes, I like it a lot. It's a great choice.' They raised their glasses, chinking them together, '*Prost!*'

'And what are we toasting tonight?' she asked.

Meaulnes and his fruitless questing encouraged Sweeney to suggest, 'The road not taken?'

Sonja looked approvingly, but before they touched glasses once more, she added, 'You can drop the line, "I doubted if I should ever come back". For here you are ... once more in Villach.'

'To the road not taken', they said together, bolder than they had intended. A man and a woman at a table across the room, both dressed expensively and possessing the quality of secure prosperity about their persons, looked over, smiling politely, if anaemically, at their loudness. Sonja put her finger to her lips, turning towards them in apology, and Sweeney also mouthed 'I'm sorry'. The man and woman nodded tolerantly and with obvious condescension.

'Congratulations on your Robert Frost. I can only ever remember the title of his poem.'

'I used to teach it to my pupils. Actually, I'm not surprised by your choice. The poem reminds me of you.' It was Sweeney's turn to raise his eyebrows. 'Seeing a crossroads, you choose your own path, not telling others where you are going.' She took a sip of wine and looked at him over the top of her glass, inviting a response that he felt obliged to accept.

'You asked me a moment ago if I didn't like the wine, but it's not what was on my mind. Have you ever read the novel by Alain Fournier, *Le Grand Meaulnes?*'

'*Der grosse Meaulnes?* Yes, why do you ask?'

He reminded her of the book's dreamlike search, a tale of painful loss and adolescent agonies. He spoke of Meaulnes thinking life seemed to be elsewhere, confessing that the character he'd found irritating when young might be the person he'd become when old. As he finished, she looked at the wine in her glass, swirled it once, set it before her, smoothed the fabric of the tablecloth and put her hand on his arm.

'We never lose our youthful vulnerability. Believe me, I have been close enough to the anxieties of young teens throughout my career, imparting adult wisdom to them when they were troubled, but only aware of my own uncertainty. Are you an adventurer like the Meaulnes character? I don't think so at all. He's uprooted like a pulled and delicate flower. Interest in men like that soon withers too. As a woman I can tell you, and despite what some men think, there's nothing less attractive than an overgrown schoolboy. It was the most annoying thing about Connolly, all that obsessive caressing of the dreams and promises of youth. I'd say to myself, "Oh be a man, Cyril".' She took another sip of wine. 'No, you're not a withered cut flower. Maybe you've become too rooted and need to get out more? And here you are, getting out more, in your Villach, my Villach, *our* Villach, in a nice restaurant, drinking good wine, soon you will be eating good food and …' she fluttered her eyelashes playfully, 'you are also in the best company imaginable. What makes you likeable is a lack of self-torturing introspection, not any French or, God forbid, Germanic, brooding.' She raised her glass to him, 'So, please, no more dark nights of the soul and enjoy life while you can. And here's how.'

Their first course, a large platter of seafood with a range of sauces and breads, was being set on the table. Seeing it, smelling it, Sweeney realised how hungry he was. They helped themselves and, like Inspector Montalbano and his perfect companion, they stopped talking to concentrate on the food. Both murmured appreciatively and ate enthusiastically. After a while she asked, 'Well, what do you think?'

'It's so good I almost forgot I was in the best company in Villach'

'That's the spirit! You must never forget the most important things in life.'

'And what you say has to be true,' again more loudly than intended, accidentally clattering the fork against the side of his plate. He saw that the man and woman didn't look over this time, but continued their meal, ignoring them with practised yet obvious disdain. Sonja noticed it too and they looked at each other conspiratorially. Sweeney asked, 'Isn't there a German saying, "*Einmal ist keinmal, aber zweimal ist einmal zuviel*"?'

She leaned over the table to say in his ear, 'Yes.'

To do something once is like not having done it at all, but to do the same thing twice is to do it once too often. Probably their dining neighbours judged him to be an old English-speaking bore in ill-matching linens, someone who was a little too fond of Austrian wine and incapable of grasping the saying's wisdom.

'At our age, you'd think we'd know how to behave better. Be careful not to make it *dreimal*,' she whispered again and put a finger to one side of her nose, 'otherwise those two will ask for us to be thrown out.'

Their main course was equally delicious, succulent steak and seafood pasta with more fresh bread. Sweeney ordered another bottle of the same wine, Sonja feigning disapproval to him, but at the same time giving assent to the waitress. Yes indeed, Montalbano would consider the restaurant a little bit of heaven outside his native Sicily.

'I don't think I have eaten so well in a long time,' he said.

'You can trust me, *Herr Professor*. Oh I'm sorry, I promised not to call you that again, didn't I?' She saluted him with a fresh glass of wine and he admitted to himself he always should have trusted her. If only he could have trusted himself. 'Thank you again for reviving my interest in Connolly. I've enjoyed looking through old copies of his work. I found a little marked passage which might describe tonight for you – and for both of us. It was a journal entry. And for once he's not lamenting his failures. He's gone to Paris where, unlike today, you could live cheaply. He's in a hotel on the Left Bank, got enough money and writes about carafes of red wine, exploring districts he's unfamiliar with, wandering along the Seine, gazing into shop windows, café crawling. It's Paris and not Villach, but you can understand his pleasure at enjoying all those simple things. And pleasure for Connolly meant plenty of good food and good company,' and she spread her hands to take in the dishes on their table, the remains of the food on their plates, 'like tonight, and like us.'

Sweeney was going to say he preferred Villach to Paris, which at his age wasn't simply politeness, but her story was too apt to qualify. He was certainly taking pleasure in everything. Their second bottle of wine was almost empty and he topped up Sonja's glass. She didn't demur and sat back in her chair. 'It was good to go back and read *The Unquiet Grave*. When you suggested toasting the 'road not taken', there's something Connolly wrote about it too. It's only a coincidence, but I remember you used to say nothing in life is *mere* coincidence. You did say that, didn't you, or have I got it wrong?'

The Fourth Day

'I did say it ... and I still say it.'

'Here's what Connolly wrote. When we look back at the stuff of disunion in the past – he means intellectual arguments, you'll be *au fait* with them in your life, all those typical academic debates – we think of them as ridiculous. The path of truth, he wrote, is forever splitting' – she stretched out wide her arms – 'which reunite' – she brought them back together again and her hands clapped softly – 'like this.' It appeared she was going to hiccup, but she swallowed instead, patted her chest and apologised.

'Do you, does he, mean the road not taken and the road taken may join together again at some point?' He considered the idea a little contrived, but was curious to discover where its logic might take her. He also noticed their two fellow diners had become visibly irritated by their behaviour, as if their sense of possession had been challenged. Were they another of Villach's 'celebrity couples'? If they were, Sweeney didn't regret spoiling their dinner.

'Connolly meant – well, I take him to mean – you can remain stuck in the middle, cultivating differences forever and being at odds for the rest of a lifetime.' She took another sip of wine, setting her glass rather too heavily on the table. 'Or you could decide to move on, try to discover where those two paths meet again ... if the two paths can meet, that is.' She looked directly at him with her bright green eyes. 'It's really a matter of choice.'

'The ones stuck in the middle remind me of most people I know.'

She pointed at him, 'I think you know too many of the wrong people' and they laughed together. Sonja held his gaze a little longer than usual, finishing off her wine in one quick mouthful. She glanced over her shoulder towards the door and then at her watch as if to change not only the subject but also the mood. 'It's almost ten o'clock. If you are leaving early to-morrow, we should really go soon.'

'Sure', he replied, his show of acceptance concealing a deep mood of regret. He looked around to catch the attention of the waitress, but she'd been hovering, unnoticed, close behind him and, anticipating his request, suddenly was beside him. Sweeney started with surprise, put his hand to his heart and the waitress apologised profusely. When she'd gone to fetch the bill, Sweeney continued to pat his chest with dramatic pretention, happy to annoy further the celebrity couple.

'At least your heart is still in working order.'

'And still in the right place, I hope.'

'The heart is made to be broken, and after it has mended, to be broken again.'

'I'm going to make a guess. You're quoting Connolly?'

Sonja clapped him silently and before Sweeney could think of a suitable reply the waitress returned with the bill. Amid all the rituals of paying – the back and forth about enjoying their meal and expressions of appreciation, the thank you for the tip, the shifting of chairs, the standing, the banalities (as well as Sweeney's childish exaggerations in order to infuriate their fellow diners) the intimacy of their conversation was lost. As they made their way out, with another thank you and goodbye to the staff, Sonja excused herself, using the Americanism, 'I need to visit the restroom'.

As he waited for her on the terrace, Sweeney mulled over the idea of two paths joining long after parting, dredging from his mind one of the few lines of Connolly's he could remember – the illusion which appeals most to our temperament is the one we should choose and, having chosen it, we should embrace it with passion. Sweeney wasn't sure if he was capable of embracing anything with passion these days, if he ever had done, but if he were to choose, he was happy with an illusion which involved Sonja. He was sober enough to accept she may not have meant anything at all by her remark. And who was he to say what illusion should appeal to her temperament?

. . . .

Re-joining him, she asked, 'What do you think? Have we been cast out of our magic domain?'

Inside the restaurant Sweeney could see candle flames reflected in the windows dancing like fireflies. The night air was fresh and Sweeney gave an involuntary shiver. 'Into the cold, anyway', he replied rubbing his hands exaggeratedly.

'Like Monsieur Meaulnes we need to wander – but not too far, only to Hotel City. OK – *Zack! Zack!* You have a plane to catch in the morning.'

'Take my arm, you can keep me warm and I can keep you steady.'

'Ha! Is that all you can offer a lady?' But she took his arm and bumped playfully into his shoulder.

Below they glimpsed the heart of Villach, its landmarks clearly visible in the misty glow of street lighting. He was hoping to see above them a silver apple of the moon, but tonight, sadly, it was a waning crescent. As they retraced their steps, chatting amiably and inconsequentially, Sweeney was conscious again of the challenge of saying goodbye and he tried to delay the moment till time was properly done. The words *finir en beauté* came into his head, but he didn't want things to end, perfectly or otherwise, and definitely not forever. The streets were silent and there were few cars, like the time he'd walked to the Hauptbahnhof that night so long ago, and he saw once more the face of the woman on the Mostar-Dalmacija Express as it pulled away into the darkness. Villach, his Villach, a town of departures, of farewells, of wistful partings.

Four Days in Villach

They reached the Bahnhofplatz much sooner than he would have liked. Business for the taxi drivers must have been slow, for a group of them stood by the leading car on the rank, talking, gesticulating and smoking. The railway station looked deserted as well. Sonja and Sweeney unlinked arms as they crossed the road and he was uncertain whether he should walk her to the hotel and call a cab from there or go over directly to the taxi rank. She decided for him, halting by the railway station subway. 'It's time to say goodbye – again.'

'Time to say goodbye – again … my trip has been all about departures.' In a clumsy attempt to lighten things, he said theatrically what was foremost in his mind, 'Oh Villach, you sad town of farewells.'

She bumped his shoulder for the second time tonight. '*So leben wir und nehmen immer Abschied.* Aha, I see you don't recognise the quote. It's Rilke, "and so we live, forever saying farewell." You could say it has become our personal elegy.' She looked at her feet for a moment and then at him. 'But these few days have been fun. I haven't enjoyed myself so much in a long time … and mostly at your expense. Do you remember talking about "the malaise" yesterday? I've felt no malaise. Only the opposite, whatever the opposite is … contentment, ease, comfort? I'm not sure what that is, but I felt it.'

He was tempted to say 'so we must be good for each other', but considered that it would sound too inane. Instead he said, 'There is something I wanted to ask you.'

'And it is?'

'Did you choose *Bacchus* for our first meeting with the story of Ariadne and Theseus in mind?'

She didn't reply immediately, smiling at him, then said. 'It would be a good story. I like the idea of the two of us inhabiting our own mythology. Let's just say *se non è vero, è ben trovato.*'

'Yes', Sweeney replied, 'let's just say that.'

The Fourth Day

Each was about to speak when an inter-city bus stopped in front of the railway station building, the high-pitched screech of its brakes making it impossible for either of them to hear or say a word. They put their hands to their ears and started giggling like a pair of school kids. When it was quiet again, Sweeney said, 'Sonja, it has been fun. It was wonderful seeing you again.'

She shook her head. 'There's no need to thank me. Remember what I told you in *Bacchus?* I wouldn't have seen you if I hadn't wanted to. And I'm certain it will sound clichéd, but your visit has been good for me. No,' shaking her head more vigorously, 'let me rephrase. *You* have been good for me. I don't need Villach, Thörl Maglern, Tarvisio or Kransjka Gora to deal with that part of my life. I needed you here to do it. And here you are. I know we have cancelled inconvenient memories, we have edited from our past painful legacies ... at least I have. Yet the pleasure of seeing you again was stronger than any tears. And if you are wondering, those are lines from an old song ... but they are true for me. I didn't expect to say them tonight, but there, I have done.' She gently poked his chest. 'You feel a need to be guilty, but it is pointless now, believe me. I can't go back. You can't go back. We are of a certain age, you and me, but I'd like to think our roads have joined once more, if only for a short time, if only here in Villach.' She paused. Sweeney was about to reply, but she put a finger to his lips. 'There is something else I want to say. It's from Connolly too. You are responsible for it with your present, so indulge me. He wrote "Green leaves on a dead tree is our epitaph – green leaves, dear reader, on a dead tree." I love that image. And let me tell you what I think. The golden tree of actual life springs ever green. Do you see what I mean? Our past is dead but miraculously – and it is like a miracle – our present has sprung newly green. I wouldn't have believed it, would you?' Sweeney couldn't find any clever words and actually, clever words were the last thing he needed. So he kept silent. 'Autumn leaves falling dead to the ground and yet against nature two green leaves grow – what do you think?'

He was delighted to think it was true and wished she was right. Because he was unsure what she truly meant, he could only say, 'Late joys are the most beautiful. They take their place between faded yearning and approaching peace.' She looked quizzical. 'It's another Ebner-Eschenbach aphorism. Remember I mentioned her to you at *Bacchus?* I thought it was one of her best.'

'Faded but not gone, approaching but not at rest – yes, I see what she means. All those anxieties we go through when younger, and the heartless, cruel things we say and do, all the *Sturm und Drang … Sturm der Liebe* indeed! And we could all do with some joy and better late than never.'

'Can we keep in touch? That would be a joy for me.' He knew it sounded contrived and her look made it clear she found it contrived as well.

'Yes, I'd like that. I've missed our conversations … and your terrible sense of humour! Here's to late joys.' She gave him a quick kiss on the cheek, 'Now, I have to get a taxi.' She took a few steps away towards the rank. Sweeney was at a loss about what to do and his failure to run along the platform beside the girl on the sleeper train returned to mock him. It was Sonja who stopped as if she'd forgotten something and turned, walked back, put her hands to his head and kissed him softly on the lips. She let her hands linger on his cheeks for a moment. 'Late joys, let's make the most of them,' and jogged over to the first taxi, a black Mercedes saloon. She spoke to the driver and got into the back seat. She blew him a kiss as the car pulled away from the square and sped off towards Warmbad. He realised after she'd gone that he was standing with his arm in the air, waving at nothing and to no one.

. . . .

The Fourth Day

Sweeney walked slowly to Hotel City. When he got to the entrance he searched in his pocket for his cigarettes. There was only one left. He lit it and leaned against the table, observing the same scene as on his first day. He'd come to Villach as pilgrim, to Sonja as a penitent, but was pleasantly surprised by his poetry of departure. He felt more alive than he'd done for a long time, as if he'd experienced a soulful restoration, one more meaningful than the moment at Monte Lussari, wishing to discern an extraordinary meaning in these few days. In these four days, he had expressed his repentance and she had extended her charity.

Those brief intimacies they'd shared – especially her final kiss – what did they mean? Nearly all of them had been at Sonja's initiative and at her discretion. She knew of his many faults, but hadn't passed judgement. Here, he believed, was the difference between her fluent worldliness and his mute unworldliness, for she made allowance for weakness while he persisted in carrying its burden. And he realised this worldliness allowed Sonja to avoid cynicism because she could accept the shortcomings of others. He, on the other hand, had found it all too easy to be cynical according to the flaws in others, but mostly in him. Or had they simply rediscovered an enduringly simple truth – as man and woman, there was pleasure enough in each other's presence, in Sonja's terms as witnesses to each other's existence? At their age, they might just settle for those late joys of compatibility and companionability. As in Klagenfurt when they had walked together under an umbrella Sweeney had a shock of recognition. It was that twenty-five years could be a mere (*mere!*) hiatus in a relationship meant to endure. And he wanted to believe the fates had brought together again what they had once chosen to divide, all too conscious the idea was too convenient as well as too self-acquitting. But hadn't she said not to be hard on himself? He smiled at the memory of his taxi journey from the airport. The cemetery at Annabichl, or anywhere else, was not the place to be. There are things worse than growing old. He stubbed out his cigarette, crushed the empty packet and slotted it into the metal bin by the door. His holiday from life was over.

When he entered the lobby the young receptionist rose from her desk, reaching across to take his key from the rack. '*Einen angenehmen Abend?*' she asked brightly, did you have a pleasant evening, and Sweeney was pleased she'd asked in German. Her look was no longer questioning and she wasn't holding back for an unexpected answer. It seemed her mind was set as to how she should think of him. He responded equally brightly, as if they were sharing a mutual discovery, '*Ja, danke, sehr angenehm.*'

Then she slipped into professional mode once more, switching to English. 'You are leaving tomorrow morning, Professor Sweeney? Have you enjoyed your stay at Hotel City?'

'Yes, I have, very much. Thank you for being so hospitable.'

'It was a pleasure.' She shuffled a few papers beneath the counter and stapled them, making ready for his departure. 'Can you please sign here' and she indicated the relevant line on the paperwork. As he did so she added, 'I hope we will see you again in Villach?'

'Yes, I will certainly be back.' He was confident enough to say it without hesitation.

Taking his key from her, he walked to the lift and as it ascended he glimpsed, he couldn't swear to it of course, a red car – it looked like an old Fiat 126 – making a turn at the roundabout by the Hauptbahnhof, heading towards the Stadtbrücke and the centre of town.

Printed in Great Britain
by Amazon